CITY OF INFERNUS

Clara—

Thank you so much for your support!!

CITY OF INFERNUS

S.M. MUELLER

NEW DEGREE PRESS

COPYRIGHT © 2021 S.M. MUELLER

CITY OF INFERNUS

ISBN   978-1-63730-837-0   *Paperback*

        978-1-63730-901-8   *Kindle Ebook*

        978-1-63730-950-6   *Ebook*

"*And above all, watch with glittering eyes the whole world around you because the greatest secrets are always hidden in the most unlikely places. Those who don't believe in magic will never find it.*"

—ROALD DAHL

CONTENTS

AUTHOR'S NOTE 9

PROLOGUE GRANDMOTHER'S TALE 13
CHAPTER 1. ALEXANDRIA 19
CHAPTER 2. THE FOREST 31
CHAPTER 3. THE TWO FRIENDS 41
CHAPTER 4. EXPLORING THE RABBIT'S HOLE 57
CHAPTER 5. MEETING ROYALTY 71
CHAPTER 6. THE TWO ALI'S 83
CHAPTER 7. REUNITED 99
CHAPTER 8. SHADOWVINES 109
CHAPTER 9. SWEET NIGHTMARES 119
CHAPTER 10. THE PROTECTOR 143
CHAPTER 11. THE SORCERERS' CAPSULE 157
CHAPTER 12. DANGEROUS DOLPHINS IN THE DEEP 173
CHAPTER 13. LAVENDER, JASMINE, AND MUD 185
CHAPTER 14. THE WAND'S MATE 199
CHAPTER 15. SKOTIA'S SECRET 217
CHAPTER 16. THE DRAKE'S CHAMBER 231
CHAPTER 17. THE SORCERER'S APPRENTICE 241
CHAPTER 18. THE DARK SORCERER 255
CHAPTER 19. WHAT COMES NEXT 269

ACKNOWLEDGMENTS 281

AUTHOR'S NOTE

A writer's mind is a scary yet wonderful place to live.

From the time I could put pen to paper, I've identified as a writer. I've always been drawn to words. If pieced together skillfully, they can capture our imaginations and create exciting new worlds. Living in a writer's mind, these worlds surround me daily; they creep into my daydreams and retell their stories as I sleep. Their citizens invite me in to hear about their troubles and sorrows, along with their triumphs and greatest feats. They call out for me to explore new depths and heights no one has seen before, yet they're right in front of me once I close my eyes.

Like I said—scary, yet wonderful.

Truthfully, I'm not sure when the lightbulb went off and I decided I was meant to be an author. While it wasn't uncommon for my family to find me with my head in a fantasy novel wondering what new character I'd become obsessed with, it was hard for me to find anyone who resonated with my love for magic.

Our world is full of magic. Most of us are just too blind to see it.

When I was fifteen, I told my hair stylist that I wanted to be an author when I grew up. She asked me what my novel would be about, and I spent the next three hours delving into my imagination for the answer to that question. One thing was for certain—there would be an element of magic in the story. A story that captured the idea that magic is right under our noses every day.

My hair may have been getting heavier with every foil she was putting on my head, but there was a lightness about me that I had not felt before. The more I talked about this idea—nothing more than a couple of teenagers on a quest to save one's brother—something inside me caught fire.

City of Infernus was born. An eclectic group of teenagers introduced themselves to me in my mind and told me the story of what brought them together, what shaped them, and how they helped shape each other along the way. Ali, Lilly, and Gavin were not normal teenagers facing normal teenage problems; they were thrown into a world that makes them question everything they've ever been taught.

My relationship with these characters grew, and they learned to trust me with their innermost thoughts and feelings. Through Ali especially, I gained access to their world. The world they grew up in is quite similar to mine: full of adults pretending to know what the right path is for their children, encouraging them to have their life's plan figured out by seventeen. But the world they abruptly find themselves in is nothing like any of us have experienced before. It is one with a dejected king and queen, a savior who fled, and caves that reveal magical stories.

Most people from our world think they have to—or they can—follow a certain path in their lifetime. But how do you plan for a child to go missing? How do you plan to be ripped from everything you've ever known, only to be thrown into a new realm that you're connected to in more ways than one?

The short answer is, you can't. Leaning into the unknown is possibly even harder than believing magic is living outside your front door.

Yet, our journeys are our own. We can heed advice from the loved, and not so loved, ones in our lives, but ultimately we're the ones who have to stroll down the path we create every single day. *Infernus* was not a part of Ali's, Lilly's or Gavin's plans as much as a pandemic was not a part of ours—yet, like these characters, we must persevere as best we can.

I knew I wanted writing this book to become a stop on my path, but that doesn't mean there haven't been bumps along the way. It's taken me almost a decade to put my pen where my mouth is and actually write the stories that have lived in my head for just as long. There have been many points along the way that helped me get here—submitting my rough (emphasis on *rough*) drafts of these early chapters as assignments in college, meeting amazing authors during my time in the Creator Institute, and learning how to give others a peek inside the story that's been evolving in my mind for all these years.

That little girl who always had her nose in a book would've never guessed how important collaboration is during the trials of writing, but her "grown up" self is immensely grateful for every conversation she's had and every connection she's made.

Falling in love with these characters wasn't part of my game plan. But *Infernus* teaches us that our game plan only gets us so far in life. This trio taught me how to see their world and make it my own. They taught me how to inject my being into every obstacle and succumb to my vulnerabilities, no matter the consequences. How they embrace their individualities and use them in the face of darkness leaves me to question what I would do in their shoes: would I turn away, looking for an escape route, or would I turn toward the evil, knowing that my chance for failure is greater than my chance at success?

Don't get me wrong, I had failures. But one cannot grow if they haven't felt the painstakingly sharp jabs of failure in their sides, begging them to quit with as little loss as possible. How these three not-so-normal teenagers handle those trials is up to them to decide.

We may not have the same evil sorcerers or magical forests around the corner, but as you're reading, I want you to ask yourself how you would react if you were in Ali's position. If you were that girl who wouldn't let herself give up that last spark of hope. Or if you were Gavin, who only feels like he belongs when he's in a world that shouldn't even be real. Or Lilly, one of the many who couldn't see the magic right in front of her.

Above all, I want to thank the nerds. The magic lovers and the quest seekers who feel like they're here for something more. The ones who look around and see the beauty in the ordinary that leads to a curiosity for the extraordinary—I see you, and this is for you. This novel is a product of many years of hiding under my blanket at night reading fanfiction by the light of my computer. Without the support from the omnipresent nerd community during those times, my light would've gone out long ago.

I hope my book has a bit of the magic we're all looking for. I hope you feel it all. Then yell at me after.

GRANDMOTHER'S TALE

———

"Grandmother, please! Just one more story," Ali begged, climbing onto the mattress in Grandmother's spare bedroom. Her eyes were threatening to close any moment now, but she would pry them open if it meant the night would last just a bit longer.

"We swear we won't tell Mom!" Carter added from the other bed in the room. Ali's brother might have been younger than she was, but they shared almost identical interests, which included staying up past their designated bedtime.

"Your mother may be my daughter, but I see more of myself in the two of you than I have ever seen in her," their grandmother chuckled to herself. Stepping back into the room, she settled herself in the rocking chair sitting between the two beds.

"I'll tell you one more story, but after that, you must promise me you will go to sleep. Deal?"

"Deal!" Both children shrieked with delight. Ali fixed her thick blankets so that her legs would be perfectly snug when it came time for the end of the story. She loved falling asleep to the sound of Grandmother's soothing voice.

"What will this story be about?" She pulled the sheets over her mouth to hide the yawn escaping from her lips. "Can we hear the one about the giant sunflowers again?"

"Not tonight, darling. Tonight you get to hear the story of three friends who lived in Infernus," the elderly woman replied. The wrinkles in her forehead were pressed together as she looked between her two grandchildren. Ali wasn't sure if it was her own exhausted mind misleading her, but there was a different gleam in Grandmother's green eyes than there had been earlier in the night. Not that it would matter; Ali loved hearing about the land that lived in her matriarch's imagination.

"The trio grew up together, running about Infernus like it was their playground." Grandmother's words were as smooth as the emerald hanging around her neck. "The boy was from the royal bloodline, granting the friends access to some of the most mysterious spots in Infernus. While they were all quite different, the three of them had a precarious habit of finding the most wonderful adventures the land had to offer."

"That sounds like something Mom would say about us," Ali joked. Her brother broke out into a fit of laughter from across the room. She knew he agreed with the statement as much as she did.

"Oh yes, that is most definitely something your mother would say," Grandmother began again. "Now, let's work on that patience skill, shall we? No more interruptions for the rest of the story."

Feeling her cheeks turning a light shade of pink, Ali sheepishly nodded. She didn't see the need for patience in a world where everything happened too quickly for anyone to understand, but she wasn't going to jeopardize their story again.

"There came a time when these three friends grew older. While they still shared their childlike wonder, it was difficult to find as many adventures as they did when they were younger."

Ali tried to picture an older version of herself that didn't enjoy running around the neighborhood with her brother, but nothing came to her mind. There would never be a time where they would stop creating more trouble than they could handle.

"Two of the friends fell deeply in love and moved into the grandest castle you can imagine. Since the boy was the heir to the throne, when the time came, they ascended into power as the new king and queen of Infernus. The castle sat upon a hill overlooking the same lands they had explored many years before. When they stood on their balcony, the two could see everything from the faraway mountains to the roaring rivers cutting Infernus into different sections." Grandmother closed her eyes while she described the scene. With a quick peek at Carter's mouth hanging open, Ali could tell he was as enthralled by the tale as she was.

"One day, they invited their childhood friend to their home. She gladly agreed, meeting them at the castle the next day. Standing outside the marvelous wooden doors, she eagerly let herself into the stone fortress. Even though they had children of their own now, the trio ran through the wide hallways and secret passages like they had always envisioned. At one point, they found themselves in a magnificent library. The walls were lined with thousands of books, and a roaring fireplace stood in the middle."

Ali glanced around the room at Grandmother's own collection of books. They were shoved away in the corner on a rolling bookshelf she had found on the side of the road earlier that year, but none of the stories in those pages compared to Grandmother's tales about Infernus. Even though she was getting older now, Ali still craved the deep lull the tales brought to her. They would carry her into her dreams where

Ali would suddenly become the protagonist of every narrative, off to explore the very world she wished she could travel to during the day.

"Once seated around the fireplace, the queen took her friend's hand in hers. Sensing that something had shifted between the trio, the visitor braced herself for the worst, without knowing what the worst could be. In a single sentence, the king and queen shared their deepest secret with their confidant."

This story had taken a turn that Ali hadn't heard before. Usually, Grandmother's bedtime stories detailed long walks by the rivers or encounters with the strangest animals Ali could imagine. This was the first time hearing about a faraway castle, and she needed to know more.

Forcing herself to stay awake, Ali tried to prop herself up in the bed. Unsuccessful, her arms gave out, and she felt gravity's strength pull her onto the pillow.

"What was the secret, Grandmother?" Carter blurted out, forgetting about the no interruptions rule. His hands flew to his mouth.

"It wouldn't be a secret if everyone found out, now would it?" she responded, laughing silently to herself. "But I will tell the two of you if you promise not to share it."

Their eyelids were drooping, but both siblings promptly nodded.

"That's settled then. The secret is that the king and queen wanted to find a way to leave Infernus and start a new life in a faraway land where no one would be able to find them. No one besides their closest friend."

"But why would they want to leave Infernus? Why would anyone want to leave the land they get to rule?" Carter asked the questions that were currently swimming in Ali's mind.

"That is a good question, dear. But, it is one that will have to be answered in our next story. It is far past your bedtimes, and, by the looks of it, your eyes won't let you stay awake another minute." Grandmother stood up from the rocking chair and moved to the doorway, reaching for the lights.

"Do you promise you'll tell us next time?" Ali groggily mumbled. Her eyes were blinking shut, and now that the lights were off she could barely keep her mind from drifting away toward her dreams.

"Don't you worry about that, darling," Grandmother cooed, coming in to give one more kiss on the forehead to each of her grandchildren. "We will finish that story another night. Sleep tight now, the both of you."

With one more click of the door closing, Ali barely had to count to ten before she had drifted off to a sleep filled with fantasies of Carter and herself running through the castle halls, looking behind every door for the trio they had just learned about. Later, Ali would think back on this night, when Grandmother finally told her something true about Infernus.

CHAPTER 1

ALEXANDRIA

––––

Six more minutes, and she would be free.

For the first time in weeks, Ali felt at ease knowing that she didn't have to wake up to her six forty-five alarm tomorrow morning. She didn't have to walk up Lorrshore High's stone stairs and absentmindedly sit in a desk while her teachers droned on about the importance of the SAT or why they had to memorize the date of the Industrial Revolution. In six minutes, it would be summer, and Ali could officially say goodbye to her junior year of high school. Not that she welcomed it into her life in the first place.

In September, Ali had subconsciously chosen a seat next to the window in all her classes, just far enough toward the back so her teachers could label her as the girl who doesn't want to get called on. In Ali's defense, they didn't want to call on her, let alone pretend that they cared about her well-being. No one had wanted to take the seat next to her that first day, either, which was perfectly fine with Ali. There was no reason to pretend anyone cared about her fun fact during those first-day-of-school icebreakers, which was why she made up a lie when teachers prompted her for one. She used to try during those awkward moments—she would reveal that her favorite color was purple or that she once went to Niagara Falls, but after years of being picked last in gym class and sneered at across the lunchroom, she didn't see the point in sharing any more personal information than necessary.

Four minutes.

The desk next to Ali stayed empty during the year. Once, a new girl walked into class and sat in the seat, not knowing the sort of social suicide she would commit if she tried to befriend Ali. She must've learned quickly, because the next day the new girl picked a different seat, and she never looked at Ali again.

Normally, that memory wouldn't have bothered Ali, but today was an exception. Today was the anniversary of the worst day of Ali's life, and waking up on this day every year made her want to create a sheet cocoon in her bed and sleep away the painful memories. But reality didn't have a habit of giving Ali what she wanted. For now, all she could do was look out the streaky window at the heat waves coming off the turf field and distract herself from knowing that the nightmares would be back tonight, as they always were.

Two minutes.

Turning her gaze away from the window and back to the classroom, Ali couldn't help but listen to a group of girls talk about how much they were going to miss each other over the summer. Each of them was getting ready to willingly be shipped off to their respective vacations for eight weeks. They usually spent that time at their grandparents' exotic houses or private yachts, giving their parents time to travel to Europe or Iceland or South Africa without the hassle of children. This group had proclaimed themselves the "Lorrshore Sisters," a cringeworthy name at best. Somehow, all six of them had been placed in Ali's history class, and she couldn't help but wonder if their parents' positions on the school board had anything to do with this minor miracle.

Time's up.

The clear sound of the bell echoed throughout the classroom, signaling her freedom. No goodbyes were exchanged as Ali briskly exited the humid classroom and let her white Converse sneakers take her out of the building and into the blinding summer heat.

Ali threw on her sunglasses and spotted her two best friends waving frantically at her from the stone wall, snapping her out of a strange space. She cracked her first smile of the day as she headed toward them, knowing that they would laugh along with her when she retold the Lorrshore Sisters' shallow conversations.

Gavin and Lilly were the only two people at Lorrshore Ali liked. Even though the rest of the school treated her as if she was a case of poison ivy, Gavin and Lilly weren't afraid to be seen talking with the infamous Ali DuBois.

As she got closer, Ali could see that neither of her best friends had bought a yearbook, only to try and fill it with meaningless signatures. While their classmates had gone around the lunchroom counting how many "friends" left them messages they'd never look at again, Gavin, Lilly, and Ali wrote each other notes on scrap paper about what they thought each other's spirit animals were and why. Gavin thought that Ali's counterpart was a raven. Lilly was convinced that she was a cheetah, but that was only because Ali had been one of the fastest runners on the track team until she quit this year. She might've been a freak, but she was a freak who could win the school a few trophies.

"Hey, loser, get over here so we can finally get away from this place for a few months!" Lilly's insults would offend most people, but Ali knew it was her friend's unique method of endearment.

Lilly's full name was Lillian, but she rarely responded to that. When people first laid their eyes on Lilly, most lost their breath but weren't sure why. To Ali, it was obvious why they were confused by her friend's beauty. It was simple—Lilly was beautiful, but she was weird. Most blond bombshells don't have an obsession with true crime documentaries or get in one-sided prank wars with their middle-aged neighbors. But, that was Lilly, and Ali wouldn't have it any other way.

"I'm so surprised you two don't want to stick around and see the Lorrshore Sisters fake cry goodbyes to each other," Ali quipped back, a smirk spreading across her face.

Both Gavin and Lilly rolled their eyes and pretended to fake cry as Ali finally caught up with them.

"Wouldn't it be great if each of them actually heard what was said behind their back? I would pay to see that."

"I bet they would do it if they got a chance to go on a date with you, Gav." Ali watched Gavin give her a sideways glance, as if to say over his dead body.

"Yeah Gav, wouldn't that be great? You could go yachting and watch them get champagne drunk before breakfast," Lilly chuckled as she tucked a lock of her golden blond bob behind her ear and adjusted her graphic tee. Today's shirt featured an alien throwing up a peace sign with a speech bubble saying, "I don't believe in humans," matched with a pair of boho pants that flared at the bottom to expose her two different-colored shoes.

"You two just think you're so funny, don't you?"

"Yes, yes we do," Ali and Lilly said simultaneously.

"Oh, both of you can shove off."

Gavin was the guy most girls ignored in middle school because he liked video games too much and didn't drool over them like most teenage boys. But now that he just had a growth spurt and his features were as chiseled as they come for a seventeen-year-old boy, the Lorrshore Sisters treated him like he was some kind of prince. Gavin was either oblivious or simply didn't care to give them the time of day, which Ali found hilarious. Even though she admitted to herself that her best friend was a pretty good-looking guy, she'd never tell him that.

Today, Gavin was wearing what Ali considered the quintessential teenage boy outfit: a pair of khaki shorts with an old T-shirt and sneakers from a basketball player's brand. Gavin's green shirt brought out his eyes—both he and Ali had piercing green eyes. Lilly liked to point out that this similarity made it seem like they were distant cousins or shared some odd family connection. Both of them laughed off the possibility, but Ali couldn't help but wonder. The only other people she had met with the same eyes were her Grandmother and her brother, Carter.

The thought of Carter sent a wave of pain through Ali's body that she pushed it aside so her friends wouldn't see the flinch cross her features.

"We must look like an interesting trio walking down the street," Ali joked, looking down at her own outfit and nudging her friends' shoulders. She was sporting a pair of ripped jeans, her Converses that were barely passing for white nowadays, and a tank top her mother thought she would look nice in, even though it was a size too big. Her Grandmother's emerald necklace hung by her neck. Ali instinctively went to grab it to make sure it was still there, even though she never dared take it off.

"Oh yeah, that modeling agency in town is going to be banging down our doors with offers any day now," Lilly countered, taking a sip of her iced coffee from earlier that day.

Ali looked around them as they walked home toward their cul-de-sac. Even though they were seventeen and could legally get their licenses, none of them had one yet. Gavin simply didn't see a need for one, Lilly was probably one of the worst drivers Ali had ever witnessed (she had almost crashed a golf cart twice the previous summer), and Ali's parents would rather have a conniption than let their daughter drive without one of them in the passenger seat. The walk wasn't too long, anyway. Only about a mile and a half until they reached the entrance to their streets.

It was nice having her two best friends as neighbors. Even though her house was on a different street from theirs, they all lived in the same stuck-up, picture-perfect cul-de-sac. Every house looked alike: stone exterior with a black iron fence lining the border. Each porch had a swinging bench in the front, inviting the residents to believe there was a sense of calmness inside the walls. Sometimes, even Ali mixed up the houses and almost walked onto the wrong porch before noticing that her navy-blue mailbox was still three doors down.

The trees lining the entrance to their roads started peeking over the horizon. In Ali's mind, these trees represented a silent barrier that divided their neighborhood from the rest of the world. As if whoever planted them years ago were telling all nonresidents to enter at their own risk.

"Hey, Al, are you okay today?" Gavin brought her out of her stupor. Ali realized she had no idea what they had been talking about for the last ten minutes, which was partially why both her friends were looking at her with concerned eyes and worry lines in their foreheads.

"Yeah, I'm fine. Well, no, I'm not. But it's the same as it is every other year. I just don't want to go home and see what they're fighting about this time."

"You can come over to my house if you want. My mom is making meatloaf for dinner, and I promise it tastes better than it sounds."

Ali had turned down every offer for dinner at Lilly's before, and she would keep declining. Lilly's mom's cooking was next level awful, but she would've preferred it to her own frozen dinner any night.

"Thanks, but I shouldn't. In some twisted way I think they like me being home with them today, even though we don't actually talk about anything," Ali sighed.

"Well, if things get too hectic, you know my parents won't question if you come bursting through our door around dinnertime."

"Thanks, Lil, you know I'd never miss a chance to eat your mom's cooking if I could help it." Ali allowed herself to laugh for just a second.

Ali looked up and saw that they were already at her street, and Gavin and Lilly still had two more blocks until theirs. "I'll see you both later. I should get going before they send out the task force."

"Call us if you need anything," Gavin said, nudging Lilly to echo his sentiment.

"Yeah, what he said!"

She gave both of her friends a sad smile before starting the last leg of her journey. The sweat had gathered underneath Ali's jeans from the June heat, and she couldn't wait for the chance to put on her favorite cotton shorts. The sun was shining down on everyone's lawn today, making them look as if they were straight out of a magazine, but Ali felt anything but sunny inside.

Today marked precisely three years since Carter had gone missing. Gone missing? Ran away? Got kidnapped? It didn't matter what label the police created anymore to explain her brother's disappearance; all that Ali knew for certain was her life had become a seemingly endless nosedive after that summer night. In her own mind, she started calling it Doomsnight, as if it were some sick holiday the world should remember.

Ali looked up at her house standing before her and took a deep breath before opening her front gate. The creaking did little to mask the sounds of her parents' voices escalating from just inside her front door. Mr. DuBois was a successful attorney at the DuBois and Richmond Law Firm, so Ali guessed that meant her father could make his own hours and "work from home" whenever he chose to, like today. Ali didn't know if her mother had ever worked a day in her life, but today her mom was taking a break from her weekly afternoon massage and daily blowout she insisted she needed.

"Oh, great, they started early this year," Ali said to no one in particular, heading down the path to the door.

It wasn't as if Ali's parents never fought before Doomsnight. Hell, they were probably destined for divorce before they had stepped off the altar. When they were younger, it wasn't uncommon for Ali to wake up from a nightmare to the sounds of her parents bickering in hushed tones through the walls. Now, the hushed tones had turned into unapologetic screams, and the nighttime arguments progressed into midafternoon rows that refused to end until one parent stormed out of the room.

As she pushed open the wooden front door, Ali heard her mother's voice get louder with each syllable, as if challenging her father to push her over the edge. Neither of them had noticed she had walked in.

"I will not cancel the search party. I don't care what the accountant or the police or the lawyers advise us to do—their son isn't missing," Mrs. DuBois profusely insisted from the kitchen sink.

Every year since Doomsnight, her mother went knocking on each door through the otherwise silent cul-de-sac, badgering neighbors to help conduct a search party for her missing son. The first time around there had actually been a large turnout, much to Ali's surprise. But as the years passed the number of supporters dwindled, and now it looked like the search party consisted of only a few unwilling neighbors who didn't have the heart to say no to the crazy woman from down the road.

"You refuse to accept the fact that no one wants to look anymore. *I* don't want to look anymore," her father groaned. Even Ali knew her dad didn't have a chance of convincing her. He stood up and started pacing around the living room, taking deep breaths and running his hands through his hair incessantly. Bumping into the coffee table, he knocked his drink over so that it was now dripping onto the sparkling hardwood floor. Mr. DuBois grabbed a handful of napkins and began cursing under his breath as he wiped up the mess.

The living room opened directly into the kitchen, where her mother was standing cleaning her dishes. Ali stood in their hallway entrance, not making a sound and desperately wanting to figure out a way to make it to her bedroom without getting roped into this fight.

"Do you know what it's like, to follow you on your wild goose chase with the smallest shred of hope that we'll find a boy we might not even recognize?"

Her mom stopped washing dishes and stared at the soapy foam gathering under her fingers. With a whisper, she squeaked out, "I will always recognize my son." Silence filled the house as Ali listened, waiting for the worst to come.

"He wasn't only your son," her dad exclaimed with a fake sense of calmness that did little to hide the rage building in his voice. "I lost him, too. I just know how to face the truth and accept the fact that Carter is gone. The next time we'll see him is when the police call us to the morgue to identify the body." By the time the last syllable spilled into the air, the underlying rage had morphed itself into a fully formed beast that was looking directly at his wife's stunned face.

"How dare you—" Ali's mom started, but before she could continue Ali's dad had already raised his voice to drown out her cries. He was barely even looking at the woman he once loved.

Ali used to wonder what it would've been like to have two parents who utterly and profusely loved each other. A mom and dad who held hands on vacations, who hugged one another in family photos, or who cranked up the radio and belted out their wedding song when it came on once in a blue moon. Now, there was no room for wonder. There was barely room to process the madness that lived inside her house.

"Do you know what the neighbors say about us? About how we are desperate, deranged people who don't know how to accept reality? About how much the value of the neighborhood would increase if we moved out? The neighbors don't answer the door when you knock anymore for those reasons. I bet people mark their calendars every year so they know which day to ignore your incessant pleas at their doorstep. We are outcasts, and you do nothing to help us regain any sense of respect that I have worked tirelessly on ever since that summer."

His heavy breaths finally abated to the point where he dared to look his wife in the eyes. Ali's mom was now furiously wringing her hands over the sink. Ali's own heartbeat was slowly escalating, even though she was desperately trying to numb the emotions clawing at her chest. She wanted nothing more than to fade into the shadows in her hallway and pressed her body against the cool wall to remain out of sight.

"We were outcasts before that," her mom muttered through clenched teeth. "If you care more about our reputation than our child, I have officially lost every ounce of respect for you. I didn't think I even had any left."

Ali's jaw clenched, bracing for her father's response.

"Don't pretend that there was any hope for this family. We're lucky Alexandria at least has those two freak friends," he said with a short laugh that didn't reach his eyes. "But knowing you, you'll probably scare them off with your absurdity any day now."

Ali winced at the sound of her full name. She hated hearing all five syllables drawn out. The only person Ali enjoyed hearing say her name had been her grandmother, and now that she was gone, she didn't even let teachers call the first attendance without correcting them.

The gray walls around Ali closed in, and her breath was getting shorter with each passing minute. Ali braced onto the stone table in their hallway and felt her legs give way underneath her. A steady sweat had spread throughout her body, and her hands shook by her side. Her parents' screams were muffled now that a severe ringing had taken host in Ali's ears. She didn't know if this was what fainting felt like, but it seemed pretty damn close.

With a sudden burst of adrenaline that distracted Ali from the ringing behind her eyes, she knew she had to get out of the house. She had been wrong—her parents didn't care if she was home today. It wouldn't stop the yelling that usually woke up their neighbors in the middle of the night. If the fights were going to happen regardless of whether she was there, she might as well make a productive decision for once in her life and get out of this nightmare.

Without a second thought, Ali's legs carried her out the front door and across the perfectly manicured lawn before her brain could decide where she was going.

CHAPTER 2

THE FOREST

———

Over the years, Ali found that the least prickly and quickest entrance into the forest was through Mr. Hill's backyard. So now she sat, hiding behind the picket fence surrounding Mr. Hill's yard, waiting for the perfect time to launch her legs over the splintered wood and make a mad dash for the trees' entrance. There was a rumor that Mr. Hill hadn't left his house in ten years. Even though Ali wasn't the biggest proponent of rumors, especially after hearing the ones spread about her throughout Lorrshore High's halls, believing that Mr. Hill was a senile old man who never left the confines of this home gave her the confidence she needed to trespass onto his property.

Ali secretly wished she had planned a better escape route before she fled her house. But after a failed attempt to collect her thoughts at the edge of her neighbor's lawn, she quickly decided that it didn't matter where she was headed, as long as the path got her away from the black hole that was her house. Her legs carried her farther away from her parents' screams, but the tears gathering in her eyes skewed her vision and the stone houses started to blend together, creating a warped wall blocking Ali from escaping this nightmare.

Ali only felt perfectly content with who she was in two places in the world: her grandmother's house and the forest behind Mr. Hill's house.

As a child, she and Carter had found solace in their grandmother's house. The chipped wallpaper, dusty trinkets, and strange smell mirrored nothing of their own home, and the siblings loved it. What they loved even more were the outlandish stories about a mystical land filled with a castle, a valley of giant sunflowers, and dolphins as big as cars. Ali's favorite part was when her grandmother described the greatest battle the land had ever seen, filled with flying sparks and thunderous crashes heard from mountaintops. The details left Ali dreaming of this land—Infernus—for days. Carter and she would whisper about escaping there, even if only for a few days, to distract each other from the mayhem at home.

After their grandmother died, there were no more stories about dangerous battles or kings and queens, but the scenes never left Ali's sleep. After a while, they started to enter her daydreams. So that she wouldn't forget them, Ali detailed the dreams in a journal she hid in a place no one, not even Gavin or Lilly, knew about. And that's where her feet were taking her now.

When Doomsnight was still fresh and the search parties took the DuBois family through every nook and cranny of Lorrshore, there was one place that nagged at Ali's heartstrings like no other, and that was the forest. God knew that they—the police, the neighbors, her parents—searched through the trees for hours hoping to find a sign that Carter had run away into the foliage, but, just like every other forsaken place on their hunt, everyone came up empty handed.

What Ali's parents didn't know was that after those endless searches came to a close, Ali still frequented the forest, even though she wasn't sure why. It was something about nature's stillness that drew her closer with each step. A certain calm existed on the forest's surface, hiding its ecosystems under the fallen branches or behind the sun-kissed treetops. It wasn't her grandmother's house by any means, but, to Ali, it was the next best thing.

The only caveat was that entering the wooded sanctuary required breaking the law first.

Just then, she heard a faint echo of a phone ringing from the house. Focusing her hearing to pinpoint precisely where the sound was coming from, a wry smile crossed her lips when she registered the noise was coming from the front of the house. The kitchen, to be exact.

"Any minute now..." Ali mused as Mr. Hill's silhouette hobbled from his living room into the kitchen. As the ringing stopped and a man's voice uttered, quite loudly, "Hello," she knew it was now or never.

With a final breath, Ali leaped over the barrier and darted as fast as her legs would carry her. After one hop over the thorn bushes and a sharp left at the birch tree, she knew she was out of sight from the neighbors' prying gazes.

"Finally," Ali sighed as she let the trees become her allies and looked for the cardinals' nest in the branches. Someone once told her that a red cardinal meant a loved one was watching you from above, and even though Ali wasn't sure she believed in a divine something, she was definitely in need of some sort of guidance. She looked down and swore under her breath as blood trickled down her ankle and into her sock. The thorn bushes had won again.

"I guess the divine don't watch out for you when you're sneaking into an old man's yard," Ali mused to herself as she used a leaf to stop the bleeding from staining her Converse.

Before Ali could block them out, the memories of her father's words came flooding back into her mind.

Ali knew what everyone thought about her parents, and she didn't disagree. While her friends got cards from their parents and the neighborhood burst with laughter at their parties, her father looked at his daughter on the morning of her sixteenth birthday and said, "Happy birthday. Your mother left you a cookie cake on the counter," before he walked out the door without another word. Ali hadn't expected to get anything special, but she always thought that a card would've been nice. Hearing her father speak about Gavin and Lilly as if they were two random strangers sparked a burning rage inside her that refused to extinguish.

The sudden crunch of a twig brought Ali's focus back to the forest. A doe and her baby surveyed Ali as if asking her why she had crossed the threshold into the trees. In a trance, she stepped forward and, as gently as humanly possible, followed the deer through the brush.

The animals were tenderly wandering through the brush, gliding across the forest floor. A few dragonflies were following close behind the doe, keeping just far away from its swishing tail to avoid being swat. Besides the gentle creatures, the forest was still today. She was only a few minutes away from the hustle of the busy street and chatty neighbors, but Ali might as well have been in an entirely new world.

The deer stopped a few paces before they reached the tiny alcove where Ali kept her most prized possessions. She could've sworn the creatures turned back and looked at Ali before heading off to their next stop, practically confirming she had reached her final destination. As if they were old friends, Ali started to clumsily wave goodbye, but the gentle beasts had already camouflaged themselves among the greenery.

The sun peeked through the leafy treetops and formed a delicate light beam on her sanctuary. What was once nothing more than a boulder surrounded by a few rather large bushes had become Ali's secret hideout for the past three years. Under a pile of leaves, twigs, and other materials the forest provided were her favorite quilted blanket, a set of fake candles, a notebook bound with twine (but still bursting with pictures of her and Carter), and the journal where she recalled her grandmother's stories.

Ali bent down to grab one of the Polaroids that had fallen out of the bundle, quickly spotting Carter's smiling face looking up at her from his tenth birthday party. Complete with a *Lord of the Rings* birthday cake in front of him, the taste of bitter vanilla icing crawled into her mouth as she remembered its terrible flavor. Even though she had not been a fan of the cake or the pointy party hat cutting off circulation with a singular string under her chin, seeing her brother's eyes light up at the sight of his cake made the day one of their best.

The sounds of the happy birthday song echoed in Ali's head as a deep sigh escaped her mouth. She clutched the Polaroid, her knuckles going white from the grip. The knot in Ali's chest swelled at the thought of never finding Carter. Her father was undoubtedly confident that this year's search party was futile, and Ali didn't have the heart to tell her mother that a small part of her agreed. No matter how much her heart didn't want to accept the reality, her brain couldn't ignore the facts for much longer.

Carter and her grandmother had always been the forces that kept her sane when it came to her family. Living through the past three years without both of them didn't feel like living in the slightest. Ali liked to think of it as surviving a recurring nightmare every time she woke up in that house.

Suddenly there were tears streaming down her face.

Ali let out a long sob before she crumpled into a ball on her blanket. Wanting to disappear altogether, she hugged her knees and let the teardrops fall down her cheeks and onto the forest ground. The trees were no longer silent. Ali could hear birds fleeing their nests and squirrels chasing each other around the bark. Her sobs were no doubt echoing into their homes and upsetting these creatures, but living without her favorite people made for a difficult existence at times, and the weight of Ali's loneliness was crushing her shoulders.

"I wish I could stay here forever," Ali whispered between heaving breaths.

If the Lorrshore Sisters saw her now, they would've had enough material to run her out of school. Since she hadn't aired out the blanket before wrapping her body in it, her clothes were dusted in a coat of dirt. Ali's journal had gotten strewn about at one point and the Polaroid from Carter's birthday had a slight tear in it.

But, above all, Ali hated feeling sorry for herself. Using a meditation technique one of her therapists had taught her, she imagined herself back in his office, lying on the couch as a voice coached her through the rising fear swelling in her throat.

"*In, two, three, four. Out, two, three four. Let's repeat, Ali. Only a few more. How are you feeling now?*"

With her breaths in a rhythmic trance, the tears stopped flowing from her eyes.

"I'll have to tell Mark that actually worked this time," she said to no one in particular, knowing fully well she would never give her therapist that satisfaction.

Grimacing at the amount of dirt gathering around her, Ali concluded it was time to go for a walk. She unwrapped herself from the blanket and reorganized her valuables so that they were once again concealed from the outside world. Carefully checking to make sure she wasn't getting caught on any more thorn bushes, Ali stepped out of her sanctuary and followed a path she had found months prior.

Even though Ali couldn't see them, she knew the animals were watching her meander through the leaves. They were always watching, whether she wanted them to or not. And just as she was wondering what the woodland creatures thought of her, Ali saw something between the branches in front of her that made her catch her breath.

There was a tree in the distance that Ali was sure never existed before. Unlike the other birch and pine trees that made up the forest's infrastructure, this tree was a magnificent oak.

"This is southern New York, we don't have this kind of oak tree here," Ali muttered as she tried to discern how this forest giant had appeared out of thin air. From the creek that was home to minnows and tadpoles to the coyote's nest that barely got any light because it was hidden under so many branches, Ali was confident that she had explored every inch of this forest over the past three years. To her, the niches had become a puzzle she was determined to solve. And this tree was a new piece that needed to fit into the final picture.

A sweeping sense of curiosity masked the sadness Ali had been feeling moments ago. Before she had a rational second to think about her decision, she jogged up to the oak's base to get a closer look.

"What the…"

The bark was more breathtaking than she'd originally thought. Hundreds of spirals were carved into the wood. They started from the roots popping out of the ground and reached as high as Ali could see when she craned her neck. Her fingers hovered over the spirals, both big and small, almost intertwined with one another in the bark. This tree felt like it had a story it was trying to reveal to her, but she didn't know how to read the language yet.

After a fair number of minutes had passed by, Ali circled the base of the tree. While stepping over roots and blocking out the animal noises that often invaded the woods, Ali looked for any break in the pattern that could explain who had carved the design. Would there be one of those lame hearts with a couple's initials etched into its side? What about a plaque dedicating this tree to a lost grandfather or parent?

Ali was on her tiptoes, staring into the treetops above her when her eyes started to strain. Blinking, she looked down and noticed her amulet had started glowing a strange shade of green the more time she spent next to this leafy enigma. Suddenly, her necklace's string was pulling away from her body.

"Agh!" Ali screamed as her feet became rooted in place, unable to run away from whatever weird voodoo was happening.

Without any help from Ali, the emerald on the end of the black twine pulled away from her neck and started to float closer to the bark's spiraled center. Even though Ali thought she was already standing too close for comfort, her necklace disagreed.

Her feet still frozen in place, Ali resisted, in vain, the amulet's pull to the tree, her face mere inches from the intricate carvings. She braced herself against the bark, pushing her palms into the wood to counter the force of the gem. With each of Ali's attempts to free herself, the green stone seemed to glow a little bit brighter and pull a little bit harder on the twine so much that Ali thought it would surely break if it kept this up.

"What the *hell* is happening right now?"

Fear started to creep into Ali's body, and she looked around desperately for something that could help her break free. Goosebumps covered her arms, and it was getting difficult to hear anything over the surge of blood rushing to her ears.

But surely, she had to be dreaming. A dream would explain why Ali had never seen the tree before, why she was starting to smell something strangely familiar, and why her necklace had seemingly come to life and had its own agenda. But no matter how many times Ali pinched her skin, she didn't wake up.

Without warning, the emerald attached itself to one of the spirals' centers, and Ali panicked. Sweat was now collecting on her palms and no matter how many times Ali pulled at the twine, trying to rip it off, it refused to go over her thick black hair.

Now it wasn't only the emerald that was radiating a bright green—the tree itself had started to emanate a soft white glow. And, if her eyes weren't deceiving her, the spirals were now moving counterclockwise and getting faster with each passing second.

"Help me!" Ali was now in a full-fledged panic. For once in her life, she wished one of her nosy neighbors knew where she was or could at least hear her cries for help.

"Ali, is that you?" She didn't know if she were imagining her best friends' voices, but Ali prayed she was hearing correctly.

"Gav, Lilly, is that you?"

"Yes! Where are you? Why are you screaming? We're coming!" Lilly yelled.

"Follow my voice!" Ali screamed back, not wondering how her friends had managed to find her secret hideout. She was desperate to have Gavin and Lilly by her side now more than ever before.

As each second passed, Ali feared that her friends wouldn't reach her in time. She decided it was time to break the string. Even though she never let her necklace leave her side, Ali definitely wasn't going to risk getting suffocated by a possessed rock.

Hearing her friends' footsteps echoing through the forest's paths, getting closer by the second, Ali pressed her palm against the swirling wood one final time. Her attempts were futile. Her hand soon became stuck to the swirling wood as if it were dowsed in superglue.

The tree wouldn't let go.

Ali's final cry for help got caught in her throat as she watched the spirals in the oak's bark slowly pull away from one another to reveal a revolving black hole. A strange yet familiar smell—a combination of lavender, jasmine, and mud—filled her nostrils and wrapped itself around her body. Before she had time to blink, Ali's necklace plunged into the darkness. Her feet, so firmly planted on the ground moments before, followed suit, and Ali felt her body somersaulting forward into the woodland beast's stomach. The last sounds Ali heard before the darkness completely shut her out from the world were Gavin and Lilly screaming her name once more, but it was too late.

CHAPTER 3

THE TWO FRIENDS

Lilly watched as Ali walked away toward a house she didn't want to go home to. Even though every house in their cul-de-sac looked the same from the outside, the tension under her best friend's roof outdid any other home on the block.

"Do you think we should chase after her?" Gavin asked. She had a feeling he wanted her to have a more creative idea, but this time around, her inventive imagination was failing.

"No, that's too melodramatic for her," Lilly sighed back. "Ali won't like that we're treating her life like some basic rom-com. She has to deal with enough drama as it is with her parents."

"Yeah, you're probably right."

"Like I always am."

The truth was, Lilly wished all it took to get their friend out of her funk was for them to run through the streets after Ali and beg her to have a sleepover at one of their houses. If that were the case, Lilly would've been much more adamant about Ali coming over for dinner even though her mother's cooking couldn't attract a starving bear.

Desperate to change the subject to something a little lighter, Lilly brought up the first thought that came to her mind.

"So, why were you late meeting me outside today?" she asked, knowing the answer already.

"I don't know what you're talking about."

"Oh come *on*, Gav. I saw you ignoring my waves when you were checking to see if the Lorrshore Sisters had gotten out of class yet. You're just lucky I didn't tell Ali because she would have ragged on you about it for the rest of the summer."

Gavin slowed his strides to a stop before answering her. Lilly was just asking to get under his skin, and it was working.

"First of all, I wasn't waiting for them all to parade out of the building. And second of all, Amanda had asked me what I was doing this summer during homeroom. When she found out I was lifeguarding at her country club, she asked for my number so her parents could text me about being the guard on duty during her brother's next birthday party. I just forgot to ask when the party was."

"And you actually bought that?" Lilly threw her head back and let out a single laugh. Boys really were that oblivious.

"Yeah, of course I 'bought that.' Why wouldn't I?" Gavin inquired, forcing Lilly to roll her eyes at his ignorance.

"Gavin, be less like a teenage boy for once and use your brain. Amanda didn't want your number for her brother's birthday party. She wanted it so that she could show the rest of that miserable friend group that she got *the* Gavin's phone number. You'll probably be getting texts all summer long now," Lilly explained.

Amanda Winters had blatantly made fun of Lilly's alien shirt today, but that was far from why she was frustrated with Gavin. As a whole, the Lorrshore Sisters had suddenly taken an interest in her best friend the past year, starting by ogling him in the cafeteria to now finding fake excuses to flag him down in the hallway. Gavin might have enough brains to get himself through high school, but Lilly had taken it upon herself to protect him from all things evil-teenage-girl during their four years.

Ali and Lilly had been friends with Gavin since middle school, which meant that the three of them had survived the good, the bad, and the ugly, especially when each of them had their turn at getting braces. Since high school had rolled around and they were starting to leave those awkward years behind, girls had started to notice Gavin now that he wasn't locked in his basement playing video games for seven hours a day. But that didn't change the fact that she and Ali had been the ones to accept him and all his geekiness way back when, which should be what counts. At least, that's what Lilly told herself.

Stumbling over his words, Gavin had started to argue with her when Lilly saw a wisp of black hair flying past them from the corner of her eye. She turned her head just in time to see Ali darting across a row of yards in the complete opposite direction from her house.

"Gavin, turn around!" Lilly urged, physically moving his head into the direction she was pointing when he wouldn't follow her finger.

"Is that...?"

"Ali!" Gavin and Lilly both shouted in their best friend's direction, but even if she did hear them, it did nothing to slow her stride.

"So, do we chase after her now?" Gavin asked with a hint of distress behind his voice.

"Yes, we chase after her now, you idiot! Come on!"

They took off down the street, their legs not quite fast enough for Ali's speed. It took all but twenty seconds for the June heat wave to catch up with them and left beads of sweat sliding down their foreheads. Lilly threw one foot after another against the pavement, ignoring the cramps gathering in her side. What had happened that forced Ali to evacuate her house so quickly? What had it been, ten minutes since they last saw her?

"God *damn* she is fast," Gavin panted as he tried to keep up with Ali's path.

"Not the car!" he yelped. Lilly saw what had caused his concern—Ali had nearly collided with Gavin's mother's precious blue convertible.

"Oh, get *over* it! You'll live to see another day if the car gets a scratch on it!"

"You can be the one to tell her what happened to her 'third child' then," Gavin heaved, placing his hands on his knees while gasping for air.

Lilly let herself come to a stop. She momentarily gave up—they had already lost sight of where Ali was headed.

"We would've noticed where she went if you hadn't been trying to argue with me," Lilly snapped. "I guess now we know why Coach Dodds begged her to stay on the team."

"It doesn't help us much that she broke the school record for the mile. Also, I was not arguing with you. I was only clarifying that I was not flirting. I can't just ignore Amanda when she's sitting at the desk next to me. What am I supposed to do, put in my headphones and pretend I've gone deaf for the period?"

"That's exactly what you're supposed to do," Lilly countered as she decidedly started a fast-paced walk.

She silently concluded that it wasn't all boys who were this oblivious to the world, just Gavin.

"Just because Amanda didn't ask you to lifeguard her brother's birthday party doesn't mean—"

"Sh! I don't care about Amanda. Look over there." Lilly was pointing again. Only this time, her index finger focused directly on Mr. Hill's yard a few houses down from where they stood. And disappearing into his backyard was a pair of unmistakable white sneakers.

"What the? Why is she going in Old Man Hill's yard?" Gavin asked, Lilly only half hearing him.

"I don't know, but from the looks of things I don't think this is her first time maneuvering around that fence."

Mr. Hill, or Old Man Hill as Lilly had grown up knowing him as, didn't leave his property much, if ever. And for as long as she could remember, his house was the only house on the block that wasn't finished with clean stone cutting and a perfectly manicured yard.

Mr. Hill's house featured dull yellow paneling all around its exterior complemented with a combination of green and blue shutters outlining his windows. His wraparound porch was just as big as some of the neighbors', but instead of featuring a shiny new set of furniture every season, the porch swing was at least a decade old. It was guaranteed to give the unlucky sitter more than a few splinters, and the chipped white paint decorating the edges didn't add to its visual appeal. The rumor was the elderly man used to tend to his garden every week when he first moved to the neighborhood decades ago, but teenagers guessed that years of loneliness or insanity contributed to its demise. Now, no more than a few weeds and some twigs spotted the yard. The nicest, and perhaps the most normal, part about Mr. Hill's yard was the white picket fence that surrounded the property and sent a clear message to all the neighbors: stay out.

Ali, apparently, didn't hear that message loud enough.

"So, what do we do now?"

"You saw the way she ran away from us. Something's wrong. It is in our job description as Best Friends to find out why. We have to follow her," Lilly responded, determined to get to the bottom of Ali's strange behavior.

"I was hoping you wouldn't say that," Gavin groaned. "Why does it have to be Old Man Hill's yard? Why couldn't it be the nice woman who gives out cookies or the new family with the pool and who invited us to go swimming? My mom has always told me that I should stay away from 'the old bat,' as she puts it."

"Your mom also tells you to stay away from anyone who earns less than six figures. No offense," Lilly added when she saw Gavin trying to defend his mother. "Anyway, Ali always said that her grandmother said to be nice to Mr. Hill. Maybe he isn't that crazy after all, and it is just a bunch of rumors. You know how the people here like to talk."

"Yeah, maybe." Gavin added with more than a hint of doubt. "Either way, we need to find a way inside that fence if we have any chance at finding Ali."

Having regained their breath, they were able to pick up their pace and jog to the edge of the white stakes. Peering over the ledge, Lilly could see Mr. Hill pacing in his kitchen, holding something to his ear that she hoped was a phone.

"He's on the phone, we have to move now. Get ready to jump," she whispered to Gavin.

"Now? What do you mean now? Are you sure he's on the phone? Lilly!"

But Lilly already had one leg over the fence and was hurdling the second one before she had the chance to doubt her instincts.

"Come on, jump over! He's gonna see you if you don't go now!"

Gavin's athletic abilities were never really something to brag about, and it was clear he probably should have tried a little bit harder in gym this year. Steadying himself on the two wooden spikes in front of him, Gavin lifted his body with the little upper body strength he had and clumsily fell, face first, onto the pile of dirt waiting for him on the other side of the fence.

"Agh!" he gasped as he landed as gracefully as a ton of bricks.

"Gavin, get *up*! He's going to hear us!"

Lilly was already halfway to the forest's entrance when she heard the sound of a sliding door opening behind her and turned to see the old man shaking his fist at a hobbling Gavin. His groans weren't as stealth-like as he had hoped.

"Hey! What're you doing in my yard? Get back here! If you broke that fence your parents are paying for it!" Mr. Hill yelled from the doorway.

Lilly couldn't help but take a second to get a few laughs in. "I'm sorry, but that was just so funny," Lilly managed to utter in between chuckles. "In my defense, I told you to go earlier. Also, your leg is bleeding."

"Dammit, those thorn bushes are way too high."

"Or you just need to jump higher," Lilly retorted, half to herself since she knew Gavin's ego had taken enough damage for one day. "Let's go. We have to find out where Ali went."

"Where even are we?"

They looked at their foreign surroundings—a vast forest filled with shadows and animals that were invisible to the untrained eye. Different shades of green plastered practically every inch of the space in front of them. From the moss trickling its way up the bark to the blades of grass hiding insects scavenging for food, Gavin and Lilly simultaneously turned to each other in awe.

"Do you think Ali knows her way around here?" Gavin wondered out loud.

"If there's anything I've learned about Ali, it's that I should never underestimate what that girl is capable of. She could have a secret lair in China, and it wouldn't surprise me."

"Well, she definitely came in here, and I didn't potentially sprain my ankle for nothing. Let's at least start to look before she gets even farther in this jungle."

As if being pulled on an invisible string, they searched a long-forgotten path. Lilly could feel the silent stares stemming from the branches as they peeked around every tree trunk and turned over old nests, but she ignored them. Acknowledging them meant that the eeriness became real. The unfamiliar soil was tearing the bottom of her pants and caking the soles of Gavin's shoes as they stepped over brush as tall as her waist. Before long, they had silently delved farther into the forest before realizing they no longer had any sense of direction.

"Do you think she's still in here?" Gavin asked, low enough it was almost a whisper.

"I don't know. At least Ali knew her way around in here. We've just been getting ourselves lost for the last half hour," Lilly groaned with frustration.

Lilly practically felt herself decide to keep going. She couldn't give up—she never did, not even the time five teachers and a guidance counselor tried telling her that she wasn't allowed to use the school parking lot as a canvas for her final art project. The next day the school walked outside and saw her painting the white lines different shades of pastels that eventually would make up her mural.

"Wait, Lil, look. Over there by those bushes, it looks like there's a towel or something." Gavin pointed with his index finger.

"Yeah, and it might belong to someone claiming the woods as their home," Lilly replied, but Gavin was already off to investigate.

She watched as he gingerly stepped over the brush into a small patch of dirt that had been cleared of all roots and unfriendly creatures. He reached down to grab the blanket that had caught his attention moments before, but before he began to rise, Lilly noticed Gavin unfolding its corners to reveal the secret treasures hidden inside.

"What are *those*?" Lilly's voice echoed against the trees, but silence followed from her friend.

"Helloo, Earth to Gavin. I said, what are those?"

"What? Oh, sorry, Lil. You gotta look at these." Gavin started passing Ali's hidden possessions over to her.

From one look, Lilly knew these were Ali's belongings, starting with the fake candles. Lilly used to poke fun at her since Ali would die to get her hands on a quality candle, but she was also weirdly obsessed with only lighting them in one corner of her room. She would never bring real candles to a forest, but the fake ones would provide her with some sense of serenity.

"Gavin, that's her favorite blanket. Her grandmother made it for her before she left," Lilly whispered as she grabbed the cloth in hand.

"After Carter died, Ali gathered some of her grandmother's possessions that were left to the family and hid them in her room. I remember seeing this blanket in the stash one night. She made me swear not to tell anyone."

"You talk about her grandmother as if she never passed away."

"In Ali's mind, I don't think she ever really did. From the way she talks about her, it's as if she's waiting for Ali to get home every day after school." Lilly had only met her a few times before she passed, but immediately she sensed there was a presence about the old woman. Her aura reminded Lilly of a warm hug or a plate of cookies, but there was a strength behind her being that far surpassed her own grandma.

The blanket was tattered, and the seams were coming loose, but Lilly could see why it was so important to Ali. The stitches held clues to a magical world Ali and her grandmother shared together. When they were younger, a glazed look would cross over Ali's face as she would describe her grandmother's tales. Especially at eight years old, she had to agree they were larger than life. The two would sit in Lilly's backyard and pretend they were the ones protecting some faraway land from the villains with their own magic sprouting from sticks and fallen branches sprawled across the yard. Now Lilly could see the stitches in the blanket sketched out these tales in incredible detail, as if by the same magic Ali and she pretended to possess all those years ago.

While Lilly was busy tracing the stitches and wracking her brain trying to remember the details of Ali's stories, Gavin was rifling through the rest of the pile. Out of the corner of her eye, she saw Gavin easily pluck out a torn picture of Carter's birthday party that was sticking out from the top.

Both looked at the image in Gavin's hands and struggled to find words. Ali talked about Carter almost as much as she talked about her grandmother, which was to say, almost never.

"I can't imagine it's easy for her to look at these pictures," Gavin added after what felt like an eternity of silence. Even the animals stopped scurrying around the tree trunks to watch what the two strange friends would do next.

"I knew I should've made her come to my house after school. I knew she wouldn't be okay going back to that house," Lilly croaked out with tears escaping her eyes. She tried to wipe them away almost immediately because she knew Gavin wasn't very good at emotions, but she wasn't quick enough. He was already awkwardly shifting from side to side.

"Hey, Lil, don't worry. You couldn't have known she was going to disappear on us like this. It's not your fault."

"No, it is. I don't mean this in a bad way, but you weren't as close with Ali and me before Carter disappeared. You didn't see how it changed her."

"What do you mean? Wasn't Ali always a slightly introverted, rage-against-the-machine type girl?"

"Yes and no," Lilly chuckled. "Ali was more comfortable around people when Carter was still around. Not a ton, but more than now. She laughed more. She smiled when she would talk about their silly fights, and she would use any chance she had to talk about how Carter was going to be a famous artist one day. He was only ten, but his drawings were like nothing I'd ever seen before.

"It didn't matter that her parents' fights were getting worse or that they were spending more time holed up in one of their rooms. She never complained about what was going on because she had someone going through it with her." By the time she had finished, Lilly was telling herself Ali's story as much as she was telling Gavin. She had forgotten what her friend was like all those years ago.

"Wow. So after Carter disappeared, that part of Ali disappeared too."

"Yeah, yeah I guess you could say that. It was only three years ago, but it feels like everything has changed since then."

A few more minutes passed as the pair carefully put back Ali's belongings exactly how they found them. Lilly knew they had just unintentionally invaded their best friend's privacy, and she made Gavin agree they would never tell Ali about the discovery. It would be a funny story once they were all old and in the same retirement home, but for now, she preferred omission.

"So, now what?" Gavin wondered aloud as he spun in a circle trying to regain any sense of direction.

"I don't know," Lilly answered. She never liked to say she didn't have a solution to a problem, but this was not a situation Lilly had ever prepared herself for. The images of a younger Ali and Carter were still swirling in her mind, and she wasn't about to give up on her best friend.

"Gav, try texting her. My phone's almost dead, but maybe she'll respond if she knows we're looking for her."

"I tried that already. There's no service here, these damn trees must block everything." Gavin held up his cell phone in search of a signal, but Lilly knew she would have to think of another idea.

"Do we call the police? Someone over there has to know how to track Ali down. Or if we give them her sock or something maybe those dogs can sniff her out within the hour."

"I don't think so. If Ali knows this forest better than anyone, she wouldn't put herself in any physical danger. The police also might laugh at us if we try to tell them Ali DuBois has gone missing on the three-year anniversary of Carter's disappearance. I'm sure Mrs. DuBois has already called the chief about this year's search party, and if we add a runaway Ali to the mix, they might think it's all a big joke."

Partially because she was energetically drained (she'd forgotten to recharge her crystals this morning) and partially because Gavin's ankle was swelling up again, she mumbled in agreement with him.

"Fine, we won't call the police. Either way, we're still faced with a major problem here—Ali is missing. Hopefully she is still in this godforsaken forest, but we have no idea which direction to start walking in."

As if on cue, a scream echoed through the trees.

"Help me!"

It was Ali. Lilly turned her head to Gavin, and her eyes widened as the reality of the situation set in—Ali was in trouble, and they were the only two who could hear her.

Gavin had apparently come to the same realization and, without warning, took off in the direction of Ali's pleas.

"Please be okay, Ali. Please be okay," Lilly begged as she followed Gavin's lead and began to blindly run toward the outcry. There wasn't a reality where Ali wasn't Lilly's closest confidant. Losing her wasn't an option.

"Ali, is that you?" The two yelled while running, fully knowing the answer to their question.

"Gav, Lilly, is that you?"

"Yes! Where are you? Why are you screaming? We're coming!"

"Follow my voice!"

"Her voice? Is she kidding me? Maybe some directions would be helpful," Gavin muttered in between gasps of air. His adrenaline was catching up with him and that wave of agility was slowly waning.

"Oh, get over it! Ali sounds like she's being attacked by a bear right now. Do you really think she can focus her energy on giving you directions?" Lilly took the lead and was trying to follow Ali's voice, but even she had to admit she would've appreciated a little more guidance.

"Ali, where are you? Keep screaming if you can hear me!" The forest had gone silent, and Lilly's words echoed with no response. Something had happened, but neither friend could place their finger on what it was.

A million possibilities ran through Lilly's mind. Had the bear gotten to Ali? Was there someone else in the forest with them? Gavin had reassured her that Ali wouldn't put herself in any danger, but what if he was wrong?

A few seconds ago, the forest seemed to have been running with them. The leaves were swaying, the birds were flying from branch to branch, and she could've sworn she saw a few squirrels keeping pace with their strides. Now, the forest was still—the branches were no longer moving, the birds had returned to their nests as if hiding from whatever was lurking in between the trees, and the squirrels had stopped trying to keep up with them. Something, or someone, was holding them back from coming this far into the forest, but Lilly and Gavin didn't have that option. They knew Ali's screams had come from this direction. What they didn't know was why they had stopped.

"Do you think someone took her?" Lilly squeaked out. "They can't have, right? We would've heard that. We're even closer to her than we were when we heard her screaming. We wouldn't have missed it if they'd taken her out of here, right?"

It was obvious Gavin couldn't come up with an answer that would make her feel any better, probably because the same exact questions were going through his brain. Instead, he trudged toward the eerie silence before stopping dead in his tracks.

"Lilly, look."

Confused by his sudden change of tone, Lilly looked in the direction Gavin was zoned in on, but saw nothing.

"This doesn't belong here. Do you see that glow? It's pulsing, like it's a lifeline."

"What are you talking about? What's over there?" she asked, concerned about her friend's mental state. No matter how much she rubbed her eyes, she couldn't spot anything out of the ordinary.

Gavin climbed the small ridge next to them and began to move his hands in a strange pattern, tracing spirals in the air.

"This bark is moving! You have to come see this. Every inch of this tree is covered in this weird, confusing pattern. I don't know where it stops or starts, what the..." He trailed off, his fingers still fumbling along the open air.

"Cut it out. This isn't the time for jokes." Lilly's voice was strong but trembled at the last syllable. One friend was missing and the other was seeing imaginary trees. This was not looking like it was going to be a good day.

Lilly's words forced Gavin to divert his attention.

"What do you mean, what am I looking at? Don't you see this gigantic glowing tree in front of us?"

Lilly looked at him like he had lost his mind. Even when she took several glances between Gavin and the clearing, her facial expressions didn't change.

"Come on, stop playing around. I appreciate you trying to make light of this situation, but I'm really not in the mood. Can you please help me keep looking?"

"Lilly, I'm telling the truth! How do you not see this thing? It's huge, it's glowing, and the wood is doing some weird *Lord of the Rings* crap. Look, watch my hand follow the pattern and tell me you don't see what I'm seeing."

Instead of waiting for him to continue to trace the invisible pattern, Lilly watched Gavin's hand get attached to the air as if by superglue. He was struggling to pull it away, but the more frequent his thrashing became the more it looked like he wouldn't be able to move from his spot.

"Oh no," Gavin gulped.

"Oh no? What do you mean, 'Oh no'?"

"I know you probably don't believe me and think I'm just doing this to be funny, but I'm really not. These spirals are speeding up, like they're...unraveling? This is...this is crazy. How do I make it stop?" Gavin began to tug on his "stuck" hand with his free one, but he still wasn't budging from his spot.

"Lilly, I am stuck to this tree, and I can't move my hand. I need you to grab my other hand and pull me as hard as possible in the other direction." He threw out his hand toward her and his eyes were pleading for help, but Lilly couldn't bring herself to play along.

"Gavin, I'm tired of this. I hope you're happy, because along with losing one best friend, you have managed to piss off the other one. Now, I am going to continue my one-man search party with or without your help. Have fun playing out your weird tree fantasy."

After that, everything was a blur and neither friend was sure exactly what had happened.

"Bla-black hole! In the tree!"

Tired of the games, Lilly had already started turning her back on him and was about to storm off in the opposite direction. In one last ditch effort for freedom, Gavin reached out and grabbed Lilly's shirt by its hem before she could get any farther, but it was too late to escape. His body had already started giving way to the tree and, before Lilly could protest and shake Gavin's hand loose, she was dragged off her feet and into the bark. Once more, the black hole started shrinking and the spirals started slowing themselves down, erasing all evidence that the two teenagers were ever there.

CHAPTER 4

EXPLORING THE RABBIT'S HOLE

Sliding toward oblivion was not how Ali had expected to die.

Not that she had given the subject serious thought, but when her mind did wander off in that direction, she imagined herself lying in a hospital bed of old, old age, gently drifting toward a forever sleep. In the end, it didn't matter because here she was a few seconds away from imminent death at the bottom of a killer tree.

And then she hit the ground with a thud.

For the next five seconds, Ali's eyes remained closed while her body waited for some type of god to whisk her away into the afterlife. It wasn't until she was sure nothing was happening that she slowly opened her eyes and blinked a few times, giving her pupils a chance to adjust to the darkness surrounding her.

Considering Ali had been convinced she was sliding to her death, she hadn't given much thought to what the inside of a tree trunk would look like. But it didn't seem like she was in a tree at all. In fact, this strange place was more like a forgotten room a princess was locked in before her destined prince came to her rescue.

Ugh, gross.

After a few more moments of silence and pinching her own skin for reassurance, Ali knew that she wasn't dead. Instead, panic began to crawl into her veins and make its way through her bloodstream.

Death was starting to sound like the better option.

The walls were closing in around her as Ali began losing track of her breath. She was back in the moment her mom told her that Carter was missing, alone with no light to turn toward. What had happened in the seconds before she fell? Even in her state, Ali pieced together that the tree had trapped her, supergluing her fingers to its bark and mocking her as she tried to pry them away. Her mind replayed the moment those swirling spirals opened into a vortex she had no chance of escaping. Her necklace led with force as it pulled Ali's body forward and uprooted her feet from the stable earth.

Her necklace.

Ali immediately reached to grab the string hanging around her neck and breathed a silent sigh of relief when the stone was still in its place. At least there was some trace of reality in this disturbed fantasy.

But, where *was* she? Ali couldn't help but feel that some part of this was normal, almost like she'd been here before, maybe traveled to it in a dream. She stumbled to her feet and shook the dust off her hands. This really was a filthy place. Dirt and grime covered the walls, as if no one had bothered to clean them for years. Under about an inch of filth, Ali was able to make out the stone edges and tried gripping them, glancing up to see how far a climb it would be to make a break for it.

About fifteen feet up was a stone ceiling that didn't leave an inch of crawling room. Well, that was a dead end. Could anyone hear her if she screamed up the chute that had thrown her to the floor? Ready to test her theory, Ali's heart sank as she saw the tunnel growing smaller by the second before closing itself off altogether, taking with it any connection to reality she had left.

How would anyone find her now? Would they even realize she was missing? Wait—Lilly and Gavin had heard her screams before they were snuffed out. Ali was questioning her sanity, but she knew that was real. Had she screamed loud enough for her friends to hear her? But, if the tunnel was closing, how would they be able to reach her?

"Help, someone please! Help!" Ali found her voice as the desperation in her pleas increased. She was almost certainly trapped down here, possibly for the rest of her life, and it was all her fault. If only she hadn't followed the siren call of that stupid tree. If only she hadn't jumped that stupid white picket fence. If only she hadn't acted on the urge to run away from her parents...

Her parents. Now, thanks to her, they had two missing children. How long would it be before her mother put together a search party for her daughter? A search party that would end in failure, causing more pain, more tears, and more fights between the two people who brought her into this world. A search party that would leave the police questioning her parents' sanity once more.

And Ali had no one to blame but herself.

The tears welled before she had the chance to realize she was panicking. She had cried more today than she had in years, but there was no point in trying to stop the waterworks. The sliver of hope Ali had been holding on to left through the tears painting streaks down her cheeks. Not only would she never get to hug her baby brother again, but she'd never get to laugh at another bad joke Gavin made or entertain Lilly's conspiracy theory rants. All the little memories she'd taken for granted were slipping through her fingers, and she couldn't grab them before they were lost to the air in front of her.

In the midst of losing all hope, one memory did come back to Ali from the deep recesses of her mind. It was just after Carter had disappeared and her parents had stuck her in therapy. Ali hadn't been able to get through her second session without experiencing her first anxiety attack. As her therapist's voice became fainter the sound of blood pulsing through her veins became louder, and Ali felt a weight slowly crushing her chest inward, leaving her no room to gasp for air. Her vision blurred and she clamped her eyes shut, furiously closing and opening her fists in an effort to feel. After an eternity passed, Ali's ears picked up a voice in the background. It was her therapist, repeating the same five steps to escape the attack. If it worked then, it was worth a shot now.

Five things she could see. Ali opened her eyes, which she didn't even know were closed, and immediately saw a pair of mud-stained Converses covering her feet.

"Okay, that's one. Now four more."

Again, Ali's left hand instinctively went to her neck and pulled out her necklace in front of her eyes. In her right hand, she gripped her cell phone and pressed its buttons, hoping for a miracle. For a moment, the light flickered to reveal a cracked screen before fading away. It was no use, the phone was busted. Emitting a frustrated groan, Ali turned her attention to the torch mounted to the right of her head.

"Wait, who lit this torch?"

Satisfied with her subdued anxiety levels, Ali tucked the phone into her back pocket and grabbed the torch from its mount in the wall. The fire was hot and wrapped Ali's body in a sheet of warmth she happily accepted. But while her bones stopped shivering, she was still trying to piece together how the flame started burning in the first place.

The panic leaving her body was replaced with that same sense of curiosity that drew her to that magic tree. A voice in the back of her mind tried to keep this curiosity at bay, but the brewing questions easily silenced that voice.

The puzzle pieces were moving around, working to connect one another and create the final picture, but something was missing. Again, Ali had the strange feeling that this place belonged to a distant memory that was buried too far down for her to recall.

"How did someone get in here?" she wondered aloud, spinning in a circle until her feet stopped but her body felt like it was still on a ship. Ali was surrounded by four solid walls and an airtight ceiling. Even if someone did somehow open the portal-like-tunnel to the forest again, there was no way they would be able to climb out in time.

Logically, nothing made sense. But Ali was slowly starting to learn that nothing about her situation was logical.

"Think, Ali, think. What would Carter do right now?"

The answer came to Ali before she could even finish the sentence. Carter, even more than his sister, was enthralled with new adventures. Much to their parents' chagrin, Carter thrived on fairy tales and could make anyone around him think they were being chased by knights on horseback. Granted, children were far more advanced than adults when it came their imaginations.

Channeling her little brother's energy, Ali set off to explore the stones that surrounded her with as much imaginative spirit she could muster. The walls looked like they hadn't been touched in ages, but that didn't stop Ali from trying to pry loose stones from their settings or scraping her feet along the floor to expose a trap door. After covering whatever white patches had been left of her Converses in a fresh layer of dirt, she decided that the trap door theory was as dead as the cell phone in her back pocket.

Over the next few minutes, the only sounds were Ali's breaths catching every so often when she thought she'd made a discovery. Key word being thought.

There seemed to be no way out of her cell. And after each failed attempt to escape, Ali was becoming acutely aware that the last food she'd had to eat that day was a pair of granola bars she'd shoved in her backpack on the way out her door that morning. At this point, the dirt was starting to look appetizing.

Shaking her head to snap herself out of it, Ali pushed the thought of food far away.

Ali, come on. You're being ridiculous. Carter would not have given up this easily.

She silently cursed her conscience. Promising herself that, if she ever got out of this literal hellhole, she would have a long talk with the voice inside her head about allowing herself to self-pity every once in a while.

And that's when things got weird.

Tripping over her worn-out laces, Ali reached to brace herself on the wall as she fell forward. Not thinking, she let the torch fall from her hand. It landed with a thud on the ground near her feet. Her shadows instantly disappeared from the four walls, and she was alone with her thoughts.

That is, until she started to notice a light emanating from her necklace. Now that the flame was gone, she could see the green pulse as clear as day. She held her breath as she thought back to the moment the string almost suffocated her. But this feeling was different. The necklace didn't have any sort of urgency attached to it, rather, Ali felt that it was trying to guide her in the right direction. Like a lighthouse points a ship to shore, leading it to safety.

Ali gently grabbed the stone between her fingers and held it closer to the wall. Her eyes grew wide as she noticed the light start to shine brighter and pulse faster the more she moved it along the rocks, silently signaling that she was on the right track. Without any help from her hand, Ali felt the necklace hitch forward and seal itself into a crevice in between two rocks she hadn't noticed before. The stone fit perfectly.

Just as it had done in the tree, the necklace wouldn't dislodge from the crack in wall. Even though something was telling her this was supposed to happen, Ali tripped on air as the floor started to shake and dust particles scrambled to settle into their new homes. She kept her eyes trained on the ground, waiting for the fault to open up. That's what happened in earthquakes, right?

But this wasn't any earthquake. Instead of a crack splitting the floor, the wall in front of Ali began to fade away. The rough edges were replaced with the nothingness of air and, even though the ground continued to quake, no stones were falling to her feet. Her necklace, still shining, fell back to her body when the stones it was lodged between started to disappear. It had done its job. As the last bit of wall faded from view, Ali looked forward into the long hallway that had been hidden by a very steady wall.

She couldn't tell how long the shaft was or where it led, but was relieved to find the path was lined with torches along both walls. They flickered against the ancient stone, inviting Ali toward their light. With nowhere left to turn, she began to walk.

"So, this is how someone got into that room," Ali mused to herself as her steps echoed down the path. She still had questions but was focusing on one at a time to keep her brain from falling into another frenzy, a second trick her therapist had taught her she would never admit actually worked. That was, if she even saw someone from her life again.

As the questions kept coming, Ali reached to the wall and grabbed one of the torches from its holder. Bits of ash fell on her arm and black smears were left as she brushed them away. Not that she minded much—her face was already covered in dirt, and her body felt like it had been tossed around in a couple of angry waves. For the first time, Ali gave herself the chance to stop and think about what had happened to her over the last few hours.

Earlier today, Ali had been sitting in her last homeroom of the year, wishing desperately to be anywhere but Lorrshore High School.

"Guess that wish came true."

But Ali was still unsure if this new, foreign land was one she should be afraid of. Even though anxiety kept crawling up her back, she couldn't help but feel that something had called her to this place. Maybe these halls belonged to an ancient cult, sworn to secrecy and destined to do their bidding from the depths of the earth. There had to be a reason that tree appeared to her today, of all days. Today, on the anniversary of her brother's disappearance. On the anniversary of when her world started to fall apart.

Before she could give too much thought to the strange coincidence, the light from Ali's torch caught something appearing on the wall. A drawing, no, many drawings, revealing themselves to her as if Ali had uttered a secret password. Stepping closer and running her fingers along the inky lines, Ali's breath hitched.

From what she could make out, the strokes were telling a story, but not the type she would've read about in her textbooks. And, like the spirals in her tree, the pictures were moving.

The images took Ali's breath away. She inched forward, running her dirt-clad fingers along the wall. Bringing the fire closer to the stone, her fingers steadied as they glided along the markings, trying to solve the mystery posed in front of them.

The etchings were moving, shifting with every glance.

The flames danced along the cave walls and gave life to the story being told. The individual lines were inching closer to one another, forming the silhouette of a striking woman with thick, braided hair down her back and a long, flowing dress wrapping around her.

At first, the woman was in some sort of castle, surrounded by blossoming flowers on either side and large crowds of people in front of her, all turning their attention to her as if her presence entranced them.

"Is this some sort of coronation?" Ali wondered aloud, her words bouncing between the walls before fading into the silence.

The transition to the next scene was slow at first. Then, the individual lines quickly rearranged themselves to from a new picture, just as clear as the last. The braided woman was still there, only this time she stood alone, surrounded by trees as tall as skyscrapers.

She held a staff in her right hand as she raised her left over her head and moved it in circular motions. Ali let out an audible gasp as she saw that the staff wasn't a staff at all—it was a wand.

There were short, jagged lines appearing on the wall where magic would've been shooting from her wand's tip. Deer, squirrels, and birds began to reveal themselves to the woman, surrounding her in a circle. Their movements began to match the wand's strokes, moving their heads up and down as her fingers did the same. The woman was practicing her magic, and they were all under her spell.

The scene ended and was replaced by another, now farther down the tunnel. Making a conscious effort to relax her muscles, Ali rolled her shoulders and carefully made her way down the drafty tunnel, afraid that if she caused too much motion, the scenes would disappear altogether. Even though she was holding the flame close, the warmth that had enveloped her body earlier was gone.

As Ali approached the wall where the next episode was coming together, her eyes grew an inch wider when she saw there were now two women. The first woman was still there, only she looked to be older. Her cloak had a few tears, and her face showed a few more wrinkles in the forehead, but there was no question this was the same person from the earlier images. The same braid trailed down her back and her wand remained in hand. The landscape had also changed—the tall trees had been replaced by sharp mountain peaks, and there were no animals in sight.

The second woman was making her grand debut on the opposing side of the mountains. She, too, had a wand in her hand and was just as beautiful as the first. Only, Ali felt that there was an air of darkness around her. Where the first woman was first seen surrounded by flowers and throngs of people, the second was completely and utterly alone. Flowers wilted as she glided toward her counterpart. Her hair was pulled into a high bun without a strand out of place, and her cloak was perfectly sewn together, no tears in sight. Both women gracefully approached the mountain's peak and pointed their wands at one another, taking a fighting stance.

The movements became faster as the next scene progressed, as if the cave itself wanted the story to reach its zenith. Sparks shooting from both women's wands exploded in midair, colliding with one another's power. The sheer force of the blows was pushing each woman back down the mountain, making it harder to aim with enough accuracy to protect themselves.

Both figures, who minutes ago seemed so calm and collected, were transformed into a frenzy of lines and dashes. Ali could hardly make out the difference between the two. What Ali gathered was that the woman from the coronation scene was using the rocky terrain around her to create some sort of shield, the stones bending and shaping to her will. Just like the woodland animals, these rocks were under the wand's spell. With her other hand, she levitated one stone at a time, stacking them atop one another until they formed a cluster large enough to barricade the side of a freeway.

From the opposing side, sharp lines were appearing from the dark witch's wand. Only, it seemed like she didn't know how to use the elements around her like the braided witch did—or, at least, she was choosing not to. Even though her magic was clearly powerful, for every three shots she fired, only one came remotely close to the target. Her feet continued to slip down the slope, taking her stamina with them.

The scene changed for a final time. Ali took a sharp inhale when she looked above the two figures, both fighting with every inch of power their bodies could spare. The dark witch didn't see the giant heap of rocks floating a few stories above her head, distracted by her adversary's constant blows. In one final effort to end the battle, the first woman emerged from behind the rock and brought her hands down in one fell swoop.

Ali could only imagine what was running through the woman's mind as she looked up and saw a wall of rock ready to attack. How could one prepare for such an ending to their life?

The dark witch shot one final spell from her wand before the rocks snuffed out whatever magic remained. Half the swirling shapes and lines disappeared from the image. Now, the picture was barely moving, and it returned to an eerie calmness. Little clouds of dust appeared where the rocks lay on top of the woman's body. The pictures began to fade into the side of the wall, but before they vanished completely, Ali saw that the single woman was now bent over, clutching her side. The last spell her opponent cast had hit her, but the cave didn't want to reveal this woman's fate too.

The wall became just a wall once again. Noticing her knuckles had turned white from clutching the torch's base, Ali loosened her grip and felt her entire body release. There was a part of her that questioned whether she had imagined the images, her mind playing tricks on her in this new environment, but at the same time she had been questioning whether any of this was real from the second the tree telepathically grabbed her necklace.

Her necklace. It was pulsing again, but Ali had not noticed because she'd been hypnotized by the story in front of her.

"Why does it keep glowing?" she asked herself, half hoping for a response from the enchanted wall in front of her.

The wall didn't disrupt the silence surrounding Ali, but in that moment a loud bang echoed from deeper down the tunnel. Ali hadn't heard any noise besides flames crackling and her own murmurs since she arrived, so the sudden noise startled her more than she cared to admit. The consequences to her fright were a bit more serious—she dropped her torch.

Whoosh.

The second her flame touched the cool ground the light extinguished. And it wasn't just her torch, every torch in the cave went out. Besides the green glow from her necklace, Ali was in total darkness.

That same panicky feeling Ali had felt before quickly started to take over her mind. Without any light, she couldn't see if someone—or *something*—was trying to sneak up on her. At least in Ali's world, she knew the typical suspects to look out for in the wild: bears, wolves, those killer mosquitos she once watched a documentary on. In this world, Ali knew nothing.

"Stop. Stop. Stop. Now."

Ali was yelling into the darkness to drown out the chaos her own thoughts were creating. A black cloud was forming over the reasoning parts of her brain, and soon there would be nowhere left for the voice inside her head to turn. Her palms began to sweat.

"One one-thousand, two one-thousand, three one-thousand, four," she repeated to herself as she tried to control her breaths, but it wasn't working. The shallow breaths were becoming more frequent, and she felt her body turning in circles, but once she stopped spinning, she didn't know what direction she was facing. If she kept walking, would she end up in the room she came from? Or would she walk directly into the wall that had just showed her some strange story for some even stranger reason?

"Maybe walking into the wall is the better option," Ali decided, unsure if she was speaking in her mind or aloud. Taking a leap of faith, Ali put one foot out into oblivion, but before it hit the floor, something caught her attention.

Out of the corner of her eye, Ali saw the faintest flickering of light in the distance. Her heart jumped back into place, and she started to regain her composure, but her mind was still racing faster than she could comprehend. This could be her way out! Back into the forest with Gavin and Lilly, where she could forget any of this ever happened.

But what if it didn't lead her to the forest? What if it was a trap, drawing her deeper into danger with no signs of escape?

Where am I?

Ali kept repeating the question to herself as she hastily walked down the corridor. She felt delirium beginning to set in as she got closer to her destination. Now she was close enough to see that the light was coming from around a corner, which meant this tunnel wasn't a one-way cavern after all. She had kept her head down while walking toward the fire to make sure she didn't trip on anything in front of her, but without realizing it, she had already come to the crossroads and the light was now burning beside her.

"Where am I?" Ali repeated to herself one final time.

"Why, you're in Infernus, of course," a familiar voice answered.

Stunned, Ali slowly turned around to see who had suddenly appeared next to her, gasping as she took in a face she knew all too well.

She was staring at herself.

"Welcome, Alexandria, to the City of Infernus."

CHAPTER 5

MEETING ROYALTY

"Lilly?"

"Gavin?"

"Where are we?"

"I have no idea."

The tree's chute threw the pair to the ground. They landed with a thud, causing a cloud of dust to rise around them and throw Gavin into a coughing attack before he could take in their strange surroundings. The dust plumed, and the dim light of the open tunnel illuminated each tiny particle. Suddenly, it looked like there were hundreds of glowing fairies dancing in the musty room that had not seen light for far too long.

Lilly was the first to stand up. Still processing what had just happened to them, Gavin looked over and saw her legs beginning to wobble and her knees caving in toward the solid dirt floor. Before gravity forced Lilly to the ground, he found his footing and grabbed her arms, steadying her until he stopped feeling the shaking in her bones. Still holding on to each other, Gavin held Lilly's gaze for the first time since falling into the tree's trunk.

"Are you okay?"

"I think so," Gavin croaked out, not daring to say more. He didn't know why, but he felt at ease for the first time all day. More importantly, he didn't feel like trying to explain why to Lilly.

"Yeah, I think I am too. No broken bones, but I am going to wake up with a few wicked bruises tomorrow morning," Lilly quipped, but her voice cracked midsentence. Normally, Lilly was the one shoving Gavin toward dangerous schemes that could get him kicked out of school, but this was different. He tilted his head back and narrowed his eyes toward the channel that had tossed them both to the ground, quickly realizing there was no way they were going to get back the way they came.

"That can't be good," Lilly whispered, following Gavin's gaze. "Why isn't there light on the other end?"

Gavin barely heard her. He moved along the walls, feeling for any signs of home along its bumps. Dirt gathered underneath his fingernails as he gripped the edges of each individual stone in the wall, desperate to find one that would come loose.

"Gavin, *why* isn't there light on the other end?" Lilly repeated, her voice rising an octave.

"I don't know," Gavin responded, startled by his own composure. "It's almost like the chute is sealing itself up."

"Well, isn't that just peachy," Lilly retorted, throwing her hands in the air. "What exactly are you doing?"

"Why do you think you couldn't see that tree?"

"Listen, are you sure there was a tree there in the first place? Maybe you were hallucinating and we fell into a really, really deep ditch instead. Maybe the cut on your leg got infected super quickly and the infection went to your brain and—"

"Lilly, I know what I saw," Gavin interjected. He might've been called many names in life, but he was not about to add liar to the list.

Lilly clasped her hands together behind her head, giving Gavin time to fathom why Lilly wasn't able to see the tree. Aside from the fact that it was the largest tree Gavin had ever seen, there was something mysterious about the woodland beast. The tree attracted him to it, doing everything just shy of calling out his name. But why had it chosen him?

"Okay, okay, so there was a tree. Can you just tell me what you saw? Maybe that will help us, somehow," Lilly replied, her voice dripping with disbelief.

So, Gavin described everything he could remember. The allure of the tree, the swirling pattern in the wood, how he lost all control over his body when he put his hands on bark. He had trouble describing his paralysis in those last few moments, finding it impossible to liken it to anything he had experienced.

"It was almost…it was like…my mind was screaming at my body to move away from the tree, but nothing worked. I know I'm not the biggest guy, but I don't think the world's strongest man would have been able to escape. There was something different, and I can't describe it. Once my hand hit the bark, some part of me knew that there was no turning back."

"Are you trying to tell me the tree was…magic?" The last word left Lilly's mouth with hesitation.

"I know it's hard to believe, but…yes."

An unsettling grimace crossed Lilly's face. Her mouth hung open and eyebrows fled to the top of her forehead. Losing her balance for a moment, Lilly brought her palms up and pressed them into her eyelids, leaving Gavin to wonder what questions were jogging around her mind.

"Lilly? Lilly! What are you thinking?" Gavin snapped his fingers in front of Lilly's eyes, bringing her back to the moment.

"I'm thinking…I don't know what I'm thinking," she answered in hushed tones. Taking a few steps backward until she found the wall behind her, Lilly sank down and brought her knees to her chest.

"I don't get it. Aren't you the one who loves conspiracy theories and aliens and all this shit?"

"Of course. I'm obsessed with those documentaries," Lilly nodded, staring at the ground in front of her. "But, this is different. Those theories, that's all they are—*theories.* They don't sneak up on me and drag me into a bizarre world, trapping me with no way out. Theories let me go to sleep at night knowing I'll wake up under my sheets the next morning. This," she gestured to the room around them, "does not let me do any of those things."

"Well, we don't know for *sure* that we're in another world. Magic was just one of the ideas I had. There could also be a perfectly logical explanation to this entire situation. In fact, there probably is some crazy science behind this that we just haven't learned about yet," Gavin rambled, trying to take back his words as his best friend began to rock on the floor. But he had already gone too far, and the wheels were turning behind Lilly's eyes.

"What if the magic from those Once-Upon-A-Time stories exists somewhere out there too? What if we're trapped here for the rest of our lives? What the hell are our parents going to think when we don't come home from school today?"

Gavin went to speak, but the words were lost in his throat. He didn't have any answers, let alone answers that would stop Lilly's babbling.

"If Ali were here—"

"Ali." Silence followed the moment Gavin uttered her name. Gavin had been too swept up in their own reality to remember why they were even in the woods to begin with. He hadn't thought of Ali since he and Lilly had fallen, but now that she was back on his mind, a new pit of worry found a home in the bottom of his stomach.

"Gav, I don't know what's going on here. I don't know where we are, and I don't know why that stupid tree tried to eat us, but I do know that we have to find a way out of here. We have to find Ali."

"I know you're right. But you saw me trying to loosen every stone in this room—there's no climbing back up there."

"Well, even if we tried to climb, it wouldn't do us any good. The chute is gone."

Lilly was right. The ceiling had finally closed itself off completely, trapping them in this dungeon. He reluctantly turned his head to the left and, for what seemed like the first time, stared down the dimly lit tunnel in front of them. With the coolness of the room now creeping into his bones, he saw that there was a faint glow from farther down the tunnel, at least half a mile away. It was nothing more than a flicker in the gloom, but it was all they had to head toward.

"Wait, where are you going?"

Lilly had risen out of the ball she was in and was trekking down the passage. This was the Lilly he was used to—do, then think.

"Well, there's no point in waiting around to be saved from our wonderful cave. Unless, of course, you would like to wait for the demonic tree to come back and finish you for the final course."

He mumbled out a feeble attempt at a comeback and reluctantly jogged to catch up.

Not more than ten seconds after he caught up to her, a heavy gust of wind whooshed past them, nearly sweeping them off their feet. Gavin felt waves of heat on his face as he found his footing, but his curiosity didn't last long. While his eyes adjusted to the newfound brightness of the corridor, he saw that the wind had lit dozens of torches on both sides of the walls. Their shadows now danced ahead of them, almost stepping away from their bodies entirely and running away from the madness while they still had a chance.

"Doesn't wind normally, you know, put out flames?" Gavin muttered from the corner of his mouth, so softly that Lilly had to lean in to hear.

"I thought so, but I also thought that trees don't swallow humans whole, so I'm going to do myself a favor and stop assuming what's real from now on."

Step by step, the pair walked in silence down the tunnel, with only the soles of their shoes echoing off the ancient dirt floor below them. Gavin took the time to run his hands across the cool stone, like he had done in the first room. The faint glow was a ways ahead of them, enticing them closer with the promise of something warm as their reward. Still running his fingertips across the tunnel walls, Gavin's hand stopped him in his tracks as it got caught on a fragment of rock jutting out.

"Damn it," he cursed and felt through his pockets for some sort of napkin to dry the blood dripping down his hand. "Just another injury I can add to today's list." Looking up, expecting to see her chuckling at his pain, Gavin was more than surprised to catch Lilly gaping at something behind him.

Quickly, he spun around half expecting a giant to be towering over him. But his intestines tightened into knots when his eyes landed on what Lilly was seeing. Images were forming on the wall where Gavin had cut his finger. They were telling a story, but this wasn't like any story he had heard before.

There was a single woman standing in a clearing with a long braid down her back. There were no signs of old age about her, no fine lines across her face, no cane in her hand and no lack of confidence in her posture. She carried herself like royalty would—head held high, moving with grace as she began to walk through the field. With every step she took, more people began to appear, growing into crowds on either side of her. They were clapping, their fists pumping the air, while children hustled to the front of the line to get a glimpse before they lost their chance. Even though no sound was coming from the walls, Gavin could feel the onlookers' cheers, praising this woman as if she were their victor.

"How are these pictures moving on their own?" Lilly wondered aloud, but Gavin was concentrating too intently on the next part of the story to comprehend what she was saying.

The woman was still the main focus, but the crowds of people were mere specks in the distance. She was with two others now: a man and a woman. And by the looks of it, they were two of her friends. The victor bowed in front of the man and curtsied before the woman before they took her into a loving embrace. It wasn't until then that their crowns became visible. While the first woman acted like a queen, the two new characters were truly from royal blood.

The royals pointed to something in the woman's pocket. She reached in and produced a very thin stick before gently handing it to the king. He turned it over in his hands like it was made of glass, both in awe of its beauty and afraid of its power. The king then passed it to his wife who mimicked the same ritual, holding it up to the light, as if that would give her a clue into its power. Her Majesty delicately placed the object back into the woman's palm, but before she sheathed the stick, she moved her hands into one swish and fireworks sprang from the stick's tip, leaping into view before fizzling out into the sky. Magic.

The monarchs clapped their hands with childlike wonder and marveled at the feats their friend could produce. Like the crowds that first surrounded the woman, they were amazed by her, but it was still unclear what she had done to win such praise. The wall wasn't going to reveal all the story's secrets.

"So it was magic," Gavin exhaled, a smile curling on his face. He knew that his instincts were right—there was magic coursing through these walls. Not wanting to miss a second, he ignored the tension radiating from Lilly's rigid body and returned his focus to the images.

It must have been the end of their meeting because the magical woman started to take one foot behind her leg in preparation for a curtsy. Before she had the chance to complete the movement, the queen grabbed her arm with such force that it left both of them off balance. Her Majesty hurriedly moved her head from left to right before leaning in to whisper something in her friend's ear.

The witch took a step back to look at both the royals in front of her. Even though Gavin couldn't read her expression, it was clear that some type of secret had just been shared among the trio. There was a quick embrace between the three of them before the woman finished her curtsy and walked away, leaving all three of their silhouettes to morph into clouds of smoke on the wall before disappearing.

Both teenagers stood rigid, listening to their hitched breaths until one of them had the courage to break the silence between them.

"I, I don't understand," Lilly began, stepping away. She shoved her hands in her pockets and began to pace. Seven steps to the right, turn, seven to the left.

"What don't you understand?"

"Are you kidding me?" Lilly stopped in her tracks. "What don't I understand? For starters, how those drawings appeared on the walls and started *moving*? Or how about when that woman brought out her wand and started shooting sparks? Or the fact that these torches lit themselves with a gust of wind? Does that clarify it for you?"

He knew her fury wasn't directed as much toward him as their situation, but Gavin had never been the best at dealing with a woman's wrath.

"Listen," he started, treading lightly with his words. "I have just as many questions as you, but do you really think us standing here, pacing, is going to get us any answers?"

Daggers shot from behind her eyes.

"Well, I personally don't think it will. The only way to get answers is to keep going that way," Gavin jutted his thumb behind them. "Come on. I won't let anything happen to you."

Her skepticism was palpable, but silence was a sign of progress in his book.

"I promise," he reassured her, hoping his words were enough.

"If Ali *did* fall down here before us, what do you think happened to her? We haven't seen any sign of her. What if the tree sent her to a different world? Or a different part of this world? What if the witch from those pictures found her first? What if—"

"Lilly, stop. We can't worry about what we can't control. We don't know if some cave-painting witch found Ali, but the longer we wait here, the more likely it is that something bad *will* happen. So, I propose we get away from the enchanted walls and find someone who can tell us where we actually are."

Instead of a response, she narrowed her eyes and brushed past him, making her way toward the flickering light and leaving Gavin confused once more.

Gavin wouldn't admit it given the current dynamic, but Lilly's questions were starting to trouble him. He felt the torches' flames flickering on his face, defining his worried angles. The slight quiver in his lower lip wasn't fooling anyone, including himself.

"Look, that light down looks different from the one these torches are giving off," Gavin observed now that they were close enough. "The shadows around it are bouncing up and down, like there's something, or someone, kindling a flame. It's also burning a hell of a lot brighter than these torches. Let's follow the light, find another living, breathing person who can get us some answers and we'll be one step closer to finding Ali."

"Okay, okay, you're right. Let's just, like, walk a little faster. I don't really feel like watching any more featured films via cave walls if I can help it."

"Agreed. Let's go."

The thought of never finding his best friend seemed inconceivable, but with each passing minute, the gravity of their current situation weighed heavier on Gavin's mind. Was this what Ali felt like on Doomsnight? Full of equal parts hope and dread? Gavin recalled helping Ali's family search through all hours of that night. Phones on in case the police called, they trudged through local neighborhoods, schoolyards, and playgrounds, looking for any sign of Carter. Even though he didn't leave Ali's side, the two didn't share more than a handful or words in those long hours. They didn't need to; there was only one thing on everyone's mind, anyway.

Their pace hastening with each step, Gavin and Lilly soon found themselves running toward the light at the end of the tunnel. Water dripping off the stalactites landed on their cheeks as they ran, and their shoes splashed in the puddles underneath them. The light was getting larger—they were closer to an answer, whether they liked it or not.

Before they could decide their next move, they were at the end. And as it turned out, the light wasn't coming from the end of their tunnel, it was coming from around the corner.

"You ready?" Gavin asked, looking down at his friend with new beads of sweat on his brow.

"Yeah. Whatever is around that corner, we can handle it. Together. For Ali."

With that final declaration, the pair walked toward the corner, preparing themselves to face a troll, dragon, or some other magical danger from their childhood fairy tales.

CHAPTER 6

THE TWO ALI'S

––––

Ali screamed. Stumbling over her own two feet, she moved backward until she latched onto something solid behind her.

"What? How? Who…who are you and why do you look like me?"

"Alexandria, everything is going to be okay, I promise. Just take a few deep breaths, and I'll answer any questions you have." This girl was remarkably calm for running into someone who was her carbon copy. Then again, she also knew her name, while Ali had absolutely no idea what was going on.

Without blinking, Ali started to regain her breath and her heart rate dropped. The chills on the back of her neck began to melt away, and feeling was coming back into her body, starting in her toes and climbing its way up every limb. Millions of questions were bouncing off the walls of her brain, but one was jumping a bit higher than the rest, demanding to be answered.

"Who are you?" Ali breathed out, uttering each syllable slowly and clearly so that she could make sure she was hearing herself correctly.

"Ah yes, an easy question. My name is Skotia." Again, Ali's doppelganger remained calm and collected, as if this interaction were part of her daily routine.

"Okay, well, Skotia, nice to meet you, I think. Next question. Why do you look like me?" Still unsure how to go about this encounter, Ali chose her questions carefully. Her shoulders were tense, and she was ready to flee at the drop of a hat, but she refused to break eye contact with the stranger.

"That one is a bit more complicated," Skotia replied, furrowing her brow while Ali anxiously waited for an answer. "How it works is this...everyone from the Upper Land has someone here who looks exactly like them—"

"Upper Land?" Ali interrupted, already confused.

"Right, apologies for not explaining. The Upper Land is what we call your world, a world full of the Unsighted. The Unsighted are people who can't cross worlds. Most can't even open their minds to the possibility that other worlds exist. They tend to believe what is in front of their eyes, not wanting to try to draw back the curtain and see what's lurking in the shadows. It doesn't take much skill to realize there's more out there in the universe, but it's easier to be an Unsighted than it is to uncover the truth."

Upper Land? Unsighted?

Ali took in the room and saw that it wasn't much of a room, but rather an extended part of the tunnel. She was at a fork in the road; either direction led toward jet-black corridors with no end in sight. In the distance, she could hear the water droplets bouncing off the floors. Otherwise, there were no signs of life.

"Anyway, every person in the Upper Land has a double in another world somewhere out there. Each individual has their own personality, own life, and own qualities that make them unique, but they will look nearly identical. The only way to differentiate between the two is to look at their—"

"Eyes," Ali cut Skotia off before she could finish the sentence. "I didn't notice it at first because, well, quite frankly, I didn't expect to see myself when I turned that corner."

And it was true. Skotia's eyes were jet black, making it nearly impossible to decipher between her iris and pupil. If someone were to glance quickly, they might think they were looking into a black hole. A stark contrast to Ali's piercing green eyes.

Ali took a few more moments to take in Skotia, trying to find any other differences between the two, but it was truly like looking in a mirror. From the way she spoke with her hands to the scrunched facial expression she made when she was trying to explain something complicated, they could've been separated at birth. Carbon copies.

Seeing this girl felt strange, like she was breaking a fundamental law of nature. Even though Ali had always wondered what she looked like to everyone else, seeing the reality sent warning signals to her brain, as if this was an experience she was never meant to have. Watching Skotia's foot rhythmically tap on the ground, she realized why her mother always told her to stay still—it was highly distracting.

"Exactly. The eyes will always be different. Here in Infernus, you might walk by someone who is the look-alike of a friend or family member back in your world, but just take a look in their eyes and you'll see that it's not truly them."

"Wait, where did you say we are?" This was the second time Skotia mentioned that name, and Ali swore she wasn't hearing her correctly.

"Infernus, Alexandria. We're in the City of Infernus."

"That's not possible," Ali stammered out. "Grandmother used to tell us stories about a land called Infernus, but they were nothing more than her stories. Just fairy tales she created to help us sleep at night."

At the mention of her grandmother, a strange look crossed Skotia's face. In an instant it was gone, but Ali was sure she'd seen something there.

"Many decades ago, it wasn't...uncommon for Infernians to try to escape to other worlds. You see, our world contains portals. They're well hidden, so it's unlikely that someone will stumble on one by accident."

Ali might as well have been thrown in front of a bus. The thoughts swirling in her head were pushing so forcefully on her skull that she was developing a migraine. Her breathing wasn't labored, but that same lightheadedness she'd felt earlier that day in her house was coming back, and her palms were slick with sweat. She slowly inched herself closer to the ground and tucked her knees under her chin, leaning against the cool wall behind her for relief.

"Alexandria, those stories didn't come from your grandmother's imagination, they came from her memories. She must have been one of the Infernians who fled, so that her family—so that you—could have a better life."

Closing her eyes, images of her grandmother flashed in front of her. Grandmother taking Ali and Carter to the park, trying not to laugh with them as they joked about their mother's horrible haircut. Grandmother teaching her to ride a bike on the weekends when her parents were too busy to take her. And when Ali graduated from bike to skateboard, Grandmother was the one who took Ali to the skatepark to watch her practice new tricks.

Then there were the times she and Carter would play hide and seek in Grandmother's house, always fascinated by the array of hiding spots that were disguised as cabinets and closet doors. Ali remembered begging her parents to let her brother and her sleep at their grandmother's house for the night, and after incessant pleading for half an hour they usually gave in. Sometimes at their sleepovers, Ali would get nightmares—a dream about a bad man breaking in and scooping her out of bed in the middle of the night. Shaking and half in tears when she awoke, Ali would run to her grandmother's bed for comfort and a warm hug. To lull her back to sleep, Grandmother would whisper stories about a faraway land in Ali's ear. A land filled with magic and awe, and certainly no bad men trying to steal her away from her family.

And now Ali was trapped in that land.

"I don't understand. How could any of this be real? You, this cave, the tree that devoured me whole?" Ali asked, turning over all of the day's events in her head.

"Alexandr—"

"Ali. Please, call me Ali," she interrupted before Skotia could finish. She still hated hearing her full name.

"Okay," Skotia started again, looking at her skeptically. "Ali, you must understand something. Infernus doesn't reveal itself to just anyone. If that were the case, many confused travelers would've found themselves here over the years. There's a reason you found that tree today. Infernus wants you here, Ali. Even though you don't know why yet. Or, do you?" Skotia asked with a glint in her eye, encouraging Ali to solve the puzzle in front of her.

Hesitating, Ali racked her brain for a single reason she might have been summoned to a new world. But, she found that she couldn't focus on that question because she was still figuring out the puzzle in front of her—Skotia.

Ali was drawn to her and couldn't explain why. Even though there were internal sirens blaring telling her to run, she forced her legs to stay where they were and see how this would play out. How could Ali not trust herself?

So she stayed put and wrung her hands with impatience at her own ignorance, but the seconds continued to tick with only silence as her answer to Skotia's question.

Then she remembered the sketches from the tunnel. Ali had almost forgotten about them from the shock of running into Skotia, but now the scenes were flooding her memory. Could those images be part of the answer?

"Back in the tunnel there were these drawings on the walls, but they weren't like anything I've ever seen before. They were moving, and I think they were trying to tell me a story, but it was hard to follow everything that was happening. Toward the end, there were two women who were clearly fighting. One dropped a pile of rocks on the other, but then the images stopped coming, so I couldn't see what happened after." Ali shook her head as she recalled the story, trying to figure out when this day would stop sounding completely ridiculous.

"Skotia, did that have anything to do with why people left Infernus for other worlds?"

Skotia slowly began nodding, avoiding Ali's gaze. She opened her mouth to start speaking, but then closed it again before composing her next words.

"Ali, I've been in these tunnels for quite some time, and I've never seen any stories on the walls. In fact, I've never heard anyone say that they've seen moving images here. You have to believe me when I say that there's a reason Infernus wanted you here, and it's not going to let you leave easily. Especially if it doesn't get what it wants from you."

She was looking directly into Ali's eyes as she said the last sentence, sending a chill down Ali's spine. Her words weren't threatening, but the idea of her identical twin holding her hostage in an alien world didn't sound appealing. She pictured Skotia leading her to one of those dingy caverns, deeper into a land she knew nothing about. But unable to see, Ali pictured herself taking a wrong turn and tumbling into a creature's nest to become its next meal.

Yup, she would have to pass on that option.

"What it wants from me? I think you're mistaken. I'm just a teenager from the suburbs who can't figure out how to get my life together. What could Infernus possibly want from *me*?"

No one had wanted anything from Ali in the past three years. She'd skillfully learned how to fade into the background, drawing as little attention to herself as possible. Ali liked living in the shadows—she belonged there rather than on center stage.

There was a long pause before Skotia spoke again. She absentmindedly stood up and started pacing in front of Ali, clearly hiding something. Skotia wasn't going to be able to hide many secrets from Ali; Ali knew better than anyone what she looked like when she was nervous. And as her therapist could attest, pacing was definitely one of her tells.

"You have to tell me," Ali continued. "You can't expect me to sit here and quietly accept that I have some job to do in a place that I believed to be imaginary up until a few minutes ago. Actually, I still don't totally believe this is happening, so the faster you start explaining, the faster I'll maybe complete this fictional to-do list and get the hell out of here." She felt her voice rising and her tongue moving faster by the time she was done speaking, but she had no intentions of apologizing.

Skotia didn't look upset that Ali had raised her voice. In fact, she barely flinched. Instead, she leaned her body against the opposite wall and let out one last sigh before continuing.

"Much like the stories you heard from your grandmother when you were younger, the story you watched unfold on the tunnel walls wasn't just another fairy tale. Those pictures were telling part of Infernus's history, a particularly dark moment of history."

Skotia paused, which gave Ali a chance to fold herself into a cross legged position on the ground and put her hands under her chin. She could hear Skotia muttering to herself, as if deciding what to divulge next.

"Skotia, are you okay?" Ali interrupted after a few more minutes of watching the pacing and muttering.

"Infernus had always been a peaceful land, no wars or mass destruction. No plagues, no droughts. People cared for their neighbors. Even though the king and queen ruled, they weren't the type of monarchs who hid behind their castle walls, only to make public appearances when necessary. They made sure their citizens were well fed, healthy, and given the support they needed. They opened their doors to the public, encouraging Infernians to come inside and meet with them and engage, really be a part of their life. They loved all their people, even those who had no love to give back." Skotia was barely looking at her doppelganger. Skotia's eyes could have been made of glass, one blink threatening to shatter their stillness.

"One individual in particular—one of the women in those drawings—was devoid of any love Infernus had to offer. Her name was Mateva, and she was the darkest Sorcerer this land has ever seen."

"Sorcerers? Like, witches?" Ali interrupted.

"You might call them witches in the Upper Land, but these wand wielders don't wear pointed hats or ride around on brooms like your folklore might presume. Infernus's

Sorcerers harbor powerful, deep magic that's rooted into their veins."

Ali's grandmother had never told her anything about the Sorcerers. If she did know anything about them, she wanted to hide the information from her grandchildren. Maybe if her grandmother had told them more, told them anything else besides the child-friendly versions they knew too well, Ali wouldn't be sitting here trying to keep her jaw from touching the cold ground.

"Mateva's training didn't go as planned. For a period of time, she was shunned from Infernus and sent into hiding, taking her knowledge and magic with her. No one knows where she went, but there was a darkness starting to envelop the land. The animals sensed it first and started to retreat to all corners of Infernus. They hid in the forests, mountains, and those that could, dove into the waters, praying they were safe beneath sea level."

Skotia's retelling reminded Ali of a dream she once had of a cloud overtaking their neighborhood, hiding any last remnants of sunshine behind its dark mass. No matter how fast she ran, the cloud towered over her, mocking her as she tried to escape its wrath. The last thing she remembered before she woke with tears and sweat trickling down her face was the shadowy beast enveloping her in darkness, leaving her blind to everything she'd ever known.

"When Mateva did resurface, she lay destruction in her wake, now combining her hate for common Infernians with her loathing for the Sorcerers who tried to tame her magic. Anyone who dared disobey her was thrust from their everyday life and punished however she saw fit. A clear warning for others to stay out of her warpath. Infernus suffered most of all as she used her newfound abilities to destroy the rich lands and abundant pastures that had sparked life for centuries. People didn't know where to turn as they watched their beloved home dying before their eyes.

"Is that why people fled? Is that why my grandmother wanted to leave?" Ali thought about what it must have been like for her grandmother to slowly watch her home deteriorate before her eyes, losing everything she had ever known to evil. Ali felt a pang of sympathy strike her core for the woman she had once looked up to more than her own mother. What other secrets had she kept from her family?

"Precisely. Those who could find a way out left without hesitation. They grabbed what little belongings they had and embarked on a journey for a new world they knew little about." Skotia mimicked the exodus by creating pairs of legs with her two fingers, kicking up clouds of dust as they ran toward oblivion on the dirt in front of her.

"While Infernians were fleeing, the king and queen closed the castle gates and barricaded themselves inside, powerless against Mateva's fury. No one could match her strength, but that didn't mean there wasn't a plan brewing. Just as it felt like all the light had gone from the world, Mateva faced a force she had not planned for. She faced her equal, perhaps her match.

"From the ashes rose Cassiopeia, another Sorcerer-in-training. After Mateva's training failed, it was evident Cassiopeia was the pupil with the most potential. She trained day and night, knowing the threat of Mateva was looming every time the sun rose and set over their heads. As her destruction intensified, so did Cassiopeia's training. After months of preparing, Cassiopeia was ready to face the reign of terror waiting outside.

"Now closer to Sorcerers than students, the former classmates met on top of the mountain. Knowing well enough that their efforts would likely decide Infernus's fate, the battle of their lives began."

Images raced through Ali's brain of earthquakes shaking Infernus and tornadoes sweeping the land. Both women were forces of nature in their own regard, compelling the land to do their bidding with one wave of a wand.

"That must've been what I was watching in the tunnel. So then Cassiopeia won, right?" Ali interjected, enthralled with the tale she was hearing. Her legs had unfolded, and she was now leaning back on her palms. It almost felt like she was a child again in her grandmother's house waiting to hear the end of the story.

Almost was the key word. Trying to put the remaining pieces together, she was painstakingly aware of the sense of dread spreading through her.

"Well, no one knows exactly what happened on that mountaintop because no one dared leave their house. After that final night of fighting, Cassiopeia made her way down the mountain and declared that Mateva had been defeated. The people could carry on with their lives and were free from the greatest threat Infernus had ever seen. There were plenty of reasons to rejoice."

Ali thought that was the end of the story, but there was still something hanging in the air between the two girls. Skotia's eyebrows hadn't relaxed from their furrowed state, and her fists were still clenched beside her as the fire crackled next to them. This story wasn't over yet.

"Don't get me wrong, I'm happy Infernus was saved from that Mateva woman, but I still don't know what this has to do with me. What's left to do if everything is safe now?" Ali broke the silence, desperate to know what Skotia wasn't divulging.

"That's just it. During those next few months when no one was afraid to speak Mateva's name and peace was restored, Cassiopeia slipped into the shadows and disappeared. The gossips claimed that the Sorcerers wouldn't let her out of their sight, afraid that she, too, might get power hungry, so they held her captive. They also theorized that she fled Infernus like those who did during the Great Uprising, but no one could fathom why since she was the most celebrated Infernian in history."

Ali's own imagination began to wander as visions of a vibrant Infernus flocked in front of her. Throngs of Infernians celebrating the one woman who had rescued them from an inevitable demise. For a fleeting second, Ali *was* Cassiopeia, surrounded by dazzling smiles and endless praise, filling her with an undying love she hadn't experienced in the longest time.

But in the end, she would always be just Ali.

"Time went on, as it inevitably does. New generations were born, and the battle became a story that people heard about from parents and grandparents. No one worried why Cassiopeia was gone or hiding from the public because Infernus was safe. At least, until recently." The last word slid off Skotia's tongue. Just then, a crisp breeze passed by them, sending a shudder through Ali's bones while briefly threatening to extinguish their fire.

"No one found Mateva's body after the battle, but that wasn't too worrisome because no one had ever seen a Sorcerer's body after they had passed away. Some thought it turned to dust, returning the magic to the land beneath them. Others thought Cassiopeia burned the body with her magic or disposed of it herself before returning down the mountain. No one possibly thought that the reason they couldn't find the corpse was because Mateva survived. And if they did think it, no one dared speak the thought into existence."

"Wait, you're telling me some people think she *survived* an avalanche of stone falling on her body? I'm sorry, that's impossible—Sorcerer or not, no person could cling to life after that."

The dread had now extended its reach to the tips of Ali's toes, threatening to numb them one at a time.

"A few years ago, two or three of the elder Infernians decided to take a hike up one of the mountains. What they saw on their trek sparked a fear in their eyes the younger generations had never seen before.

"The men were making outlandish claims that Mateva was back, that they had seen her practicing her dark magic, and no one was safe. Their outcries sparked fury and terror in the same breath. Those who were old enough to remember the Great Uprising slandered the men for bringing those ideas into everyone's heads with no concrete proof."

"Proof doesn't matter when people are afraid," Ali mumbled, feeling her own features turn dark. The police never found proof that anyone harmed Carter, but it didn't stop the terrors from slinking into her sleep.

"Exactly." Skotia met Ali's gaze, trying to read her expression. But Ali wasn't about to let her in that easily, even if they did share a face.

"Since then, more reports have surfaced claiming that Mateva is back. People and animals have started disappearing from their homes. Some people report that Mateva has a power that she didn't have before, something so strong that even if Cassiopeia were to return, she wouldn't have a chance at victory this time. Every day hope is fleeing our people.

"A couple of months ago, I started having these dreams. Dreams about you, Ali. That you, my look-alike, were going to somehow get to Infernus and help us stop Mateva before she became too strong. A few weeks ago, the dreams started becoming more vivid. They told me that I had to get to the mountainside because you'd be showing up here. I've been roaming these tunnels for at least a week looking for you in case you had already arrived, but it turns out that I didn't need to—you found me instead. I don't know why Infernus picked you, Ali, but it did. You have to stop her."

For the second time today, Ali swore she must have misheard Skotia.

"I'm sorry, but your dreams told you the wrong thing. I've never punched anyone or anything besides my pillow. The idea of me facing some dark Sorcerer sounds like a death wish if you ask me."

At this, Skotia laughed. "Dreams are rarely wrong. People just have a habit of ignoring their real messages."

"Listen, I am absolutely not equipped to fight someone who somehow survived a pile of boulders falling on their head. Even if I could think of a way to defend myself, let alone an entire city, I did not sign up for this. Tell whoever you need to that I, Ali, hereby rescind my imaginary application to save—"

"Sh. Do you hear that?" Skotia interrupted.

After overcoming the shock of being shushed by the girl who just told her that she had to essentially save this strange world, Ali complied and listened. A few moments passed before she heard what Skotia was alluding to. There was the sound of footsteps echoing from the tunnel Ali had just come from, and they were gaining speed, clearly headed toward the pair of girls. Skotia cocked her head to the side and stared toward the opening, steadying herself to stand at a moment's notice.

The footsteps stopped and were replaced by the murmurs of voices resounding off the stone walls. It was impossible to hear exactly what they were saying, but Ali couldn't imagine where this group could've come from. There was a dead end at the end of that tunnel that she had been trapped in, and she saw the chute that spit her out into Infernus close behind her. Defenseless to any possible threat, Ali clenched her fists and clamped her jaw as she watched two shadows round the corner to where she and Skotia were camped.

Ali's eyes widened and her breath hitched as she looked into the eyes of the impossible: Lilly and Gavin had somehow gotten into Infernus, and they were standing in front of her.

CHAPTER 7

REUNITED

———

"Oh my god."

"That's not possible."

"Lilly? Gavin? How are you two here?" Ali jumped up from where she was sitting and wrapped her friends in a bear hug, squeezing them together until she assured herself they weren't figments of her imagination. She released her grip when she felt Gavin gasping for air.

Out of breath from being hugged a little too tight, Gavin took a few inhales before explaining,

"After we heard you screaming in the forest, we tried to follow your voice, but you were gone by the time we got there," Gavin began, slowly getting his breathing under control. "After that, it was pretty much a blur. I put my hand on this tree and this black hole started to open. Lilly didn't believe me that it was actually happening, so she tried to pull me away, and then—"

"Wait, what do you mean she didn't believe you?" Ali questioned. Turning toward Lilly, she asked, "Didn't you see the tree?"

"Well, no, I didn't." Lilly barely met Ali's eyes. "I...I don't know why I couldn't, but how was I supposed to believe him?

One moment, my feet are on the ground, and the next I'm lying on my back in some musty cave. It's kind of a lot for a person to take in at once, don't you think?"

Ali thought back to her first few moments in Infernus, which now felt light-years behind her. She had been panicked, lost, and confused, each emotion wrangling for their chance on top. She couldn't blame Lilly for doubting this new reality. Hell, she could barely understand it herself. But why wasn't Lilly able to see the tree?

"She didn't see it because the Unsighted can't see any of Infernus's magic," Skotia interjected, practically reading Ali's thoughts. "They're ignorant to what's happening before their very eyes. I'm actually not quite sure how you two got in."

This was the first time Skotia had spoken since the trio reunited. Ali had been so startled at seeing her best friends that she had momentarily forgotten Skotia was a few feet behind her watching the friends discuss this strange, new world they'd found themselves in. Even though Skotia was at home in Infernus, she was now the outsider.

Stammering to put together a cohesive sentence to explain what they were seeing, Ali released a long, grateful exhale when she heard Gavin ask what she knew they were both thinking.

"So, who's your friend?" he asked with his head cocked to the side, slowly looking Skotia up and down without blinking.

"This is—"

"I'm Skotia," she interrupted, holding out her hand before retracting it when neither teenager shook it. "I'm Ali's look-alike from Infernus, and she's mine from the Upper Land."

"Excuse me? You're her *what*?" Lilly retorted, her skepticism palpable the longer she looked between Ali and Skotia.

Confused at Lilly's disbelief, Skotia slowly responded, "Well, you see, the two of us look very alike, and where I'm from they call us look-alikes."

Ali stifled a laugh as she watched Lilly refrain from rolling her eyes. She assumed that rhetorical questions weren't as common in Infernus.

"Skotia," Ali cut in, "I think they can both see that we're basically identical. Maybe if you could explain the story you told me about the Upper Land and the Unsighted and everything else, that would help." Remembering how her knees felt hearing the story minutes ago, Ali turned to her friends and ushered for them to take a seat on the hard, steady ground.

Skotia began with the same information she had revealed to Ali. She explained that they were no longer in their world, which they had suspected, and instead had landed in Infernus, a world full of magic and power, both light and dark. Lilly held her knees close to her chest and fidgeted while Gavin kept his head cocked to the right, mouth wide open, occasionally pinching his forearm when he thought no one was looking.

As Ali listened to the story for a second time, it dawned on her how ridiculous it all sounded. Where she had come from, the closest thing to magic was when the DVD player worked on the first try. Now, she was supposed to wrap her head around the notion that there were other worlds that had been hidden her entire life, silently lurking in the nooks and crannies of her neighborhood. Even if she could accept that bombshell, now she had Skotia trying to convince her that it was her job to save Infernus from a violent, wicked Sorcerer who nearly destroyed everyone's livelihood decades ago. If her grandmother knew Infernus was real, why hadn't she told her?

Thinking of her grandmother sent an arrow of sorrow into her heart, followed with scattered splinters of betrayal. Ali blinked away tears welling in her eyes before anyone had the chance to see, but the tightness in her throat remained. Grandmother was her best friend, but now she felt that she didn't know her at all. What kind of life had she lived in Infernus? Did she ever try to come back after fleeing to Ali's world? Why would she treat Infernus like it was some children's story, when it was really the story of her life?

What if her grandmother didn't want her to know about Infernus because she thought Ali would go looking for an entrance? Up until her grandmother's passing, Ali loved hearing the adventurous tales time and time again. Toward the end, it became clear that it was taking more energy for Grandmother to remember the details—her face wasn't lighting up quite as brightly as it used to, but her grandmother never stopped sharing, nonetheless. If she had divulged a little bit more, maybe a few more stories, Ali would know what to believe right now. Maybe if she had shared a few more forbidden secrets, there wouldn't be a seed of doubt sprouting in Ali's stomach, growing with every thought that crossed her mind.

"You're telling me that Ali is destined to help you save Infernus from a vicious Sorcerer because your dreams said so?"

The sound of Lilly's voice brought Ali back to reality, and she quickly cleared her throat, erasing all signs of her emotion from her face.

"No, no, no. Not help *me*, she has to do this on her own," Skotia clarified. "I knew that I had to find Ali, but now, it's up to her to accept the task."

"But why exactly do you trust these dreams so much? Do all Infernian look-alikes dream of their other half, or is it just you?" Ali probed, determined to find something to disprove Skotia's theory. If she couldn't save herself, how was she supposed to save an entire world?

"No, not necessarily," Skotia began, pausing to choose her next words carefully. "These dreams, they align with one of Infernus's ancient prophecies. There's a legend that an Upper Lander will come down to save Infernus from its ultimate destruction. When these dreams began coinciding with the rumors surrounding Mateva, I realized it had to be more than a coincidence."

With no words left at her disposal, Ali simply shook her head in disbelief and absentmindedly made her way to a firm, unwavering wall that could hold her balance. Meanwhile, Lilly switched between hanging her mouth open in disbelief and closing it in reflective contemplation before Gavin interjected.

"Lilly, you're the one who's always going on about how aliens built the pyramids and promoting every other conspiracy theory out there. Why couldn't this be another conspiracy theory come to life?"

"Yeah, but that's our world. This is different. This world isn't even supposed to exist." She turned toward Gavin, her face reddening by the second. "Are you saying you believe her? You really believe that Ali's meant for this?"

"I…I don't know, honestly. What I do know is that you're the one who told me to stop assuming what's real when we were in that tunnel, so that's what I'm trying to do. I'm trying to be like one of your beloved aliens that crash-landed on a new planet, careful not to judge anything here too soon."

Nodding in reluctant agreement, she turned and walked over to where Ali stood against the rigid cave wall. Placing her hand gently on Ali's shoulder, she gave her a knowing look that only best friends could share.

"We both know it doesn't matter what the two of us believe in the end. Where's your mind right now? Do you believe you could do this?" Lilly asked in a hushed voice.

"I know that I can't do this." Ali laughed, leaving a sliver of spite lingering in the air. "My grandmother might have lived in Infernus and told us some stories, but there's absolutely no way I'm meant for this.

"I'm sorry, but I think you have the wrong girl," Ali said, turning her attention to Skotia. "Why can't one of the other Sorcerers help? You said there were four of them originally. Where are the other two who have trained for this?"

"After realizing that Mateva had returned and Cassiopeia wasn't coming back, the last two went into hiding as well. Rumor has it they knew they were no match for Mateva, especially with this new weapon she's said to possess. A new power source that'll leave her invincible if she can figure out how to use it properly."

"Something she didn't have last time? Like one of those magical wands you were telling us about?" Gavin asked, raising his eyebrows in confusion.

"No, from what the walls were showing me, she definitely had a wand last time. She used it to fight Cassiopeia. Skotia, where do people think she's generating her strength from this time?" Ali asked, peeling herself off the wall and taking a few steps toward her look-alike.

For the first time since they'd run into each other, Skotia was tongue-tied. She tried to stammer out a few incomprehensible sentences but then turned her back on the trio, her fingers fidgeting at her side. Ali strained her ears but couldn't make out the conversation Skotia was having with herself.

Her shadows danced across the cave walls as she continued to pace, but just as Ali was about to grab her by the shoulders and shake an answer out of her, she answered their question.

"There's something I haven't told you yet."

"Well, yes, we figured that much out for ourselves."

"Lilly," Ali snapped back, shooting Lilly an icy look. "Let her talk."

"As I was saying, there's something I haven't told you. But, if you stand a chance against Mateva, then you should know what you're going up against. If what everyone's been saying is true, then it's quite inhumane. And they don't know for sure if it's real, but the recent stories have been almost identical to one another. No matter who is claiming to have seen her, they all say the same—she has a child she's been using to derive her power."

"Her own child?" Ali interrupted, disgusted with the notion that this woman would use her own child's innocence for evil.

"No, this child isn't her own blood. It's been said that three years ago, a child found their way into Infernus through one of the portals. A boy. Mateva was the first to find him, sadly, before anyone else could help him find his way back home. She must've found something very intriguing about him because she's been keeping him captive ever since."

Ali felt her face turn pale.

"Thr-three years ago? Has anyone said how old he was? Or what he looked like?"

"Yes, three years ago. Now that I think about it, it was around this time of the year too. The golden berries had just started sprouting, like they are now. Infernians know it's the same child every time because of his dark, curly hair. The latest reports have said that he looks about fourteen or fifteen now, so he must've been about eleven or twelve when he showed up here."

Drops of sweat were falling from Ali's forehead mixed with the tears falling from her eyes. Gavin and Lilly each grabbed an arm as they slowly brought her to the ground. Her body was shaking uncontrollably, and her vision was blurred. She couldn't make out the faces in front of her, so instead she tried to focus on her shoelaces because they were the first things her eyes landed on. Lilly gently rubbed her back like they were back in elementary school again and she had just fallen off the monkey bars, but Ali didn't want her to stop.

"Ca-Carter. She has Carter," she finally choked out. The lump in her throat was making it hard for her to form complete sentences, but the tears had stopped blurring her sight for just long enough that she could make out everyone's petrified faces, silently waiting for her to burst into hysteria once more.

"We don't know it's definitely him," Lilly soothed, continuing the circular motion with her palm.

"I'm sorry, who's Carter?" Skotia whispered to Gavin since he wasn't the one taking care of Ali at the moment.

"Her brother. Carter went missing three years ago, just like you said. The police never found any clues into where he went, but if he ended up here…"

"They would've never found any trace of him," Ali finished. "If Carter fell through the same tree that we all did, there wouldn't be any clues left behind. Think about it. Gavin, you found that tree minutes after I fell into it, and you didn't see anything that proved I was there."

Silence ensued. The two friends didn't want to confirm Ali's speculations, but they didn't have to; Ali already knew she was right. And now she knew Carter was here, trapped in the same world she was. Trapped in a world their grandmother had told them about all those years ago.

Knowing that Carter was so close yet still out of reach flipped a switch in her mind that had been off since her world fell apart. The hope she'd thought was lost was suddenly spreading throughout her body and giving her a new skin, letting her shed the old one that was filled with loss and misery. She hadn't seen her brother in three years, and now Ali had the chance to bring him back home. They would have a second chance to play games and be each other's confidant, making up for all the time they'd lost.

But first, she had to find him.

"All right, I'll do it. If you can take me to wherever Mateva is keeping Carter, I'll go with you."

"Ali, wait. Think about what you're signing up for. How are you going to fight an evil Sorcerer when you don't know the first thing about fighting *or* magic?" Usually, Lilly was an advocate for the reflexive decision-making, so Ali was less than pleased that she was trying to bring some rationality into her thought process.

"If it means getting Carter back, then I'm in. I'll figure out the fighting part along the way."

"Great!" Skotia exclaimed, her eyes brightening at the sudden turn of events. "Shall we get started, then?"

"Hold on. We first need to figure out a way to get Lilly and Gavin back home."

"We're coming," they chimed in simultaneously.

For the first time since she'd fallen through that portal, Ali felt the corners of her mouth turn upward into a true smile. She didn't want to say goodbye to her friends just yet, but she also didn't want them to face whatever she had just agreed to. Thankfully, she didn't have to make that decision because, judging by the way their lips were pressed together and arms crossed across their chests, their minds were made up.

Skotia didn't look thrilled at the idea of having two extra people along for the ride, but it seemed like she quickly figured out that was a battle she was not going to win.

The trio watched as she walked over to a corner of her cavern they hadn't explored yet and reached into a knapsack that had been camouflaged into the wall. Ali stood on her toes to see if she could sneak a peek at what she was searching for. After a few moments, Skotia pulled out a few pieces of tan cloth and held them out in both of her hands.

"Time to change."

CHAPTER 8

SHADOWVINES

Ali and Lilly exchanged a quick look as they glanced down at their new outfits. Skotia didn't have extra shoes, so Ali was still in her white Converses and Lilly in her mismatched shoes, but other than that, they looked like true Infernians.

Lilly hadn't been as lucky as Ali, and Skotia's outfits didn't fit her quite right. Her flared pants, made of something that resembled cotton, were a tad too long on her and were already collecting dirt at the bottom. Apparently Infernians didn't have a very wide color palette because her shirt was almost the exact same color as the pants. It hugged Lilly's hourglass figure a little too tight at the hips but was still comfortable enough that she had full range of motion.

Luckily for Ali, being Skotia's look-alike proved to be useful. Over the years, their bodies had developed the same. Ali's pants were the perfect length, and her shirt didn't hug at hips like Lilly's did. Instead, it gave her just enough wiggle room to breathe while still being light enough that she didn't find herself sweating through the material.

"Sorry, I didn't pack any clothing that would work for you," Skotia apologized to Gavin, grimacing at his shorts and T-shirt combination. "If we run into anyone and they ask you where you're from, just pretend you can't understand what they're saying. I'll think of something while we walk."

"Thanks. I'm guessing you don't have any basketball players in this world?" Gavin joked, pointing to his sneakers and giving a light laugh.

Ali could tell that joke went directly over Skotia's head by the way she was glancing between both the girls, waiting for someone to fill her in. Not caring to explain the concept of basketball to her, Ali decided to jump in.

"If I'm going to do this, we're going to get started now. How do we find where Mateva is holding Carter hostage?"

"From the rumors, it sounds like her hideout is somewhere in this mountain. I haven't seen any signs of her since I've gotten here, but I *have* had the chance to do my fair share of exploring. The tunnels can get confusing, but I think we should keep going in that direction. I haven't explored that yet." Skotia pointed directly behind the three friends, and they all turned around to see what their path looked like right now.

Darkness.

Hearing that Carter was even closer than Ali thought made her heart skip a beat. She imagined what it would feel like to run up to her little brother and squeeze him so tight he'd be begging her to let go for air. If only she'd done that three years ago, then she wouldn't have to wonder what that felt like today. Then she wouldn't be off to face a dangerous Sorcerer who had infinitely more power in her pinky than Ali could ever wish for.

"Did you ever think to make a map at all during your exploring?" Lilly butted in from Ali's right side.

"I can remember just fine," Skotia snapped. Lilly looked dumbstruck, like she had gone to pet a friendly-looking stray dog, and it had suddenly turned to bite her. Skotia turned her back and walked toward her knapsack, gathering her belongings in the final few moments before their departure.

This gave Ali time to talk to her oldest friend. She grabbed Lilly's shoulders and turned her body so the two were at eye level. Leaning in closely, she whispered, "We have to trust her. She knows more about Infernus than we ever could, and she's my best chance at finding Carter. Please."

Meeting her gaze, Lilly begrudgingly nodded and the tension in her posture deflated.

"Fine, but just because she looks like my best friend, doesn't mean I have to trust her. Deal?"

"Deal."

With their pact solidified, the two turned back toward their small group and watched as Skotia smothered the fire with a blanket she'd packed away.

"Shall we?" she asked, looking up with a fiery spark in her eyes and a determined smirk to match.

For the next half hour, the group traipsed through the darkness. The new passages were just as musty and damp as the first tunnel was, but there was something different about this escapade from the first. A current of energy flowed through Ali's veins. Her fingers felt like they had been pricked by hundreds of tiny needles, and her feet were desperate to pick up and run toward the void in front of them, eager to put less distance between herself and Carter. She threw her hair into a ponytail, jutting out her lip to blow away the baby hairs that were too short to fit.

The electric flow overpowered Ali's static muscles and kicked them into overdrive. Before she realized what was happening, she was running through the darkness, keeping her eyes focused on the few feet in front of her she could see.

After a few seconds, she heard the others fall into line behind her. Their pace picked up until the only sounds Ali could make out were the echoes of their steps bouncing between the walls behind her.

But the only noise occupying space in Ali's mind were Carter's screams, begging his sister to save him. Ali told herself they weren't real, she *knew* they weren't real, but it didn't matter. Visions of her feeble brother trapped in a sunless, grime-ridden cave flashed before her. When Ali saw his helpless eyes staring back at her, she lost control of her body and found herself falling over a pile of rocks that had camouflaged themselves into the ground.

"Ali! Are you okay?" Lilly caught up to her first, bending down to inspect Ali's scraped knees.

I was hallucinating about my missing brother, she thought.

"Yeah, yeah I'm fine. Just lost my balance," Ali lied. "We should keep going. I'll be up in a second."

"I don't think we should keep going," Gavin whispered.

"Don't be ridiculous—" Ali started. But her words got caught in her throat when she saw the reason behind Gavin's suggestion.

A door was materializing into existence out of the stone wall in front of them. It had a large iron handle on its right side, but it was decorated with the same spiral pattern she'd seen on the tree. Instead of being carved into the bark, these spirals were welded into the stone. At first glance, they were difficult to make out, but as the door became more pronounced, so did the pattern.

"It's the same design," Gavin softly exclaimed, wide-eyed at the new discovery.

"I think we're supposed to go this way," Ali said. If her inner voice had arms and legs, they would have already pushed her through that door. "Skotia, what do you think?" She wanted another opinion from a voice that wasn't living inside her head.

Skotia looked as confused as the rest of them. She gingerly ran her palms across the iron handle before taking a step back to observe the wall the door had appeared in. There was no gap between the stiff ground and the ceiling to give them any clue as to what lay on the other side. Pursing her lips together, Skotia hesitated before nodding to motion that they should pull the massive handle.

"But first, find a rock that we can prop the door open with. I don't know if we'll be as lucky with finding a way out of whatever's on the other side of this thing."

Thankful for the foresight, Ali grabbed the heftiest rock she could find and signaled for Gavin to open the door. Grabbing the iron in both hands, a grunt escaped his lips as he pushed his feet into the floor and heaved the door toward him. Once open, Ali ushered the other three inside before wedging the rock in between the door and the damp wall.

She didn't know what she had expected to see on the other side, but it certainly wasn't this.

The four teenagers all stood gazing at the ceiling, which seemed miles away. There was nothing in front of them except for an empty room. If it hadn't been in the middle of a mountain and composed of dark, rough stone, Ali would've said it looked like a ballroom.

At one time, this room could have accommodated throngs of merry partygoers, enjoying themselves to the finest celebrations magic could promise. But now, the room was anything but joyous. The ceiling seemed miles away, with thousands of tiny glowing insects lighting its roof and giving the room a faint glow. Its walls were barren, but Ali felt souls lost in the room calling out to her to join them in their invisible void.

Ali tried to find any sign that Carter had been there. Any piece of clothing, markings in the ground, a secret message that screamed that Ali was going in the right direction. But after a quick sweep of the room, there was nothing that suggested her little brother was there. A few ounces of irrational hope left her body as quickly as they'd come.

"This place is giving me the creeps. I never thought I'd say this, but I think I'd rather be back in that dusty tunnel than here right about now," Lilly's voice quivered. Ali couldn't help but also admit that she didn't see a point to being in this cavern for a second longer than necessary.

"Agreed. Let's turn back."

A loud thud boomed through the cave. Ali spun to see what had caused the noise, and when her eyes landed on its source her heart sank into her stomach. Gavin was standing next to the entrance with the rock in his hand, and the door shut tight behind him.

"Gavin, what did you do?" Lilly's words came out slowly, enunciating each syllable. The rage hiding behind her eyes was tangible, and Ali said a quick thank you that she wasn't Gavin.

"I…I was just moving it so that I could open the door, but then I lost my grip and…and it shut before I could stop it," Gavin rushed his response, putting one foot on the wall and pulling on the handle with every ounce of strength left in his body. But there was no use. They were trapped in the cryptic ballroom.

"If we figure out how to make it out of here alive, I am going to kill—"

"Sh! Does anyone else hear that?" Skotia interrupted, bringing her fingers to her lips so that everyone would fall silent.

Ali quieted her mind and focused on the walls surrounding her. She couldn't see any movement, and after Lilly's threats faded into the crisp air, there were no voices left.

Then, she heard it. There was a low, rumbling sound coming from under Ali's feet. She bent down to press her palms against the floor and felt the vibrations coming to meet her fingers. Without speaking, the four travelers exchanged puzzled glances from across the cave and started walking toward one another, as if that would provide them with some sort of answer. Ali's eyes were still darting around the room, looking for another exit they could use as an escape. Without warning, the ground crumbled beneath Ali's feet, throwing her off balance as she scrambled away from the forming abyss.

The floor was falling apart.

Gavin had just leaped off the ground he was standing on in time to watch it fall into the black hole below him. The perimeter of the floor were the first to go completely. Ali looked toward the door and realized, even if they could figure out a way to open it, they'd first have to figure out how to leap across a ten-foot gap to reach it.

Ali couldn't tell how far the bottom was because every time another piece of stone collapsed, she couldn't hear any sign of it hitting the ground beneath their floor. That was enough to encourage her legs to run toward the middle of the room where the floor was still intact. The other three followed Ali's lead until they were all back-to-back, legs shaking as they anxiously awaited their fate.

Ali peered over the edge and immediately regretted her decision. There was nothing below her, which was arguably worse than seeing a creature rise up from the depths. At least if there was a creature, she knew there was a bottom.

Suddenly, the stone stopped collapsing. They had about two feet to spare before their dinky island would've been next, so Ali said a silent thank you to whatever force had spared her life. Could it be Infernus itself protecting her?

Before she could dwell on that question, another one took its place. How were they going to get off this rock?

The others must've been thinking the same thing because Gavin asked, "Skotia, got anything in your backpack that could help us right about now?"

"Can't say I know of anything that helps someone jump a fifty-foot gap. Now, if you hadn't let go of that— Wait, what are those?"

Three words Ali did not want to hear. Filling her lungs with air, Ali took another step toward the edge to see what was lying beneath them.

She lied. Having nothing below her was definitely better than what was awaiting them.

"What? What's down there?" Lilly demanded with a distressed edge to her words.

Ali's voice caught, her mouth dry. She stared hopelessly down in horror.

Slithering up to meet them were hundreds of vines. They were making their way through thin air, some wrapping themselves around the rock column beneath their feet to reach their next victims. Dark thorns protruded from their stems, and at the top of the vine was some sort of black rose. The rose itself had the typical layers of petals Ali was used to seeing, but none of the beauty. The petals were moving in and out of their formations, always coming back together in the end to create that unmistakable rose pattern. Before her eyes, she could see the vines multiplying, sprouting new limbs from its buds that were more viscous than the next.

The vines were fast. Ali gulped as they finally rose to meet them at eye level, incredibly aware that she didn't even have a knife to protect herself. The vines looked hungry, desperate for a feast they'd been deprived of for far too long.

"Shadowvines," Skotia stated, her voice cracking at the last syllable. "I've only read about these. I didn't think they still existed. They were one of the methods ancient Sorcerers used to ward off invaders from Infernus."

"And what exactly does that mean for us?" Lilly blurted out, her eyes frozen on one of the wicked roses swaying in front of her face.

"These vines are said to wrap around you and slowly dwindle the life out of your soul, leaving you to rot as a shell of yourself for the rest of eternity. Let's just say these are one of the reasons Infernus didn't have many wars. No one wanted to fight against these things once they realized what they were capable of."

The anecdote did absolutely nothing to ease the nausea rising up Ali's windpipe. She grabbed Lilly and Gavin's hands, interlocking her fingers in theirs. They both gave a squeeze back. She was the reason her best friends were here, the reason they were about to reach their demise, and there was nothing she could do to stop it. An invisible, crushing weight landed on Ali's shoulders, making her want to jump into the arms of the shadowvines and sacrifice herself if it meant saving her friends' lives.

But before Ali had the chance to become a martyr, the vines lurched forward, wrapping themselves around each teenager. Ali felt thorns digging through her clothing, eager to puncture her skin. Suddenly, her fingers were torn from Gavin and Lilly's hands, and she was airborne. They all were. There was a flurry of legs kicking the air, trying to reach the black roses that were controlling the vines' movements. It was useless. Each of them was playing a losing game against an opponent that thrived off their struggling. As if it made their deaths more enjoyable.

The last thing Ali saw were her two best friends dangling in the air with blood running down their limbs. The thorns had pierced Lilly's thigh and left a gash in Gavin's neck, leaving cuts that were already too deep to save. Suddenly, Ali's vines wrapped themselves around her eyes, blindfolding her before plunging their way down into the deep, taking Ali into a darkness her nightmares could never imagine.

CHAPTER 9

SWEET NIGHTMARES

———

When Gavin opened his eyes, he was standing on the freshly trimmed lawn in front of his house. No longer trapped by shadowvines, he waved his arms in circles and kicked his legs into the air. He was free.

But where were his friends? And how did he get back home?

"Ali! Lilly! Where are you?" he shouted, cupping his hands around his mouth to make his voice carry.

There were a dozen voices shouting over one another in Gavin's mind. He pressed his palms to his forehead to drown them out, but his efforts were futile. There were too many questions that needed answers, and Gavin didn't know where to start.

Suddenly, he heard voices coming from inside. He spun around to see if it could be the two girls but saw his parents and little sister through the front window instead. They were sitting on the couch, enjoying each other's company and laughing at a joke his dad just told. The sun bounced off his mother's ginger curls, while his father's balding head reflected the rays. His sister, who shared their mom's vibrant red hair, was sprawled against the cushions, taking up the entire sofa with her tiny frame.

Relieved that his family was safe, Gavin jogged to the front door and walked into his front hallway. Everything looked the same as it had when he left for school that morning: his parents' keys sat in the round, glass tray on their stone table, and his sister's bright blue sandals were propped up against the gray wall, just underneath the oversized mirror hanging at eye level. The chandelier hung above his head and not a speck of dust was caught in its lights, leaving it to shine perfectly for all who entered.

His mom's laugh rang out like a bell. He rounded with a wide smile across his face, eager to relax on the couch with his family.

"Hey everyone. Sorry I'm home late, you'll never believe what happened to me. To us. Lilly, Ali, and me, we were in the woods behind the neighborhood, and I saw this massive, glowing oak tree. Lilly couldn't see it, but when I went to get a closer look, my hand got stuck and—" he cut off midsentence. Not one of his family members had turned around to listen to his story. Come to think of it, they hadn't skipped a beat since he walked in.

"Mom? Dad?"

"Honey, do you see that news anchor's outfit? Who told her that was okay for television?" his mom asked his dad, who merely grunted in agreement.

Between stories, his sister mindlessly doodled on her marble notebook, rolling her eyes at her mom's comments while perfecting her figures' shadows. Taking off her headphones, she creased her eyebrows and quickly scanned the room.

"Is Gavin still not home?"

"I'm right here," he replied, now stepping in front of the group and waving his arms frantically in front of their faces.

"Um, honey, when was the last time you saw your son?"

The last time they saw him? He hugged them goodbye this morning after breakfast.

"Probably about a week ago? Maybe more?" his father answered, barely looking away from the television. "But who cares? We have Ashley home, and that's all that really matters."

His mother smirked, and Ashley released a cruel laugh that sliced through Gavin's heart as much as it did his ears. She put down her colored pencils and went to sit in between her parents on the couch, almost brushing against Gavin's shoulder as she stood.

"What, what do you mean…who cares?" Gavin whispered. A large lump was swelling in his throat, making it difficult to swallow the pain.

"You know you're our only true child, right sweetie?" His mother coddled his sibling between the plush couch cushions until she submitted and fell into the wide arms awaiting her.

Gavin always had a suspicion that he was different, even though he wasn't sure what that meant. From a young age, his olive skin didn't match either of his parents' pale complexions, and his dark hair stood out in all family photos. When Gavin was barely five years old, his parents sat him down to share the news.

"Sweetie, we have something to tell you." His mom gave his hand a tight squeeze. *"You're adopted, which means that you didn't come from Mommy's tummy. But that doesn't mean we love you any less."*

A few months later, she revealed Gavin was going to have a little sister—one that did come from her belly. He didn't completely understand what the difference was, but when he first saw how his sister's skin matched his parents' pigmentation, he knew something was different.

Growing up, his parents always made it a point to assure him that they were loved equally. They always had the same number of Christmas gifts, birthday parties were equally grand, and their bedrooms were the same exact size, even though his sister owned twice as many clothes as he did. He always had a nagging suspicion that their actions were a facade. For the past seventeen years, he'd been able to convince himself otherwise.

But after hearing his family's words, Gavin saw his gut feeling was right about the one part of his life he prayed it would be wrong about.

His family didn't care that he didn't come home from school that one afternoon. They weren't like Ali's mother forming a neighborhood search party to try and locate their missing child. His parents were content with the one child they had left. More content, it seemed, than they were when both teenagers were under their roof. Gavin was struggling to keep his balance, resting his weight onto the arm of the couch. His family didn't need him—no, they didn't *want* him. But if they didn't want him, who would?

A cold, numbing sensation ran through his veins. Those days he spent wondering how his family could love him if he wasn't really their child came rushing back. Gavin was hiding under his plaid covers, wondering if his birth parents were ever going to come crashing through their front door in the middle of the night, challenging his mom and dad to a duel for their son. The scene played out every night before his eyes blinked themselves to sleep, stopping just before he found out which set of parents won. Each morning he'd wake up in a cold sweat, jolting himself up from underneath his blankets before reminding himself that it was all a dream. Frantic, jagged breaths would follow him into the kitchen until he'd had his bowl of cereal in silence, the cold milk providing some relief to his perspiring body.

Gavin could use some of that cold milk right about now, but his feet couldn't find their way to the kitchen. Instead, he had the sudden urge to get as far away from the house as quickly as his legs would carry him. Maybe he could go back into the forest and find the enchanted tree again? This time, he would know what to expect when he touched his fingers to the bark, and he could get back to Ali and Lilly. Maybe they were still stuck in Infernus, trapped somewhere in that horrible cavern, wondering where he was. They were his best friends; they had to be worried about where he was.

At least, that's what he told himself.

Sidestepping around his living room furniture and away from his nauseating family, Gavin made a beeline for his front door. The chandelier wasn't shining as perfectly and after sneaking a glance in the mirror, he saw that his eyes were puffy and brimming with tears. He quickly brought his wrist to his eyes to wipe away any signs of his dejection. Whether or not his family could see him, they didn't deserve his tears.

He flung the door open and stepped onto their front porch, letting the wood slam shut behind him. A fury of red clouded his vision. He had no control over his adoption, so why was he being treated like he had a choice in the matter? He never asked to be stuck in a house with a sister who didn't want anything to do with him or parents who, evidently, felt that he would never be enough. So why did he have to deal with the consequences?

Scanning his yard for answers, Gavin made the only decision that was coming to his mind that moment—he walked across the freshly cut lawn and started kicking up tufts of grass.

"Take that!" Gavin screamed to the wind. His breath hitched with every kick and his fists were shaking at his sides, but the destruction felt right. It gave him the sense of control his body craved. Like a wolf who had found its first meal of the winter, he leaned into the rage and continued to ruin the perfection that lay under his feet.

Looking at the results of his wrath, a flicker of satisfaction settled inside Gavin, but his frustration still dominated. Turning the yard to shambles had been a quick release, but he needed something more that would yield the answers to questions he'd suppressed for so long. Kneeling on the ground, he picked at the strands of grass left intact and twirled them between his fingertips.

"Where can I even go if I can't go home?"

Without warning, the remnants of his yard began to quake underneath his feet. Confused by the sudden shift, Gavin tried to stand, but the tremors knocked him to the ground, his hands sprawled out in front of him.

"Not again," he whimpered, remembering how the cave floor had given way under his feet. The ground began to swirl beneath him, like a merciless whirlpool forming at sea. He clung to the clumps of earth that were in his fists and closed his eyes, silently pleading for the tremors to stop.

Eyes still pressed shut, Gavin felt the earth open and suck him into the swirling vortex, leaving him wishing for his parents one final time.

* * *

Lilly huddled under her blankets like the caterpillar who would rather put off their metamorphosis another day. Slowly gathering her bearings, Lilly propped herself up and scanned her bedroom.

"Wasn't I just with Gavin and Ali?" Wiping sleep from her eyes, she recalled being lost in a strange world but couldn't put her finger on exactly what had happened to the trio. As more sunlight crept into her bedroom, the memories blurred together until they formed a giant blob of unrecognizable names and faces.

"Huh, must've been a dream."

Lilly glanced at the clock and a shot of adrenaline struck her chest. It was her last day of junior year, and she was going to miss first period if she didn't finish her routine in record time. She launched out of her bed, both feet landing simultaneously and threw open her closet doors, only to find that her colorful wardrobe had been replaced with hideous, gray school uniforms.

A row of pleated skirts hung underneath a dozen white blouses with L & S embroidered into the right arm. Lying across her drawers were sets of black neckties and a pair of tights neatly folded into a perfect pile. Gray and black were not typical staples of Lilly's wardrobe. Pushing past the skirts and blouses, Lilly rummaged for any of her normal outfits. Where was her alien graphic tee? Her boho pants? Her mint green blazer she made work with any and every outfit?

But time was doing its job and ticking down, leaving Lilly only a handful of seconds to question who had replaced her closet with a boarding-school student's attire. With many grunts and a few curses, she managed to pull up the tights without tearing a hole in the seam and tucked the blouse into her skirt.

"I am a vision of lackluster beauty," Lilly mumbled, looking at her new outfit in the floor-length mirror while fumbling with the necktie. "How does this thing even work?" She gave up the fight, throwing the accessory on her unmade bed. Hurriedly grabbing her backpack and slamming the bedroom door, her footsteps thumped on the staircase leading to the kitchen. Not noticing her parents sitting at the coffee table, she threw open the refrigerator and took a large bite out of an apple before having the chance to wash it.

"Eh, a few pesticides never hurt anybody," she said to herself.

"Lilly dear, don't you look nice. Why are you in such a rush?" her mother asked, taking a moment to look up from her crossword clue.

"Um, because I have history first period and at this rate, Mr. Melgar will have taken attendance by the time I get to the parking lot? Wait, why aren't you two at the studio, don't you have to prepare for the gallery?" Lilly froze mid bite. She took in her parents' outfits. Their own vibrant wardrobe had been replaced with blouses and suits. Suddenly losing her appetite, she placed the fruit on the counter.

"What gallery? Dear, do you know what she's talking about?" Mrs. Lamboll turned to her husband and placed her hand on his forearm to bring his attention out of that morning's paper.

"What?" Her father raised his head ever so slightly out of the "Stocks" section. "No, no idea what you're talking about, sweetie. Why don't you call Addison and see if she's left for school yet? Maybe she can give you a ride."

"Also, I thought you had a free period? Remember, I called the principal at the beginning of the year so that you would have history with Rachel this year—that way you two could work on all your projects together." Lilly's mother must have mixed up her morning vitamins (as she liked to call them) because the last time she spoke with either Addison or Rachel was in eighth grade when they were comparing their art projects to hers, and she barked at them to leave her station. Literally, barked. As a collective, the Lorrshore Sisters left her alone after that.

"No, I've had history first period all year. Wait, Dad, are you reading about *politics*?" Lilly let the word drip off her tongue like a spoiled swig of milk.

"Of course, if I'm going to beat out Tom Rutledge for County seat, the people have to think that I'm one of them. Just like everybody else, I read *The Journal* one article at a time."

If there was any food left in Lilly's mouth, it would've been on the floor by now. This was not the household Lilly grew up in. Her parents hated anything to do with regulated government and would much rather hide in their art studio for hours, working on their latest abstract commission that would help pay the bills. If it hadn't been for the birthmark on her mother's left cheek, she would've debated whether these were impostors.

"I don't know what's going on here, but I'm going to call Ali or Gavin to see if one of them can get me to school. Lord knows one of them is always running ten minutes behind," Lilly muttered, rummaging through her bag for her cellphone.

"I'm sorry, who did you say you were going to call?" Lilly's mother's voice cracked at the end, feigning composure.

"Ali DuBois and Gavin Briondelle? My best friends? The ones I spend essentially all my time with when I'm not here? Why are you two acting so weird today—and what happened to my closet?" Lilly's arms slammed on the countertop below her.

"Honey, are you sure you feel all right? Maybe you should take the morning off from class today. It's the last day, your teachers won't mind. Plus, I'm making beef wellington for dinner tonight—your favorite!"

Lilly had been a practicing vegetarian for three months, which was a suggestion originally made by her mother.

"I think I'm just going to walk to school and beg Mr. Melgar to mark me here as present when I eventually show up. I'll see you both for dinner, and I'll just take a salad."

The second Lilly shut her front door behind her, she ripped out her cellphone and scrolled through her contacts. Ali's number had disappeared from her phone, and so had Gavin's. Luckily, she had Ali's number memorized from all those nights using her landline to make secret calls under her comforter.

With bated breath, Lilly dialed the ten digits and waited until the ringtone stopped playing.

"Hello?"

"Ali, thank god you answered. Are you at school yet? If you're not, can your parents pick me up on their way? I'm having the weirdest morning—you'll never believe what's been going on. By the way—"

"I'm sorry, who is this?" Grateful to hear her best friend's voice, Lilly breathed a sigh of relief. But why did Ali ask who was calling her?

"It's Lilly, obviously."

"Lilly Lamboll?"

"Um, yes? What other Lilly would be calling you this early in the morning? What other Lilly do you even know?"

Silence.

"Ali? You there?" The hairs on the back of Lilly's neck were standing up. Why was Ali acting like she was a complete stranger?

"Well, I hope you had your fun. I don't know how you got my number, but don't call again. Tell your other Lorrshore Sisters they can screw themselves. Or don't, I won't care either way."

With that, the line went dead.

"What's…what's happening to me?"

Lilly felt tears starting to well in her eyes. There had to be an explanation to the absolute absurdity of her morning, but wherever she turned, she hit another dead end. Theories swirled in her brain, but each new one was more ridiculous than the last. She scrolled through her phone to see if there was anyone else who was worth calling, but the only names she recognized were those of the Lorrshore Sisters, and Lilly couldn't imagine why she would have ever saved their numbers.

As reality set in that the most important people in her life—her parents, Ali, Gavin—didn't know a single thing about her, Lilly's heartrate picked up, and she frantically scanned her neighborhood for an answer. But no matter where her eyes fell—a convertible driving along the perfectly paved street, squirrels chasing each other up a tree, the balcony that jutted out from her parents' room—nothing looked amiss.

With no other option, Lilly began to walk.

"If I keep moving, I have to find some answers eventually, right?" An answer to why she was wearing a hideous uniform, why her parents had suddenly changed career paths, and why her mother had suddenly forgotten that she was a horrible chef and was going to try to cook beef wellington.

A car honked behind Lilly. She had drifted into the road, but she quickly made her way back to the sidewalk. Losing her balance, Lilly tripped and fell onto the yard next to her, ripping her tights and staining her skirt a putrid green color. She raised a particular finger up to the passing driver and went to go rip her tights off clean but stopped when she noticed that the road looked like it was...moving?

As if it were the ocean, ripples started to form into the blacktop. Carefully propping herself up from the yard, Lilly took two steps closer to check whether or not her eyes were deceiving her.

They were not.

Lilly's eyes went wide as the road started to disappear and was replaced by a hollow crater with no bottom in sight. The winds started to pick up around her, whipping her hair in front of her face and blinding her from seeing that the black hole was now almost at her feet, leaving her with little time to run.

"No, no, no, no!" Lilly shrieked. Turning her head on a swivel, she saw that the neighborhood was empty. No one would hear her calls for help.

With one last gulp, Lilly's petrified feet unfroze from the ground, and she turned on her heels. Adrenaline propelled her limbs forward faster than she could've asked for. But it was no use. The sunken pit wanted Lilly as its victim and was not going to lose.

The wind was pushing against Lilly, forcing her closer to her doom. Closing her eyes, Lilly used one last effort to throw herself forward and dig her fingernails into a yard in front of her, but there was no escaping. She felt her feet go first, giving in to the relentless pull that seemed to be growing as quickly as the hole itself. With one last scream that no one would hear, Lilly's fingernails unlatched from the earth, and she tumbled backward into the black abyss.

Skotia lifted her head off the damp grass and found herself looking directly at the front steps of her grade school. The striking teal building stood out against the mountainous vista, but the bell swinging from the top of the building echoed for miles, calling for children from across the land. The blooming, flamboyant flowers at the front of the building had grown to the tops of the second-floor windows and would continue to sprout through the year until they reached above the rooftops.

"Huh?" She brought her fingers to her head, expecting to feel a large bump forming on the back of her skull. But there was nothing there.

That's when everything came flooding back. The shadowvines sweeping them off their feet, sending waves of adrenaline through her body as her feet dangled helplessly in the air. There they all were—Ali and those other two—most certainly moments away from death. But she wasn't dead—she was at school.

Scrambling to her feet, she heard a jumble of whispers from behind her. She scanned the schoolyard for the source, and her eyes landed on a younger version of herself making her way to the front door of school.

"No, no, no!" Realization dawned on Skotia as she pieced together what was happening. The vines weren't going to *just* leave their bodies to rot in a void for eternity; they were going to trap them in their minds as well.

"For Infernus's sake!" She stormed toward the little girl. By her outfit choice, she clearly still enjoyed wearing the frilly handmade dresses her mother loved to choose for her. The plaid pattern started at her neckline and stopped just above her knees, but the two braids falling down her back were the perfect complement to her first-day-of-school outfit. With both hands clutched to her bookbag, the younger Skotia walked through the tall doors toward her classroom.

Teenage Skotia wasn't far behind, taking in the four walls she had long forgotten. The chalkboard hung at the front and twenty desks made from the finest Infernian wood were scattered throughout the room. Crystals hung from the ceiling, and sunshine floated in from the dozen windows creating rainbows when the rays hit their edges. For a moment, everything was flawless. But Skotia knew better.

The child took her seat next to the window, pulling at the seams in her dress and wiping off specks of dried dirt while the other children filed in, laughing with one another as they recounted their adventures over the long break.

Skotia remembered this day. She had sat in her chair wanting nothing more than to pull out her braids and run far from the class and from the children who weren't even glancing her way. Skotia had never had a first day like this one: instead of trekking to her last school with her hand tucked in her older brother's, she was now enrolled in a new school filled with strange faces and expensive clothes.

"You'll do great, sweetie. No one will notice anything different. Just try to make a friend."

Even now, her mother's advice from that morning rang in her ears as the lessons began.

"Kids are just as cruel as adults, Mother. They just have an imaginative way about their punishments," teenage Skotia spat.

In the blink of an eye, the classroom began to spin. The rotations grew faster, throwing her off balance, but none of the children noticed the sudden shift. She held on to the desk in front of her and slammed her eyes shut as her legs threatened to give way beneath her.

But before she was thrown off her feet, the spinning came to a stop. When she opened her eyes, she was in the schoolyard again, practically standing on top of her younger self.

"Skotia! Do you want to come to the creek with us?" Perry Ember asked, breaking free from the pack. Four children stood behind Perry, staring at both girls.

"Oh, er, um," Skotia stuttered, staring at the inch of grass between her feet. "I-I don't think I can today. Maybe next time?"

A frown had barely started to form on Perry's face before Skotia turned and ran. Her little legs carried her quickly away from the others and toward her home.

Truthfully, Skotia wasn't sure why she had said no that day. Her mother had asked—no, pleaded—with her to make a friend. But the moment the opportunity arrived, she jumped at the chance to say no. Maybe things would've been different if she'd said yes.

She watched her younger self's braids fly behind her. The plaid dress was blowing in the breeze and the knapsack full of papers bounced behind her. Skotia cursed before the scene began to spin once more. This time, she didn't close her eyes. Instead, she left them wide open to watch her younger self grow smaller on the horizon. As the girl disappeared entirely, Skotia felt a single tear fall down her cheek before it was lost entirely to the wind.

Skotia knew what scene was next before it finished developing. They were in one of the sunflower fields next to her house. The flowers had barely reached three feet off the ground, but Skotia loved to hide among them on her worst days. Their brilliant yellow sheen promised Skotia better times if she would only stay there for a few more minutes. She gladly let the soil cover her arms and legs as she bent down to smell each flower, breathing in a sigh of relief.

"Come on, we have to get out of—" teenager Skotia began. Sweat was gathering on her palms, but when she grabbed the younger girl's hand, all she felt was air.

"Skotia, where are you?" Her father's voice boomed from their window. "Don't think just because you're off at that new school that you'll be excused from cleaning these pots! You're still the same as the rest of us!"

"Please, no," the child whimpered. "I can't go back there, not yet."

The child looked down at her dress; it was covered in the same dirt her limbs were.

"No, no, no. Not the dress." She grabbed the fabric in her hands and tried to rub the filth from its stitches.

"That's not going to work!" Skotia screamed. "You're only making it worse!"

"I have to get this out," the girl cried. "I can't go home like this."

Without another word, she was off to the only place she could think of—the creek. Skotia remembered this moment, thinking the water would wash away all her problems, leaving her with nothing but wet hair that would dry on the walk home. Her throat tightened realizing how wrong she had been.

Once they reached the water's edge, the child dove straight into the icy water. A shiver ran down Skotia's spine as she recalled how the sharp coldness had stayed in her bones for hours, laughing at the sun's rays when they tried to warm her frame. She stood on the bank, waiting for her head to break the water's surface.

"Oh my *goodness* was that chilly," Skotia gasped. She ran to the bank and began to wring out her dress, shaking her hands dry as quickly as she could. Her father wasn't going to wait for her much longer.

Something in the water caught the child's eye. Its end stuck out from the ripples, calling out Skotia's name in every wave.

"Please don't touch it. Please go home," Skotia whispered from the bank. Her dark eyes were burning from the salty tears resting on her waterline.

"What is this?" the girl gasped, pulling a thin, smooth branch from the brook. It couldn't have been longer than her forearm. She held it out in the sunlight, letting the light define the tiny carvings etched into its side. The current had erased anything that might've been legible, but that didn't deter her curiosity. To Skotia, this was a hidden treasure piece she would make her own.

Without a second thought, Skotia lifted her discovery high in the air and began to twirl in a circle. She waved it in front of her, pretending that she was parting the waters and creating a pathway to a secret world only she could enter. A world that promised to love her despite how many—or how few—pots she cleaned at dinner.

"Everyone, look at this! Skotia thinks she has a magic wand!"

Her eyes flew open. Standing on the other side of the creek were her classmates, staring at her with growing eyes as they surveyed the sight in front of them.

"Seriously, what *are* you doing?" they jeered, pointing at the object in her hand. The child instantly dropped the object and kicked it away.

The older Skotia was still standing a few feet away. She took in the child's appearance. Her wet braids drooped loosely next to her face and the seams from her dress were halfway undone. The water had cleared some of the mud, but there were still splotches of dirt caked onto the print. Compared to her spotless classmates, the young girl might as well have been working on a farm for the last eight hours.

That day was the last Skotia would be invited to the creek after school. Perry was the last to leave, giving the girl one regrettable glance before running off to join the others who were still giggling among themselves.

With her fate ultimately sealed, the child held her head in her hands. Forgetting the reason she was at the creek in the first place, she spun on her heel to start her hike home. Before she took two steps, her father was waiting for her on the hill's crest.

"You!" he shouted, making his way down to her. "What do you think you're doing? And what did you do to that dress? Do you know how long it took your mother to sew that?"

Skotia had enough. If she was going to live out the rest of her days in this nightmare, she was at least going to cut off her memory here. She took two steps forward before diving into the water, waiting for the ice to seep into her body like it had once before.

But she felt nothing. At the last second, the water turned into a swirling void that opened to a depth that Skotia couldn't see. She opened her mouth to cry out, but the sound was caught in her throat, leaving her flying headfirst toward the black hole below her.

* * *

Ali was sprawled on her front lawn, as if she were about to start doing snow angels in the middle of summer. She sat up, then hauled herself to her feet. Turning to face her front door, a flood of memories rushed through her brain, sorting themselves until they aligned into chronological order.

"What just happened?" she pondered aloud, twirling in a circle and running her hands from her feet to her shoulders to make sure she was still whole.

"How did I get back home? Where are Lilly and Gavin? What happened to Skotia?"

From where she stood, nothing looked out of order, but everything felt different. The lofty trees that lined her street were still soaring as high as ever, and the summer evening air was sticky against her skin, but her front door was painted its old shade of jade green instead of its current deep red, and both of her neighbors' cars were in their driveway. Those neighbors had divorced three years ago, and Ali hadn't seen either car since.

"Three years ago..." Ali murmured to herself, slowing letting the gears click into place.

"Ali! Carter! Get down here *now*!" Her mother's voice rang from inside the living room.

"Did she just say Carter?"

Ali's body jolted awake from its fog and carried her through the front door, only to see that her brother was plopped on the living room couch and a younger version of herself sat next to him.

Her black hair wasn't nearly as long, and Ali still had braces plastered to her teeth, but there was no confusing that Carter was sitting next to her. His hair was almost as black as Ali's, but instead of it being pin straight, it curled around his face and blocked his green eyes from sight at times. His skinny frame was leaning against the arm of the sofa and his youthful skin was glowing against the furniture's dull exterior, but all his focus was on their mother. Ali stood frozen, her hands shaking as she slowly moved closer to her brother. Clutching onto a table for support, she focused on evening her labored breathing one exhale at a time.

Once her legs felt a little less like rubber, she ran to the couch. Barely noticing her former self sitting there, she reached down to envelop Carter in the hug she had dreamed about too many times to count. But as her arms swooped down to where he sat, they went through his body and caught the air behind him.

No one knew she was there. She was a ghost floating through space and time, forced to watch the remnants of a past life.

That didn't stop her from doing everything in her power to make her brother notice that she was standing a few feet away. She waved her hands in the air high above her head, stomped on the hardwood floors, and even strung together a slew of choice curse words. As predicted, nothing worked.

"Yeah, Mom? Why'd you call us in here?" Carter asked, his voice higher than Ali remembered it.

Their mother was looking between Carter and her younger self with frowning eyes, causing chills to run up Ali's arms. She remembered this conversation.

She remembered what day this was.

Glancing down, the newspaper on their coffee table confirmed her suspicions. The date on the top right corner read June 24, 2004. To Ali, this wasn't just another day on the calendar: it was Doomsnight.

"I called you both here because I need to know what happened to the upstairs bathroom. When I walked in today the Egyptian cotton towels were torn to shreds, the floor was covered in bath water, and my makeup was sprawled over the counter. It was absolutely disgusting, like we live at an animal farm." She scoffed, her perfectly coiffed hair frizzing in the summer heat.

"Your father doesn't know about this mess yet, but when he does, he's going to absolutely have a fit. Now, we can prevent that from happening if you two tell me the truth. Which one of you destroyed the bathroom?"

"I don't know what you're talking about," younger Ali said from the couch, arms crossed defiantly across her chest.

"You might as well have 'liar' painted across your forehead, dear. Carter, what do you know about this? And don't try to lie like your sister."

Watching as an outsider, Ali could see the moral dilemma that was playing out in her brother's mind. He was fidgeting with his hands, looking down between them, and his tapping feet. Their mother had never been a fan of lying, especially when it came from her own two children. She knew that the two of them wouldn't have had time to think of a plausible story before she called them downstairs, and now was her time to strike. At the time, Ali had been trying to send telepathic briberies into her brother's mind, desperately pleading with him to quickly come up with a lie they both could improvise.

"What do we say about lying in this house?" Her mother was directing the question toward Carter, breaking him down with her piercing gaze.

"Ali did it because she was mad at you for reading through her diary and telling her she couldn't hang out with Lilly this weekend!" Carter blurted out in one breathless sentence.

"Are you *kidding* me?" Ali screamed into her brother's face even though he was an arm's length away.

"I'm...I'm sorry Ali! I didn't know what to say, I—"

"Sweetie, you did the right thing. You can go to your room. Alexandria, you're grounded for the next month. And I *will* be looking through the rest of that notebook of yours. There were some disturbing images in there that we need to address."

Her mother's voice had returned to its normal pitch now that she'd gotten the answer she wanted. It was some sick game she enjoyed playing, pitting her children against each other until one cracked.

Ali cringed as she watched her younger self storm off in protest, ignoring her brother's apologies. What she didn't see the first time around were her brother's silent tears running down his face. He quickly tried to wipe them away as they flowed, but he could have been possibly more upset than his sister.

The knot of guilt she had been trying to ignore in her stomach the past three years was at its breaking point.

"I can't believe you were so stupid, Ali! Why couldn't you have been less selfish for a second? Just one second?" she yelled at herself, looking in the mirror they had hanging in their living room.

Desperate to change the past, Ali ran up the flight of stairs toward her bedroom. She slid her body in the crack between the doorframe and the wall and sat down in her desk chair, watching her younger self cry into the pillows on her bed. She remembered the salty tears gathering on her lips and mucus running from her nose. Not to mention the utter betrayal from Carter, possibly the worst blow of them all. She trusted her brother not to let their mother wedge herself in between them, but that trust was broken. Now Ali was the one facing the consequences.

There was a knock, followed by a small hand pushing open the door and a head full of curly hair popping itself into her bedroom.

"Ali? Are you okay?" Carter's voice was so small, as if raising it an octave would shatter the glass windowpanes.

"Do I look okay to you?" she shot back, lacing hurt into every syllable.

"I'm sorry that I told Mom about the bathroom, I really am! I know you didn't want her to find out, but she was going to one way or another, and I didn't want her to get Dad involved. You know what he's like when he gets mad. I thought maybe, while you're grounded, we could hang out some more. We have a couple board games we haven't played yet, and this will give us plenty of time to start rewatching some of those DVDs we had lined up," Carter said, trying to shed light on an otherwise dreadful punishment. His voice slowly filled with excitement as he outlined their plans.

The corners of her mouth crept into a sad smile. She had forgotten how often her brother would slink into her room, only to go over the laundry list of activities he'd created for the both of them. His eyes lit up when he mentioned something he knew his sister would like, eagerly waiting for her approval. When school finished, they could spend hours in their basement, finding a hidden gem around every corner, only to do it all over the next day.

Until Ali ruined everything.

"Carter, does it look like I want to spend my summer vacation inside this house with you, watching stupid movies and playing board games that are meant for seven-year-olds?"

"I'm just trying to help," Carter said, his voice shaking. The curls on his head deflated and he tried to walk over to Ali's bedside before she cut him off.

"Well, you're actually doing the complete opposite. You know what would help? If you stop talking to me, turn around, and leave me alone for the rest of the summer. In fact, you can just get out of my life while you're at it!"

With a single sob, Carter turned and fled, shutting the bedroom door behind him. Ali could hear his footsteps echoing down the stairs and eventually out the front door.

That was the last time she saw her brother.

"Go *after* him! *Please!*" Ali begged her younger self. But like her previous attempts, there was no sign that she was even in the room.

"Ugh, you idiot!" she yelled one last time, lips quivering with every word.

Taking it upon herself to follow Carter's footsteps, Ali flew down the stairs two at a time and bolted through the open door. Stopping for a second to see which way he'd run, she wasn't surprised when she saw a black-haired dot sprinting down the street.

"Carter! Carter, wait! I didn't mean it! Please don't go!" Her voice was cracking as she called out to her brother, hopelessly watching his tiny dot grow smaller as he sped away from their front yard.

Determined to save her brother from whatever fate he experienced the first time around, she tried to lurch her body forward, to no avail. Her legs felt like they were stuck in an aged molasses that had been sitting in the hot sun for far too long. Cursing her helplessness, Ali gaped at the ground beneath her as she realized what was happening. Her front yard was no longer the perfect, cookie-cutter lawn it had been moments ago. Now there were divots in the grass that were coming together to form one vast crater. With one last look in the direction her brother had run, Ali didn't fight gravity as her body fell into oblivion.

CHAPTER 10

THE PROTECTOR

———

Ali woke with a start, gasping to fill her lungs with the oxygen they desperately needed.

"Ali! Are you okay?"

She looked up and saw Lilly rushing toward her with arms wide open, ready to envelop her in a bear hug. The force threw Ali onto the floor with the weight of Lilly's body on top of her.

"I think I'm okay now," she answered, still piecing together what she'd just witnessed.

Gathering her thoughts, she tried to put together the timeline of events. The last thing she remembered was being pulled into the depths of the darkest blackness ever created. A shudder coursed over her bones thinking of those vines wrapping around her body, winding her limbs together and sucking her into the void.

With Lilly off her, Ali sat up and took in their new surroundings. The four of them were safely on the other side of the ballroom, their makeshift island now lost to the bottomless pit. The same mixture of soil and dust swarmed her nostrils, and she had to squint while her eyes adjusted to the dim lighting. The insects were still glowing, but their light had certainly dimmed since she first entered the cavern. Lilly and Gavin flanked her on either side, but Skotia was standing a few meters away, hastily searching through her backpack.

"After the shadowvines got to us, what happened to you?" Ali asked, afraid to reveal what she'd seen.

Gavin began to answer before he shoved his hands into his pockets and went mute. Digging the toes of his shoes into the dirt, he was muttering something under his breath that Ali couldn't hear.

"Gav, we can't hear you. What happened to you?" she asked, suddenly noticing the newly formed bags under his eyes.

"I don't know…it was strange. After those things tried to suck the life out of me, I think I passed out. The next thing I knew, I was on my front lawn back in Lorrshore, my family inside the house like it was any other day," he started, struggling to get the words out. Ali waited for the rest of the story, but it didn't come.

"And?" she pushed. "What happened next?"

"When I walked in, they couldn't see or hear me. I was a phantom in my own home. My parents began talking about me like I had been missing for weeks, not a few hours. Only, they didn't seem to care—they treated my sister like she was the only child they ever needed," Gavin trailed off, looking past his two friends toward the blank wall behind them.

"You know that's not true, right? They love you just as much as her," Ali proclaimed when she saw a lost, glassy look overwhelm his features.

"Yeah, yeah, I guess. It just felt so real, like my worst nightmare come to life."

"Wait, I think that's exactly what those vines did to us— they showed us our worst nightmares." Lilly perked up, returning her arms to her sides and pacing about the cave.

"It was like any other day in my house, only I was living a life that wasn't mine. My entire wardrobe had been replaced with drab, hideous uniforms and my parents were into politics and crossword puzzles. My house had been shined to perfection, and we didn't have art in any of our rooms. They didn't even know what gallery I was talking about." Lilly wrinkled her face, pursing her lips together until they turned white.

"Worst of all, I wasn't friends with either of you," she continued, quietly this time. "Ali, I tried to call you, but by the sounds of it, you hated that version of me. And honestly, so did I. I would've preferred it if those shadowvines actually sucked the life out of me, instead of throwing me into a reality where I was one of the Lorrshore Sisters."

Ali listened to her friends' nightmares and realized that they hadn't been thrown into the past—they'd been thrown into an alternate reality. The magic in those shadowvines had seeped into their souls, creating a life filled with darkness disguised as normalcy. Nightmares that had always escaped during the late hours of the night, coming to fruition in daylight with no escape.

"Ali, what did you see?" Lilly asked, quietly. By her hushed tone, Ali could sense that she was afraid to hear the answer. And frankly, she was afraid to admit it.

"What do you think I saw, Lilly?"

Mateva could've shown up right then and there, and Ali would've preferred it over the suffocating silence that followed.

"Mine was my worst nightmare, but it wasn't anything that I had to imagine," Ali sighed, the guilt from her outburst already creeping into her veins. "When I woke up, it was the night Carter disappeared. Like Gavin, no one could hear me or see me, no matter how loud I screamed. The last thing I saw before I woke up back here was his curly hair bouncing away down the street, running as far away from me as he could." Ali couldn't meet her friends' stares. She wished she could will her body to melt into the stone beneath her, where she would be free from answering any questions circulating in their heads.

If she were honest, Ali would've admitted that seeing her brother again was the only thing she had wished for every day since he left. Reliving the moment she ruined the chance to have three more years' worth of memories crushed her windpipe, threatening to take all life out of her.

"I don't care who Mateva thinks she is. She's not stopping me from getting my brother back," Ali stated to no one in particular, but there was a fierce certainty to her words.

Looking between her two friends, she realized that she hadn't asked the question that had been staring them in the face since they'd awakened.

"Wait. If those shadowvines were supposed to leave us to rot for eternity, how did we escape?"

"That would be my doing. You're welcome, by the way," a deep voice boomed behind her. She narrowed her eyes, barely making out a shadow's edges against the dark cave. The shadow took a few steps toward the trio, and in a matter of seconds a full-fledged figure emerged.

Ali's breath hitched as she took in the boy in front of her. She guessed that he was eighteen or nineteen, not much older than herself. From the dark skin that wasn't covered by clothing, she could see scars running across his forearms and one small line creased into his face, like it had been there for years now. His shoulders were broad and defined, giving room for his chest to protrude against his shirt. There was a narrow, curved knife sheathed into his waistband, forcing her to imagine what other weapons were hidden.

"Damn," Lilly whistled.

"And, who are you?" Ali asked, trying to speak over her friend's whistle.

"Vulcan. I would say it's nice to meet you all, but usually my first encounters don't involve me risking my neck to save a bunch of strangers, so it's not very nice, after all."

"Excuse me?" Ali questioned, standing to try to meet this stranger's eye level. She was shorter by more than half a foot, but at least now she wasn't on the floor like a sitting duck.

"You were wondering how you escaped those vines, right? Well, you *didn't* escape—I saved you. I heard your screams echoing in the tunnel I was in, and I haven't seen anyone else since I started camping out here. I repelled down from up there," he gestured up with both hands, and they all saw that there were dozens of tunnels built into the walls, at least two stories above their heads.

"By the time I found you all, the shadowvines had already taken you under, and their friends were looking for their next meal. After some pesky dodging and a few cuts with my knife, they let you all go, and I was able to bring you back up here." Vulcan chuckled, leaving a glint in his eye as he recalled the fight. "Not sure what you all were doing in the first place. Only a fool would wander these caves without a weapon."

There was a smugness painted across Vulcan's features, starting with the smirk gracing his lips to the way his eyebrows were creasing together. Ali curled her fists as he talked about his victory with such ease, as if they should've been able to save themselves while they were getting thrown into an endless nightmare.

"We would've been fine," Skotia chimed in, enunciating each word so that her message could not be mistaken. Regrettably, Ali had almost forgotten her look-alike was among them since she'd been so quiet.

"Skotia, what was your nightmare?" Ali asked, turning to her right.

"Well, I...I didn't have one. For me, everything just went black. But we would've been fine. I had everything under control." Skotia was biting her nails while she recalled what happened—another one of Ali's tells when she was lying. Why didn't she want them to know what she'd seen?

Vulcan let a brief laugh escape his mouth.

"She wouldn't have been able to do anything without a weapon. You were pretty much at the point of no return, destined to live out your lives as joyless corpses swaying in the wind." He whistled and swayed his body to show what the three teenagers would've looked like.

"Also, why do you two look exactly the same?" Vulcan asked, pointing between Skotia and Ali.

If he was an Infernian, why didn't he know about the look-alikes? Ali whipped her head to look at Skotia, but she was pointedly avoiding her gaze, going so far as to turn her body away from Ali and toward the newcomer.

Now was not the time to probe her doppelganger; she couldn't show Vulcan they were incapable of protecting themselves *and* fighting among each other.

"Why don't you answer some questions for us first? Like, why were you in these tunnels in the first place? And even if you did save us, why should I trust you?" Ali hadn't meant for the "I" to slip out in her last question and cursed her tongue for speaking too fast. She wanted her questions to be for the good of the group, not reflecting her own trust issues.

"Fair, fair. I'll answer some questions for all of you." Vulcan held his hands up in surrender, but the sly grin was still glued to his face.

"I'm here because there have been rumors of Mateva coming back and hiding away in this mountain. I'm sure you've heard of her, yes? And it's been my family's job for centuries to protect Infernus. I made a vow to my parents that I would carry on their legacy once the time came."

"What do you mean it's been your family's job to protect Infernus? I've never heard of you," Skotia interjected, narrowing her eyes and raising her chin toward Vulcan.

"Let's just say we like to fly under the radar. There's a reason you haven't heard of us, and that's for the better." Vulcan's mouth was smiling, but a dark glint flashed across his eyes.

"I've only been stationed here a few weeks, but so far no sign of her. This place is massive, almost like it's creating new tunnels every day to steer me in the wrong direction. But, I can't go home until I find her. I can't face my parents until I know I've done my part." At the mention of his parents, Vulcan's collected composure cracked, and a fraction of vulnerability peaked through his hard shell.

"And now, there's been talk of a child with her this time—a boy, a few years younger than myself. I don't know what Mateva could possibly want with a child, but if I find him, then I find her, and I'll be damned if I can't locate a powerless child after my training."

"His name is Carter. And that *child* happens to be my brother," Ali stated matter-of-factly.

Until now, any time someone had mentioned Carter, a lump of sadness lingered in the back of her throat. Hearing Vulcan speak about her brother like he was just another pawn in his chess match replaced that sadness with something new, something she hadn't felt before. It was raw, and a primal instinct to protect him consumed her body. When she opened her eyes, she felt flames dancing in her pupils. Squaring off her shoulders, she grew two inches taller and was ready to defend her brother to the end, even if she wasn't with him yet.

For the first time since he'd saved them, Vulcan's eyes widened with genuine surprise. Clearly, he wasn't expecting Ali to be a component on his quest, but she could see the wheels spinning in his mind, figuring out how he could use this new information to his advantage.

"Well, can't say I saw that coming. No one told me the child—Carter, sorry—had a sister. So, I'm guessing you're here to save him too?"

Ali slowly nodded, careful not to reveal her lack of Infernian knowledge. Vulcan had regained his cool composure, leaving his surprise far behind.

"And how do you intend to save him? Are you going to tell me your family is full of secret Sorcerers too?" Skotia interjected from behind Ali, her voice dripping with sarcasm. It reminded Ali of how the Lorrshore Sisters would use their words to make the first-year band kids feel as small as possible. Only, Vulcan didn't play the flute and he was six inches taller than Skotia.

"I don't need magic when I have these," he scoffed, flicking his wrist and producing an array of weapons Ali had never seen before. There were several knives, a set of what looked like nunchakus, a long dagger, and something that looked like it could take off her head in one graceful sweep. "For centuries, my family has protected this land without magic, and I intend to do the same."

Skotia scoffed but said no more.

"So, now it's my turn for some questions, eh? Let's go back to my first one—why do you two look the same? And, where are you from? Because, obviously it's not Infernus," Vulcan pointed to Gavin's outfit with the tip of his knife. Skotia's plan of lying low with strangers wasn't working out so well anymore.

As much as she didn't want to admit it, Ali knew that she'd need Vulcan one way or another to find Carter. Even though their motivations were different, he had some experience navigating the mountain, and his weapons alone were more power than the four of them would ever have. If she did decide to fight the most powerful Sorcerer Infernus had ever seen, she was going to need some help. And to get that help, she needed to share some of their secrets.

"Fine, we'll tell you what you want to know," Ali succumbed, quieting Skotia's protests with a single look.

Once she launched into the story, the words couldn't be stopped. In no coherent order, Ali told Vulcan about how she had fallen into Infernus earlier that day and found her way to Skotia's encampment, with Lilly and Gavin following shortly after. She recalled the cave drawings she'd seen and how her grandmother had always told her about Infernus, but failed to mention that it was her childhood home. When Vulcan said he had never heard of look-alikes, Ali paused.

"Skotia, why hasn't he heard of the look-alike rule? Doesn't everyone from Infernus know about this?" Ali pried, trying to keep her tone as casual as possible.

"Well, not exactly." An uncomfortable stillness hung between them.

"What else are you hiding from us?" Lilly demanded. Usually, Ali would've tried to calm Lilly's outburst. Now, she didn't even bother to try.

"Lilly, give her a break! What was she supposed to do, give us her entire life story when we met?" Gavin cut her off, giving Skotia a small smile while avoiding Lilly's scowl.

"I'm technically *not* supposed to know about it, either," Skotia admitted, shifting her weight back and forth. "One day, I heard one of my mentors discussing it in secret. She didn't realize I was around the corner, but the longer I stood there, the more I needed to know what she was talking about. If other worlds did exist, and there was my double out there, I deserved to know." For the first time since they'd been rescued from the pit, Skotia looked into Ali's eyes. Ali saw pools of regret and guilt swirling in her dark pupils, begging for a sliver of forgiveness.

Arms folded across his chest, Vulcan glanced back and forth between Skotia and Ali. Ali had no words for her double. She understood Skotia's need to uncover the real story—it was the same itch she felt when she asked herself why Grandmother hadn't told her the truth all those years ago, but she couldn't help but feel a hint of doubt twisting in her stomach.

"So, anything else I should know about?" Vulcan chimed in, snapping the tension in half.

"Not one thing," Ali responded flatly. She still wasn't convinced that she was the right person to stop Mateva, but now that Vulcan wanted to take that job, she wasn't necessarily itching to stop him, no matter what Skotia's dreams were telling her.

When she was done, she let out a long breath and watched Vulcan process the hand he'd just been dealt, waiting for him to throw a joker into the mix. Without looking at Ali, he nodded slowly and began pacing in a tight circle.

"Like Skotia said, Infernians have always heard rumors about the other worlds. I was never sure if I could trust them, but now it looks like there's some proof in front of me that I can't ignore," he said, slowly looking Ali up and down. She fidgeted where she stood, not used to being stared at quite so intensely.

"You said that your grandmother was an Infernian. You must have a powerful lineage if you were able to open a portal after being surrounded by the Unsighted for years. If Mateva knows that about your brother, it might explain why she's kept him by her side these past few years."

"That's just hearsay. Anyone with Infernian blood can come through a portal. And, in this case, they can bring friends." Skotia pointed to the two teenagers standing off to the side, pressing themselves against the wall. Ali guessed the pair were a tad too traumatized to be near the edge again, and she didn't blame them—she could feel more bruises forming where the thorns had jabbed her side.

"Maybe. But, then again, maybe not," Vulcan replied, a bit more ominously than Ali liked.

"Either way, if you're going to find Carter, it looks like you need my help. Plus, you all owe me for saving your lives, so you don't really have a choice," he added, chuckling to himself as he gathered his things together.

"On the other side of that door, there's going to be a set of stairs camouflaged into the stone that will take us to where I've based myself these past few days. You can all come with me, and we can get some rest for the night. We'll regroup in the morning." Vulcan's words sounded more like an order than a suggestion. He gestured to the wall that Ali's friends were leaning on. Sure enough, when she took a closer look, she could make out a handle carved into the edge of the rock, just big enough to grab. Gavin gave it a firm tug, and specks fell from the top of the door as it creaked open, sprinkling Lilly and him in bits of gravel.

"What do you mean there will be stairs on the other side? We'll just be able to walk to where you were, no killer vines hiding behind a wall or two?" Ali questioned, half kidding but with enough edge to convey she wanted real answers to her questions.

"I told you, this place has a mind of its own. It creates what it chooses, we're just here to fill in the maze."

And with that, they grabbed their few belongings and followed Vulcan through the door. Before he took the lead, he threw Gavin one of his knives.

"You never know when you're going to need a good knife," he said with a wink. Gavin fumbled the weapon in his hands before ultimately dropping it with a clang.

"He could've at least given me a heads up," Gavin muttered, retrieving the blade. The result of Gavin's blunder echoed around the group, leaving Ali grateful they were leaving the cursed ballroom behind.

Ali hadn't thought of sleep in a number of hours, but as soon as the idea crept into her brain, she couldn't get it out. Her muscles suddenly ached in crevices she didn't know existed, and her eyelids were drooping with every step she took. There was no telling what time it was, but she figured it had to be nighttime in her world, close to when she would be shutting her eyes in the comfort of her own bed.

Once they reached Vulcan's campground, he spread out a few blankets and created makeshift pillows from the bundles of clothes he had lying around. No bugs scattered the ceiling, but the top was almost smoothed into a dome, like they had just walked into a bleak snow globe and were about to be shaken off their feet.

"Want to share a blanket?" he whispered so that only Ali could hear. She chose to ignore him, and instead set her camp up on the opposite side of the room. Making herself as comfortable as she could be on the bumpy pillow, Ali let herself stare at the dark ceiling for the next few hours while the others closed their eyes for the final time of the day. She said a string of silent prayers that the next day would bring her one inch closer to finding Carter, but the voice in her head couldn't help but laugh at her useless wishes as a wave of sleep finally overcame her body.

CHAPTER 11

THE SORCERERS' CAPSULE

———

The night did not bring a very productive sleep. Ali tried to find the most comfortable spot on the rocky, uneven floor, but her tossing and turning were a result of the nightmares that were flooding her subconscious. Scenes of the shadowvines pressing their thorns into her ribcage flooded Ali's mind. This time, Vulcan wasn't there to save any of them—instead, she was forced to spend the rest of eternity floating through the cavern as a soulless corpse.

After the fifth time those visions replayed in her head, she groggily pried her eyes open and forced herself to stay awake. Lifting herself off the jacket she had fashioned into a pillow, Ali looked around at the sleeping bodies. There was no outside light she could use to judge the time, but her internal alarm clock was begging her to go back to sleep. Refusing to listen, Ali scraped the sleep from her eyes and delicately moved her blanket from her lap. Getting to her feet, she folded the covers neatly and decided to explore.

The previous night, Ali had been too exhausted to take in Vulcan's abode, but now she was ready to pry. Even though he was only the second Infernian whom Ali had met, Vulcan seemed to have a better plan of action to find Mateva than Skotia did. At least he had a knife.

Gingerly stepping over his knapsack, Ali made her way to the stairs they had climbed the night before. Her eyes were adjusting to the shadows, and she could make out the stone borders of the room. It was surprisingly spacious for hosting just one person, but it didn't seem that Vulcan was the type to decorate. Besides his few belongings, the space was vacant, daring Ali to explore its secrets.

When they'd come to the fork, Vulcan had directed them to the leftmost tunnel, but she felt drawn to the other corridor, like something was calling her name. Even throughout her nightmares, Ali's inner voice was nagging at her, reminding her to explore the first chance she got. With one more push from her mental guide, she took her first step toward the new ground.

Dragging her hand along the wall, Ali waited for something to feel familiar.

"If my family is from here, why can't I feel a damn thing?" she wondered aloud, scanning the tunnel for any more signs of magical stories or drawings.

Did Carter feel this lost when he got sent here, or did he actually have a clue what he was doing?

"I just want something to make sense," Ali raised her voice on the last word, frustrated with her incompetency.

Suddenly, a bright light flashed on her right. Turning quickly, she saw that a torch stuck on the wall had lit itself, sending beams of warmth toward Ali's body. Only now realizing how her skin had grown accustomed to the cold, damp air of the tunnels, Ali moved toward the flame and let the heat wrap itself around her body in a welcoming hug.

"How did you do that?"

The heat immediately left her body. Ali spun on her heel and raised her fists toward the intruder. Her heart skipped a beat when she saw it was Vulcan, black hair still tousled from his sleep.

"What're you going to do, fight me? With those?" he joked, motioning toward her fists. Ali relaxed her grip and brought her hands down to her sides, scowling at him in the process.

"Shouldn't you be catching up on your beauty sleep?" Ali retorted.

"Shouldn't you? I'm not the one who almost died yesterday—several times," Vulcan quipped. He was quick to remind Ali that she had him to thank for her life, which wasn't a debt she was fond of having. Those who owed their life to someone else rarely lived a flawless existence.

"Also, you still haven't answered my question. How did you light this torch?" Vulcan strutted to the torch's base to inspect it, grabbing the handle out of its holder and twirling it in the air. Sparks flew from the top of the flame and disappeared into the drafty tunnel. When he reached out for the hilt, his fingers grazed Ali's shoulder, sending a shiver down her spine.

"What do you mean? I didn't do anything," Ali questioned, regaining her composure before Vulcan noticed her behavior. She silently wished he hadn't moved the torch so she could bask in its warmth a little longer.

"Yes, you did."

"No, I didn't." Ali's temper was slipping through the cracks. She could feel the tone of her voice changing with every sentence, struggling to keep it even.

"Listen, I'm not going to stand here and argue about this with you. You can either join me, or feel free to turn around and go back to the others. No one's stopping you." Ali felt a twinge of remorse sending him back to the group, which was why she offered the option to join her. Secretly, she was hoping she'd be left alone for just a few more minutes.

"I appreciate a little company myself," Vulcan replied, strutting past Ali with the torch in hand, continuing down the tunnel as if it were his idea to investigate originally.

Muttering a few indistinct swears underneath her breath, she followed the light of his torch.

"How did you know it was me who got out of bed and not Skotia?"

"I can easily tell the two of you apart," Vulcan said matter-of-factly. Ali waited for him to elaborate, considering even she had trouble telling the difference at times.

"And not for nothing, you seem to tolerate me a little bit better than your twin over there," he added, causing Ali to fight back the urge to laugh.

"Don't be so sure," she said. At this, Vulcan let out the smallest of laughs, and his mouth crept into the first authentic smile Ali had seen since they'd met. A smile looked better on him.

It wasn't that she hadn't noticed Skotia's less-than-friendly behavior toward Vulcan, but if Ali had trust issues, she figured it wasn't out of the realm of possibility for Skotia to have them as well. Even though Skotia had spent her life in Infernus, it seemed like she hadn't been exposed to many others, or to anyone. From the way she interacted with Vulcan, Ali gathered the Great Uprising must've taken a larger toll on her family than Skotia was letting on.

Ali stole a glance at Vulcan and noticed the shadows dancing across his face, highlighting his defined cheekbones and illuminating his features. There were bags under his eyes that Ali hadn't seen before.

Maybe Vulcan hadn't slept as well as she'd originally thought.

"The reason I followed you here wasn't because I had nothing better to do, by the way. I need to talk to you about your look-alike."

There was a change in Vulcan's demeanor, but Ali couldn't put her finger on what had caused it. She could see the tension gathering in his broad shoulders and the muscles clenching in his jaw, but there was no guessing his thoughts.

"I've never met anyone in Infernus like her. Usually, my family and I have a pretty good handle on the older families—the ones that hold the real power here. She speaks like she's from one of the influential lineages, but I've never heard her name come out of my parents' mouths."

"Is it possible your family just missed one person this time?"

"Not likely," Vulcan replied with a sad laugh. "My family may not be the most...traditional in their methods, but they're effective. They haven't missed a beat in decades, and with word of Mateva returning, they're on higher alert than usual. Not to mention, they have a little help from our allies." His jaw flexed, so quickly that Ali questioned if she had imagined it. She wasn't sure what to say, so she didn't say anything at all.

"In Infernus, especially now, you have to be careful who you're talking to. Even the trees are listening."

"Careful about what? You're telling me Infernus has people who actually supported Mateva the first time around?" Ali tried to fathom the idea of anyone rooting for the woman whose mission centered on destruction.

"You'd be surprised. Magic is a privilege Mateva was granted, and some believe that those with that power should wield it a bit differently than Infernus intended. It works to have powerful friends, and Mateva was the most powerful of them all. I won't lie, the idea is attractive." Vulcan told the story as if this was a lesson he learned during his schooling, drilled into his memory with no room to form his own opinions on history.

"Since then, my family has taught me to be wary of who I meet on my travels, let alone who I allow accompany me. You and those other two, I trust. Not Skotia. And neither should you, if you ask me."

"Well, it's a good thing I didn't ask you," Ali retorted, her guard now raised on all fronts. Who did he think he was? Vulcan was as much of a stranger as Skotia was. At least she could tell when Skotia was lying.

And with that, they walked in silence for the remainder of their expedition through the tunnels. The only sounds were the prickle of ash falling from the torch's grip. At one point, Vulcan suggested that they head back to the group and Ali nodded in agreement, not wanting to break her vow of silence yet.

A part of her was upset that she didn't have more time alone with Vulcan. She wanted to crack his code as much as he wanted to understand hers, but it was far more difficult to do that if he spent the entire day sneaking looks at Skotia.

When they rounded the corner where she'd originally started, Ali was surprised to see that the other three were wide awake and standing in front of one of the cave walls in a far corner, looking intently at something in front of them.

"What's going on?" she asked, walking over to join her friends. Lilly's eyes moved between her and Vulcan, asking silent questions that Ali quickly shut down with a shake of her head.

"When I woke up, I saw you both were gone, so I decided to do some investigating of my own. I didn't want to wake these other two," she said, gesturing to Gavin and Skotia. "I started at the farthest corner I could find. The rock was, like, glowing, and then this showed up."

Ali inhaled sharply as she looked up. In the stone, a large, magnificent *I* was protruding from the wall layered on top of another letter, *C*. The letters were at least double Ali's height, and they were imposed on a giant swirling pattern, like the ones from the tree in their world. Where it looked like there should be ragged edges at the seams, Ali ran her fingers over the design and felt it was smooth as a precious gem.

"That's...never been here before. I scoured every part of this cavern before setting up camp. I would've definitely noticed this," Vulcan interrupted from behind Ali, sounding as mystified as she felt.

"Didn't you say yourself that Infernus creates what it chooses? Maybe this has been here the entire time, but Infernus is only revealing it to us now," Lilly reasoned, still gaping at the new find. Ali studied her friend's expression, searching for the same doubting look she had when Skotia first told them about Infernus. It was nowhere to be found.

"This symbol, it feels so familiar. I know it's ancient, but I've only seen it in the old books. No one's used it in years. I can't remember what it means..." Vulcan trailed off.

"It's the Mark of the Sorcerers. They used it to mark their territory, among other things. It's all but forgotten nowadays. Like he said, no one's used it in years," Skotia piped up, her black eyes burning a hole into the side of the wall.

"Finally," Ali whispered to the wind. "A sign that we're supposed to be here. They were here before us."

"Ali—your necklace!" Lilly cried from behind her.

Her necklace was pulsing its familiar emerald color again. This time, instead of the initial fright she'd felt the day before, the glow felt like a welcome beam of sunlight after a week of nothing but thunderstorms.

"Wait, your necklace *glows*?" Vulcan asked, unable to take his eyes off the stone hanging around Ali's neck.

"Oh, well, yeah. Did I forget to mention that?"

"Must've slipped your mind," he dryly replied.

Every other time her necklace had started to glow, it was guiding Ali toward the right path, having her open her eyes a little bit wider to see the full picture. Even though she knew the other four were watching her every move, she might as well have been alone in Infernus. The stares on her back melted away, and a light surged in her mind's eye, moving away the debris cluttered in her brain and paving a clear path for her to follow. The emerald's pulse quickened as she moved her hands along the smooth wall, but when her hand found a break in the pattern, the stone was beating as rapidly as a hummingbird's wings.

A notch no bigger than the palm of her hand was removed from the carving, but when she pulled, nothing gave way. She moved her other hand to the opposite side and felt what her mind told her she would find: a matching indentation. Eyes still closed, she took a deep breath and pulled down.

Click.

Ali opened her eyes and took a step back. She had pulled some sort of trigger—the enormous symbol began to rotate counterclockwise, shaking the room. Not wanting to take her eyes away from the carving, she almost missed the long, delicate box that was slowly inching out of the wall. The teenagers lined themselves up on either side of the object, hovering on their toes to get a better look at the new discovery.

It came to a halt as soon as the spirals stopped moving. The group lined themselves up on either side before inspecting their new discovery. Ali's heart skipped a beat when she realized the box had a shape eerily similar to a casket.

"Do you think there's someone in there?" Lilly asked the question Ali had been trying to avoid. She could only imagine what a body would smell like after decades, possibly centuries, stuffed into a wall. Bile rose in her windpipe that she quickly pushed back down.

"No, Infernians don't memorialize their deceased in this way. We burn the bodies, thanking their souls for their journey in Infernus." Skotia shook her head, cautiously tracing the container's edges one finger at a time.

Gliding around its perimeter, Ali looked underneath to see if there was a piece of code or key that could unlock their strange find, but when her head was looking toward the underside she heard Vulcan unsheathe one of his knives.

"Gavin, you still have that knife I gave you? Take it out and follow my lead."

"O-okay," Gavin said, shakily removing the blade from his waistband. Holding it out a foot in front of him, he carefully removed the knife from its holder and held the two pieces up in his hands, looking to Vulcan for his next move.

Tipping the blade into the seam of the bin, Vulcan motioned for Gavin to do the same on his side. With a bit of wiggling back and forth, the artifact let out a long groan as air hit its contents for the first time in many moons.

The girls worked to remove the top and carefully lean it against the wall, leaving room for them all to crane their necks over the side and get their first look at the treasure.

Ali reached in and began pulling out handfuls of documents, careful not to grasp them too tightly in fear of them disintegrating at her touch. The writing was faded, and she was barely able to make out the sketches in the margins, but from the cursive handwriting, she quickly determined that they were letters.

"There must be hundreds of letters in here, but I can't make out who they were written for, or what they were writing about. But look, in this one you can make out the Mark of the Sorcerers in the bottom corner," Ali gasped, delicately tracing the symbol with her forefinger. Even though it had aged, she could still feel the indentation from where the pen pressed into the paper, the ink running over itself as the scribe made sure the mark was visible.

"Wait, I can make out Mateva's name in this one. Here, in the second paragraph," Vulcan inched closer until he was pressed against Ali, pointing to the name that was barely visible after years of being pushed to the bottom of the pile. That same shiver she felt earlier threatened to return, but Ali felt herself inching closer to Vulcan rather than stepping away.

"What could they possibly have been saying about her? Were they warning the others?" Ali pondered, running through each plausible and implausible scenario, one after the other. She bit her tongue against her cheek and impatiently tapped her foot against the cool floor, flipping through the letters to find any patterns in the calligraphy.

"There has to be something else here, something that will tell us who these people were." Ali hastily pushed through the remaining letters that were scattered across the box's bottom. She needed something that would give her more answers than questions.

Without warning, her fingers brushed up against something long and solid, knocking it over so that it rolled a few inches. Clearing the debris that was covering her find, she lifted the item and blew the dust away, her eyes instantly watering.

"It's a wand," she whispered reverently, in awe of the magical object. Gripping it in her hand, she let her fingers run over the lines etched into the wood, wrapping themselves from the base of the wand to the tip. Ali could've sworn she felt a fluttering from its center, almost like the wand were alive. She envisioned the sparks from the drawings shooting out of the end, creating a fiery circle around them in one motion.

Everyone gingerly placed their documents into the box, their eyes glued to the wand. Ali held it out for them all to see. Skotia's hand flew out to grab it, but Vulcan's reflexes were too quick.

"Hey!" Ali protested, not realizing how empty her hand would feel once the wand left her grasp.

"Don't yell at me. We need to be careful with this." Vulcan held the wand high above his head, where no one had a chance of reaching it. He eyed Skotia's pout and moved an inch away from her, avoiding her glares.

"I don't think you realize what you've just found. This is a Sorcerer's wand. Look—on the bottom there's that same symbol that's on the wall," he informed them, spinning the piece of wood so they could get a good look at the minuscule symbol imprinted on the circular base. He was right—it was the Mark of the Sorcerers.

Why would a Sorcerer leave their wand behind? Did they not feel the need for their magic once they thought Mateva was gone? Or did they leave it before her fall from power and fled, giving up any shred of hope for Infernus?

It looked like this new discovery was, in fact, opening the door for more questions than answers.

"It's almost like the Sorcerers left this here to be found, like a time capsule for future Infernians to find and take with them," she observed, not taking her eyes off the wand in Vulcan's grip. "We're reawakening the knowledge they left behind, and judging by the dust that's floating around us, I'd say they left it behind quite some time ago."

"It's great that we found a wand and everything, but how do we get it to work?" Gavin asked plainly, knocking Ali down a few notches. She hadn't thought about how they would actually use the wand to help.

"We can't just *get it to work*," Skotia scoffed. "It's not like it has a switch where we could turn it on when we please and off when it's an inconvenience. We'd need magic, which none of us have."

Skotia's black eyes looked a little darker than normal. Her arms were folded across her chest, and she was leaning into her right hip, but hadn't taken her gaze from the wand since Ali had found it. For a moment, Ali's mind soared back to her conversation with Vulcan earlier that morning, warning her not to trust Skotia. To be fair, she hadn't wanted to let go of the wand either—Vulcan's explosive reflexes were simply unmatched.

"Geez, okay. Just a non-Infernian here trying to come up with a plan." Gavin rolled his eyes and raised his hands in surrender. "There has to be something else in here then. If this is a time capsule, the Sorcerers wouldn't have only left two things. That would be totally lame."

"I think this might help." Lilly had been shuffling through the contents and, like Gavin predicted, was holding up a piece of parchment that looked nothing like any of the other letters.

"If I'm reading this correctly, it looks like a map of these tunnels. There's a faded *X* right here," she continued, pointing toward the upper right corner of the document. "This must be where we are."

"Can I see that?" Vulcan asked politely. Ali opened her mouth to voice her surprise at his sudden manners, but quickly realized he was already deep in thought, inspecting every inch of the map.

"This checks out from everything I've been tracking so far, and this even goes farther into the places I haven't reached yet. Here. There's a fire burning in the center of the map, but some of the markings are faded around it. There's no one clear path to get there. I'll bet this wand that if Mateva's hiding in these tunnels, that's where she'll be. In the core."

"That means Carter will be there too," Ali interrupted Vulcan's rant and locked eyes with both Lilly and Gavin. Suddenly, the bags under Ali's eyes didn't feel so swollen, and the muscles in her back weren't as sore from sleeping on the jagged cave floor all night.

"We have to go. I'm not making my brother wait a minute longer than necessary to be freed from that wretched woman."

It looked like Vulcan was in a different world from the distant look in his eyes, but as Ali spoke about starting their journey toward the newfound core, he absentmindedly nodded.

"I'm so close…" he said, speaking softly under his breath. Being the closest to him, Ali was the only one who could make out his words.

"What do you mean?" she asked, trying to piece together if he was speaking to a voice inside his head or the group in front of him.

"Huh? Nothing, it doesn't matter," he said, shaking off Ali's question and rolling up the map until it was small enough to fit in his jacket's inner pocket. The powerless wand was already nestled tightly against his chest. "If you want to get started right away, we need to clean this place up first. Lilly and Gavin, you two get these letters back into the capsule and put it back into the wall. We have everything we need from it. Skotia and Ali, you two help me clean up camp. Make sure nothing gets left behind. We don't need someone else stumbling through here and realizing that they aren't alone in this mountain."

The thought of another person taking refuge in the tunnels sent an unnerving tremble through Ali's body, but they obeyed their orders, each doing their part to clean the site. While her heart sank a bit watching the time capsule being shoved back into the wall, she knew Vulcan was right—they didn't need anything else from it. If anything, carrying the indecipherable letters with her would only fuel her frustration.

Within the next half hour, there was no sign that five teenagers had ever slept in the cavern. They smudged the footprints left in the thin layer of dirt, leaving the stone floor as grimy as when they arrived. With a little bit of luck and a lot of patience, they fit everything inside Skotia's and Vulcan's backpacks, except the map and wand. Vulcan wasn't letting those go, especially after Skotia asked if he wanted her to hold the wand in her bag.

"According to this map, we have to head southeast if we're going to reach the core. These tunnels should do the trick. Are you all ready?" Vulcan commanded more than asked, barely looking up to see everyone nodding in unison.

Now that the time had come, a mixture of dread and eagerness swept through Ali's bones. The logical side of her was screaming to pause and take more time to evaluate the situation, to maybe get a closer look at the map herself. But the fleeting, hot-blooded emotional side was in control, and it was telling her to sprint down through the dingy tunnels because every minute she hesitated was a minute she wasted without her brother.

Letting her emotional thinking reign supreme, she took a deep breath and followed the four others into the unknown, not daring to look back at the Mark of the Sorcerers they were leaving behind.

CHAPTER 12

DANGEROUS DOLPHINS IN THE DEEP

———

They had been walking for almost an hour, but there was no sign of life the farther they trekked into the tunnels. Stalactites hung above, dripping moisture onto their heads and threatening to break off from the ceiling at any moment. The sounds of their shoes bounced off the walls, creating a rhythmic tune that mocked their journey.

For once, Ali welcomed the silence. She usually preferred to be distracted from her thoughts, but this gave her time to process everything they had found in the time capsule. Acutely aware that the wand was still pressed against Vulcan's chest in his pocket, she tried to think of any way the group could activate the wand. If Vulcan was going to try to fight Mateva and help her save Carter from the Sorcerer's grip, it would be nice to have an ounce of magic on their side. It may be a raindrop fighting a forest fire, but it was the only hope they had.

At the head of their single file line, Vulcan held his hand up, silencing their footsteps.

"Do you hear that?" he asked, turning to face them all but making direct eye contact with Ali.

She cocked her head to the side, trying to focus on the sound Vulcan was alluding to, but all she could hear was the flutter of insects throughout the tunnel.

Then, a distant burbling made its way to her eardrums. Closing her eyes, Ali carefully followed the noise's pattern, making her way to where Vulcan was standing at the head of the pack. The sound had grown louder, and after a minute or two had passed, she was confident in her guess.

"Water," she mouthed, returning Vulcan's stare. The familiar sound of the rushing current sent a single chill through her. Ali was trying to avoid imagining what else was hiding from them in these tunnels, but the idea of creatures hiding in the water's depths added an unwelcome layer to the terrors lurking in her mind.

"Water," he repeated, nodding slowly and pulling out the map from his pocket.

"Skotia, did you ever see any signs of streams or brooks when you first got here? Maybe you heard a current or two before you set up camp?" Ali questioned.

"No, I've seen plenty of streams, but none here."

"How could water be flowing within these tunnels? Wouldn't it have flooded the caverns after all this time?" Gavin asked.

"Not if the tunnels were built around the water," Vulcan answered, pointing toward a small blob on the map. "Remember how I said parts of the map were faded? Well, it looks like I missed this line here. It's so faint I still can barely make it out, but based on where we were and how long we've been walking, it looks like we're just about to cross it." Vulcan squinted at the map, holding it an inch away from his face.

"But this line is different from the ones they used for the tunnels—the tunnels are shown with heavy markings and a straighter line. This one is a bit finer, with little ripples drawn on either side of it. I think we're about to cross over some water once we reach the end of this corridor."

"Do we have to go over the water? Is there any other path we can take?" Ali's voice cracked. It wasn't that she hated the water. In fact, in the forest she used to watch the deer drink from a few brooks during the evenings, quenching their thirst after a long day scavenging for food.

But that was when she was in her world and knew what to expect when she looked through the ripples and saw her feet resting on the pebbles underneath the water's surface. Wiggling her toes in her sneakers, she swallowed as she imagined what would be waiting under the waves in this new land.

"Not unless you want to walk a couple of hours with no guarantee we'll be able to find our way out," Vulcan answered, flatly. Ali rolled her eyes in defeat, wishing he didn't always feel the need to be so blunt.

"It'll be all right, Al. I'm a lifeguard, remember? If anything goes wrong, I can jump in to save somebody," Gavin chimed in, sounding much more confident in his diving abilities than his knife-wielding skills.

Ali was never one to give in without a fight. In her world, everyone around her recognized that. But now, against her better judgment, she nodded and gestured for Vulcan to take the lead once again. While they continued toward the squiggle on the map, two versions of herself battled internally. One side—the side Ali had known all her life—wasn't ready to give up the urge to defend herself before anyone had the chance to judge her. But this new Infernian Ali was questioning everything she had ever known. How could she defend herself if she didn't know who she was?

"Hey, you okay?" Lilly had slowed her stride to fall in step with Ali, who had resumed her position at the caboose.

"I'm not sure," she started. "Everything about this—this world, finding Carter, seeing Skotia, discovering that wand—it feels like I'm watching it from someone else's body. Like the real Ali is hovering over me, silently giving her disapproval while an impostor makes fatal mistakes at every turn."

"Listen, this isn't exactly normal for any of us, even Skotia and Vulcan. They've never met anyone who wasn't from this world, and we never knew their world existed, until yesterday. You have to give yourself a break once in a while." Lilly comforted her friend, giving Ali's hand a tight squeeze.

"And remember, we're in this together. Gavin and I don't need to see visions of you in our dreams to know you're important to us. We've known that for years," she added, matter-of-factly.

Except for a handful of times, Ali and Lilly never talked about their feelings. They'd become best friends over the years simply because they didn't need the constant reassurance that they mattered to one another, among other reasons. But now, hearing Lilly's words reassured her that she wasn't in this journey alone. These past few years without her brother might've made Ali feel like the only person in the world, but now she had two people she trusted with her life on this journey with her, whether she had originally wanted them here or not.

Returning Lilly's gaze with a slight nod, Ali released her hand and almost walked straight into Gavin, who had abruptly stopped in his tracks.

"Whoa," he breathed out. "This is a little different from the neighborhood beach." His low voice was a few octaves higher than usual.

Ali peered around Gavin's large head and saw what had caused his surprise. Lying in front of them wasn't a simple brook, but a fully formed river, and the murky water hid its secrets. It was only about thirty yards across—maybe swimmable on a good day, but today wasn't one of those days. The current was picking up as the seconds ticked by, and it was impossible to decipher how deep the river was from their angle. Ali could only assume what was awaiting them down below.

She prayed her assumptions were wrong.

"Did your parents ever teach you how to cross a rushing river?" Skotia asked, scoffing before turning to Vulcan.

"Other than by swimming? Afraid not," he flung back. Ali could see his mouth clamp shut, clearly restraining himself from saying more.

"Lovely." Skotia turned away from Vulcan. Her lips were pursed tightly together, and a flicker of fury flashed across her face, equally as irritated with her fellow Infernian.

Not caring to hear any more of their bickering, Ali scanned the current for any signs of life. She felt her feet start to take her down the edge of the wall, where the water was rushing up to splash along the rock and leave beads of mist suspended in the air. Bending down to feel the water's temperature—a little warmer than ice—Ali noticed that there was something sticking out of the wall underneath her.

When the swell died down, she pointed her foot into the murky depths and came in contact with something solid, wide, and rectangular—stairs.

Focusing her gaze on her submerged foot, Ali was starting to make out a few more stairs past the first one she was standing on, plunging deeper into the river.

"If there are stairs down, there must be a way—" she cut herself off, catching her eye on something directly across the river. "Up."

"Hey! What do you think you're doing?" Vulcan was behind her in a second, flinging her body backward and away from the water.

Ali's legs went limp when she felt his powerful grip on her arms, but she quickly recovered her footing.

"For your information, I think I might've found a way to get us out of here. I was just figuring out the kinks before I interrupted your extremely useful quarreling," Ali shot back, finding the fuel to her own fire.

"See these stairs that look like they lead down to the bottom of this river? If you look across the way," she pointed with her forefinger, "you'll see a staircase rising out and onto that ledge. Maybe this wasn't always meant to be a river. Maybe Mateva used her magic to fill this, stopping anyone from being able to find her."

"I don't think she'd be able to do that." Skotia was the first one to answer, dismissing the theory without question. Ali waited for her look-alike to elaborate, but she wouldn't meet Ali's eyes. Instead, Skotia scuffed her feet into the damp floor, waiting for one of the others to interrupt the silence.

"Weren't you the one telling us that she's the most powerful Sorcerer Infernus has ever seen?" Ali's patience was thinning by the minute. The sound of blood rushing through her ears was becoming louder, but she managed to stop her eyes from shooting icicles into Skotia's black ones.

"Well that's correct, but—"

"So then it's perfectly logical for us to assume that Mateva was able to conjure this river, or at least intensify it from a stream into this," Vulcan stepped in, gesturing to the flowing current in front of them.

"If I had the bounty on my head that she does, I'd do anything in my power to stop us from reaching her." Vulcan's defensive tone was a bit stronger than usual. Normally Ali would've stepped in to defend Skotia, but after her doppelganger's quick rejection, Ali decided she'd let Vulcan's tone speak for itself. For once, she was thankful for his candor.

"So, I know that I said I'm a lifeguard and everything, but this water looks a little bit rougher than the county pool," Gavin cut in, narrowing his eyes toward the river and taking a few steps closer to the sturdy wall behind him. "I mean, I'll definitely still swim across if we decide to, of course," he added hurriedly, glancing between each of the unfazed faces in the group.

"Wait. Shouldn't we come up with some sort of plan first before any of us dive headfirst into that cloudy torrent?" Ali wasn't the type to ask for every detail to be planned out before she jumped toward a new excursion, but in this case having one scrap of a plan would ease the knots developing in her neck.

"No point. We might all have to swim across if this keeps up. Look, the water is rising," Vulcan groaned, cursing under his breath as he searched his pockets for what Ali could only hope was an inflatable raft.

Vulcan was right. The waterline was steadily rising, and soon enough it would reach their feet. Ali didn't know what had caused the sudden shift in the river's temperament, but she had a sneaking suspicion that the closer they got to Mateva, the more their surroundings would be pushing them away, encouraging them to turn their backs and never return. Pulling her hair into a high ponytail, Ali wracked her brain for anything they could use to stop the current from swelling. By her mental calculations, they only had a few minutes before it was above their heads.

A glimmer across the riverbed caught her eye. She squinted to see what was reflecting back at them and saw that there was a rusty lever protruding from the opposing wall.

"That lever over there, maybe if we pull it down, the flooding will stop, too."

Vulcan was already taking off his shirt, arming himself with a dagger in one hand and a whip in the other. New sets of faded scars revealed themselves, lining his perfectly defined stomach.

"What do you think you're doing?" It was Ali's turn to ask the question.

"I told you the only way I knew how to cross this thing was by swimming," Vulcan muttered, with a wink in her direction that she wished she could hate. He dove into the water without another word.

The four remaining teenagers stood there with their mouths open, looking for any sign of his body under the dark waves.

But Vulcan wasn't the one they saw come up for air.

A sea creature bearing a resemblance to a massive dolphin soared out of the water, baring its two sets of razor-sharp teeth before descending back into the depths. Faded scars ran across its hide, but Ali barely noticed those once she met its eyes. They were the color of blood, guaranteed to incite a new level of terror in any unsuspecting prey. Its barbed tail was the last piece to descend out of view, lashing out once more and splashing cold water on them all.

Before Ali had time to process what she had just seen, four more vicious dolphins leaped out from the water, seemingly following the first's path. While they may not have been the leader of the pod, each one was as terrifying as the next. Ali inhaled quickly as she saw some of them were foaming at the mouth, hungry for their next meal.

And Vulcan was about to become that meal.

Without thinking, Ali shook off her shoes and leaned back against the wall, preparing herself to sprint forward into the unknown. In three steps, she was off and diving into the monster-infested waters.

"Ali, no!" Was the last thing she heard before water rushed into her ears and the noises from above became muffled.

Surprisingly, the water underneath was as clear as could be. As soon as she opened her eyes, she saw Vulcan ten yards from her treading water, being circled by the vicious creatures that had surfaced moments before.

When Ali was above ground, she hadn't noticed how much brighter this room was compared to the last. Beams of light shone in from above the river, accentuating the other underwater beasts surrounding her. Her eyes went wide, and her muscles were momentarily paralyzed when she saw the world of sea creatures that had been hiding below the waterline. Minuscule jellyfish with lightning shooting from their tentacles, piranhas as large as her torso circling the bottom of the river, and one large shark with a narrow snout, jagged scales, and fins as sharp as a dagger swimming through the currents. There was a stone bottom beneath them, but her feet were treading far from the floor.

Vulcan's eyes lit up when his gaze met Ali's, turning his body so that the monsters wouldn't notice her. Not yet, at least. Their barbed tails were moving back and forth in the water, as if they were waiting for the perfect time to strike the foolish boy who dared cross into their territory. The pod had every angle covered. With every circle, they inched closer to Vulcan. He looked helpless in the water. His rugged body paled in comparison to the muscular creatures taunting him. The dagger and whip that had looked so mighty on land hung lifeless in his hands.

Ali's breath was already running out, but she had to try to save him. She had to distract them. Kicking her legs out, she swam straight for the group of jellyfish that had sparks traveling between one another.

The first one felt like a pinch on her hand, like she had just stuck her fingers into an outlet. She couldn't say the same for the next fifteen. While the water was crystal clear, the jellyfish were clouding her vision, gathering in groups in front of her. Their shocks forced her eyes closed to cope with the pain, doing everything in her power not to scream and let the water fill her lungs.

Even though her body was a current of lightning, her plan was working. The electricity was flowing through the water, turning the dolphins' attention away from Vulcan and toward their new target.

The first killer dolphin deviated from the group and was swimming toward her to see what the commotion was all about. Ignoring the numbing in her arm, Ali tried to guide both sets of creatures toward the wall she had dived in from and as far away from Vulcan as possible. Even with her blurred sight, she could tell Vulcan was losing his strength—his arms were slumped by his side and his legs weren't treading as quickly, dragging his body weight farther toward the bottom with each passing second.

Soon, there was only one dolphin left for him to fend off. But no matter how many of its friends had turned their attention to Ali, their leader couldn't take its soulless eyes away from Vulcan.

Losing her own breath, Ali pushed her body toward the surface. Once she breached the water, she filled her lungs with oxygen and dove back down, barely hearing her friends' pleas for her to swim to them.

The entire right side of Ali's body had started to fail her. Like Vulcan, her legs weren't kicking as quickly, and she struggled to breaststroke through the river. She clutched her right arm, ignoring the jabbing pain in her side, and met Vulcan's eyes. With a single look, she knew what had to be done.

Using the limited energy she had left, Ali swam toward the monster circling Vulcan. Its barbed tail was swinging faster than before. Seconds Ali didn't have to waste were ticking away, the lingering creatures hot on her trail. Ali launched herself onto the dolphin's tail, its barbed edge cutting deep into her sides as it thrashed against her.

The moment Ali attached herself to the beast, Vulcan used his last bit of vitality to lunge forward and stab the dolphin, digging the dagger into its side until Ali felt its entire body go limp. Vulcan pulled the dagger out. Beads of blood were floating in the glassy water, but she wasn't in the clear yet.

Ali's own blood was seeping out of her abdomen. No longer able to hold back the pain, Ali shrieked and watched the bubbles rise from her mouth. Fire was enveloping every nerve she had left, spreading throughout her body like a forest fire lit with a thousand matches at once. With the dolphin's venom spreading throughout her bloodstream, she let her body start to sink, arms flailing loosely above her head. Losing consciousness, Ali's last thoughts were of Carter. Watching him run away from her house that last day, never to return.

Before blackness engulfed Ali's mind, an energy she had never felt before coursed through her bones, reaching from her skull to the soles of her feet. She couldn't control it—the energy had a mind of its own, but it felt good. It was powerful, yet weightless. Spontaneous, yet tame. Like it could've left a larger footprint, but it wanted to give Ali a taste of its potential first. A bright light flashed around her, burning the inside of her eyelids but enveloping her body in a cloud of warmth. Cracking her eyes open, she could see all the creatures that had threatened the teenagers were swimming away from them, like they suddenly had no use for their fleshy bodies. The light was protecting her from the threats still lurking.

Even though she was free from any further harm, Ali's body was too defeated from its battles to give her the last push she needed to reach the surface. Succumbing to her fate, Ali let her eyes close one last time as she fell deeper into the abyss. She swore she felt something desperately tugging at her limp body in those last few moments, but her mind had already wandered to a distant land before she could get one last glimpse at her life.

CHAPTER 13

LAVENDER, JASMINE, AND MUD

———

Ali gasped for air as her eyes flew open. Rolling onto her side, her hand immediately flew to her stomach and tried to pinpoint the site the venom had entered her veins. But when she pulled her hand away, there wasn't any blood dripping from her fingertips. Ali slowly felt alongside her back and sides, trying to locate any dips or new scars on her body, but there were none.

In fact, her body felt better than it had in weeks. Her legs weren't fatigued, and her feet weren't rough and calloused. Her shoulders weren't carrying the tension of the world, and the crick in her neck had worked itself out. It was like she was back home, waking up from the best night's sleep she could've possibly wished for.

"Hey—" she started, but stopped once she realized she was completely alone. She'd left the group, but where had she gone?

Ali realized she wasn't in Infernus anymore. There was something different about the atmosphere, maybe it was the absence of magic that made the air feel dry, like an element had been stripped from every molecule she was breathing. The room she was sitting in was painted a blinding light, but someone had decided not to put any furniture in it yet. The only contrast against the four walls was a wooden door directly in front of her with a smooth, bright red doorknob.

"Well, here goes nothing," she exhaled, getting to her feet and turning the doorknob in one graceful motion.

As soon as the door creaked open, three scents flooded her nostrils: lavender, jasmine, and mud.

The last time that combination overwhelmed her nose, she couldn't place where she knew them from. Now, the memories came flooding back to her. She knew where she was.

Flinging open the door, Ali stepped into Grandmother's house. Everything was exactly how she remembered it—the crooked pictures on the wall, the paisley rugs lying in almost every room, and the ornate grandfather clock in the corner of the living room, pendulum keeping time like nothing had changed.

And sitting on the periwinkle leather loveseat was the second person in the world she thought she would never see again.

"Grandmother!" Ali ran to the loveseat, enveloping the matriarch in her arms and letting tears fall onto the leather.

"Oh, my Ali," her grandmother cooed, returning the embrace. Her grandmother's bones weren't as feeble as she remembered—they weren't bending or popping against Ali's tight squeezes. Instead, they felt sturdy under her grasp.

"Grandmother, how are you younger?" Ali pulled away, sniffling. The wrinkles on her grandmother's forehead weren't as pronounced, and the veins in her hands were hiding under healthy skin. The last Ali remembered, her veins were protruding from her ghostly skin, threatening to burst at any moment if they encountered a sharp edge. The woman had to be at least twenty years younger. Growing up, Ali had never seen this youth in her eyes.

"Time works in fickle ways, darling," she responded, looking at Ali with a twinkle in her eyes. "I am neither older nor younger, yet I get the chance to be here with you. And that's all that matters."

Ali stepped back, taking in the woman in front of her. For a moment, a rush of hysteria flooded her mind as she remembered the last time she was ripped away from Infernus, dragged toward oblivion by the shadowvines. But this felt different. She wasn't exactly in her world, but her grandmother's house was as real as could be. But how did she get there?

Her grandmother patted the cushioned seat next to her, motioning for Ali to sit. Sinking into the cushions brought back a peace of mind Ali had been missing. Serenity spread throughout her body, loosening her muscles and slowing her heart rate. For a moment, everything was perfect.

And then that moment ended. The air left Ali's lungs, leaving her gasping for the words she needed to get out.

"I've missed you," Ali's voice cracked on the second word, not wanting to show how weak she'd become over the few years.

Her grandmother returned her gaze with a sadness about her, almost like she was holding back tears herself.

"Why didn't you tell me Infernus was real?" Ali couldn't resist asking. These past few days, all she could think about were the secrets that had been kept from her. Secrets that might have prepared her for the journey, instead of adding more pieces to the puzzle.

"All those stories you told Carter and me about this far-away land, treating it like it lived only in your imagination. Why didn't you tell us it was real? That it was your home?" The last word caught in Ali's throat, the hostility starting to bubble with each syllable.

"I'm so sorry darling, I thought I could protect you," she started, taking Ali's hand in hers. "I was wrong. By the time I realized I should've told both of you the truth, it was too late. I wasn't strong enough, and there wasn't enough time to explain everything."

There was a single teardrop running down her youthful face. Even though a part of Ali's soul was on fire, telling her to pry further and dig for the truth, another part was shattering for her grandmother. The woman who had stood so tall in her world was breaking, and there was nothing Ali could do to stop it.

"I see you're still wearing the necklace," she smiled, her fingertips brushing the emerald around Ali's neck.

"Of course I am," Ali whispered, touching her neck to meet her grandmother's fingertips. "I haven't taken it off since the day you gave it to me, like you said."

"Good girl. It belongs more to you than it ever did to me."

Ali couldn't take it anymore. The secrets, the lies, whatever her grandmother wanted to call them—she wasn't going to sit here and let them continue. Ali stood and turned her back to the woman, making her way toward the clock's pendulum ticking away.

"Grandmother, I know that you thought you couldn't tell us before, but now that I know about Infernus, and now that I know Carter is trapped there, can you please tell me more?" Ali begged, not meeting her grandmother's gaze. Instead, she looked around the eclectic room she had so dearly missed, wishing for a second that she could have another sleepover there like she did as a child.

"Please," she squeaked out. "You don't know what it's been like these past few years without you both. I can't lose him again."

"All right, I'll tell you. But please, forgive me, Ali. Even the wisest of the old have much to learn from their life." She rubbed her temples, closing her eyes before taking a long breath to begin.

Ali gave a quick nod, hoping that was enough approval for her grandmother to start her story.

"In order for you to know and understand Infernus, you need to understand the Sorcerers. Without the Sorcerers, there is no Infernus. Without Infernus, there are no Sorcerers. The two cannot exist without the other." Wrinkles were appearing across her forehead as she spoke. The stories were visibly aging the matriarch.

"Infernus had always been a peaceful land for its people. The land itself has been around for as long as anyone can remember. Whether it sprouted from the world you grew up in or whether that world is a product of Infernus is a mystery that will remain unsolved for years to come."

Ali tried to imagine Infernus birthing her world one day, taking a giant hand and removing a piece of its body. It made Ali's world its neighbor, never too far from reach.

"Since its inception, Infernus has been magical. While most Infernians don't possess magic, they can feel it everywhere they turn—in the soil that produces a bountiful harvest every year, in the constant breeze that keeps everyone cool on the warmest day, and in the water that rushes between children's toes by the ocean, bringing them beautiful conches and treasures if they ask nicely."

A smile crept onto her grandmother's lips as she recalled Infernus's natural beauty. Even though Ali had only seen the inside of dingy tunnels, she could picture the summer breeze blowing through her grandmother's hair as a young girl.

"You sound like you regret coming to our world," Ali spoke softly, careful not to derail the story.

"Oh no, no I don't. It was the right decision to make at the time. Looking back, I know that now." She cleared her throat and shifted her position on the couch before continuing.

"The land itself gifts a handful of Infernians with magic. They call themselves the Sorcerers. At some points in history, there would be two or three students trained to assume their new roles, sometimes no one was chosen. The last time, about fifty years ago, there were four students chosen to start their training."

"Why were there years no one was chosen?" Ali interrupted, confused why these people wouldn't always want someone to protect the land if it was that important.

"Because the Sorcerers weren't the ones choosing their successors. If that was the case, more likely than not the same families would wield the power for centuries, turning the keys over to one another when someone was too tired to fulfill their role," the matriarch explained to Ali as if she were in grade school. It reminded her of how Skotia and Vulcan talked about Infernus's nuances with such simplicity even though they may be the most complex of concepts.

"Even though they possess magic, the magic lived and died with them. They had no way to transfer it to another person. Infernus has always been and will always be the one who chooses who will defend it. When the time is ready for the next cohort to be prepared, the training begins," her grandmother went on. With every detail she recalled, there were new specks of pride in her voice Ali had never heard before.

"Out of the four chosen, there were two boys and two girls, not much older than you. Upon getting the call, each left their home to fulfill their destiny, knowing their lives would never be the same once they learned how to control the power brewing inside them. Once they reached the Sorcerers, they were handed their wands and the training began."

"Grandmother, I think I found one of their wands! It was in a time capsule we discovered in one of the caverns. Engraved on the bottom was a symbol my friend told us was the Mark of the Sorcerers." Ali perked up, welcoming the single sliver of familiarity.

"Yes, I saw that. I was very proud, darling," her grandmother nodded.

"You saw it? How did you see it?"

"I see many things, Ali. I'm with you even when you cannot see me."

Ali tried to picture her grandmother standing next to her when she was first dropped into Infernus, using nothing but pure adrenaline and a little bit of luck to escape that stone room. Maybe she wouldn't have felt so alone if she had known there was another person there, tangible or not.

"If the Sorcerers were meant to protect Infernus, how did Mateva's training go so wrong? Why did no one try to stop her early on?" she questioned. Her fingers started drumming on her thigh, eager for answers.

"I see we're still working on our patience skill, hmm? Don't worry, Ali. I'm not done with my story yet," her grandmother said with a little laugh, but it was countered by a dark flash passing across her face.

"When Mateva was chosen, it was the talk of the land. Infernians couldn't comprehend why she was chosen. Her family didn't have much, but not because they couldn't afford it. They chose to isolate themselves on the outskirts of the city, rarely socializing with their nearest neighbor four farm lengths away. Mateva and her siblings had a hard time making relationships with anyone besides themselves, often getting mocked by any traveler or daring teenager who would sneak onto their property at night."

Even though she knew how Mateva turned out, Ali couldn't help but sympathize with the younger version of her.

"So I guess teenagers are cruel no matter where you grow up," she mumbled.

"When word got out that Mateva was a future Sorcerer, it's safe to say there were more than a few envious Infernians in the city. It's rumored that during Mateva's training, she was interested in learning the history of the land. What would've happened if the Sorcerers hadn't stepped in to protect Infernians for all those years," she stalled, raising her eyebrows to ask if Ali had any questions.

She did, but determining which to ask first was proving difficult.

"You're telling me that Infernus has never seen a drought, a plague, a tsunami?" A land full of peace, and there were still people struggling to survive. Go figure.

"Thanks to the Sorcerers, no. If there was the smallest of hints that a disaster was threatening our home, the Sorcerers stepped in, and the threats would disappear. But Mateva didn't understand why it would be her job to protect the same people who had taunted her for years. Infernians had never done anything for her, so she felt no need to do them any favors."

After years of being taunted by the Lorrshore Sisters, Ali couldn't imagine being responsible for protecting them. Isolation can make the most faithful into a heathen.

"The elder Sorcerers tried to remind Mateva that her powers were given to her to do what was best for Infernus, not act on her own petty emotions. Magic was a gift that came with a price."

Her grandmother's complexion was becoming a bit more…translucent? Ali moved back to the couch, grabbing her grandmother's hand in her own. Afraid that their time was becoming more limited, she gave the hand a gentle squeeze with her own. There was still much to learn.

"Mateva did not argue. Instead, she became a fierce student, flying through her trainings at a remarkable rate. Some say she would wander around the training grounds at night, studying spells on her own so that she could show her mentors the progress the next morning," Releasing her fingers from Ali's hand, the older woman pretended like she had a wand of her own, tracing invisible shapes in the air.

"Where were the training grounds? Did anyone ever stumble upon them practicing?"

"Ah, another one of the Sorcerers' secrets. No one knew where they trained, not even their families. The trainees were truly stripped from everything they had known and forced into their new life."

A feeling Ali was a little too familiar with.

"Her teachers were so stunned by how quickly she was tuning into her magic, they gave her access to books that hadn't been touched in decades. No one had shown enough prowess to master the spells inside their pages, but this new student was different. That decision is said to be the first of many regrets." The last word scratched out of her throat with a hitch.

She must've noticed that her granddaughter was tuned into her inflections because she quickly blinked the emotion out of her eyes.

"Please, don't fret, Ali. I just haven't told this story in many moons. I had forgotten what it felt like to recall the details that were only shared with us through whispers."

"I trust you, Grandmother," she said with a reassuring smile that didn't reach her eyes.

"Mateva conquered the new spells with ease. She began to explore the chapters of the book the Sorcerers hadn't intended for her to read, blowing dust off their pages. They contained spells that the Sorcerers either forgot about or didn't know existed because they were not for Infernus's greater good. Awakening her innermost desires, Mateva craved this new magic and practiced in secret."

Ali pictured the Sorcerer-in-training rushing through the quiet grounds at dawn, trying to reach her quarters before anyone would notice she was missing from her bed.

"Naturally, she excelled at these new ventures. Convinced that the other Sorcerers would be impressed with her new-found abilities, Mateva called them all together. While they were in awe, they were also terribly frightened."

"If they were so scared, why didn't they fight her themselves?" Remembering the battle she'd watched on the tunnel walls, Ali shuddered thinking about the magic Mateva must have chosen to show her mentors.

"The student had clearly surpassed her masters, but instead of risking their own lives and fighting her, the elders reminded Mateva that this new magic broke the Sorcerer's Code—it did not protect Infernus, therefore she was forbidden from ever using it. They demanded she forget the spells she learned."

"Are you serious? They were too *scared* to fight her. If protecting Infernus was their job, how could they possibly think that just asking nicely would work?" Ali flung her hands in the air with an audible grunt. She didn't feel sorry for criticizing the Sorcerers' choices.

"Like I said, age does not equate to wisdom. As you can guess, Mateva wasn't as willing to compromise this time around. Furious at their lack of appreciation for her abilities, she made them a proposition. Either she would stay and continue to practice these new spells within the confines of their grounds, sharing them with her fellow students, or she would leave, never to return."

Knowing the next part of the story from Skotia's tale a few days earlier, Ali didn't have to surmise how the tale ended.

"The Sorcerers let their own egos make the decision. A common mistake, but one filled with irreparable consequences. They told her to leave." Her grandmother exhaled slowly and sat back into the velvet cushion, letting her limbs go limp at her sides. She must be exhausted, to have to dredge up tales she'd rather forget entirely. Ali hadn't seen her in so long, and here she was making the woman uncomfortable.

"And shortly after, I fled Infernus. A few others and I, we set out to find one of the portals that led to other worlds, never looking back."

With a quick calculation, Ali deduced that when her grandmother fled, she would've only been a few years older than herself. Some days, Ali could barely make it out of her bedroom without anxiety's shrill voice dragging her back down toward the blankets. How had her grandmother done it? How had she left her birthplace for a world she wasn't even sure would exist on the other end of the portal?

"Did your family come with you?" Thinking back, Ali could never remember her own mother speaking about her grandparents growing up. Did she even know about Infernus?

"My family?" her grandmother echoed, tears brimming in her eyes. "No...my family stayed. They were convinced that they were safe, not believing the rumors I was hearing. I didn't see them after the day I walked through that portal."

Ali may as well have been slapped across the face with the throw pillow next to her. Even though her family wasn't the most loving, she could never imagine willingly leaving them—leaving everything she knew—behind, without knowing what awaited her in a new world.

"Ali," her grandmother started, invigorated with a new energy. Even though she still felt distant, her green eyes beamed as bright as ever. "I know you're scared, and you have every right to be. But you belong in Infernus. It's your birthright."

She may have thought that it was Ali's birthright, but Ali still felt like a foreigner traipsing through Infernus's tunnels. If she ever did make it out of the mountain, she wasn't sure if she would ever truly belong.

"Listen to me very carefully, darling. You have a fight coming. Getting Carter back won't be easy, and there will be times it seems near impossible. But you have to save him from her. You don't know how detrimental to Infernus it will be if you fail."

"Detrimental? What do you mean, detrimental?" Ali felt the panic rising. Sirens wailed behind her eyes, but she couldn't get them to stop. She knew that she wouldn't be able to survive if she lost Carter for a second time, but why would Infernus suffer?

"There's no time to explain. We only have moments left together, and there's too much left to say. I need you to promise me one thing, Ali. Promise me you'll trust your eyes."

With every word, her grandmother's grip was loosening. No...fading away, until Ali would be left clutching air. But it wasn't just the woman in front of her—the objects in the room were vanishing too. At some point, the grandfather clock had stopped ticking and was frozen in time, its pendulum hovering just to the left of its center. The sirens were growing louder, pushing Ali to wrack her brain for anything she may have forgotten.

"Grandmother, please! Don't go yet. I still have so many questions!"

"It's not me who will be going, dear. But I need you to promise me. Say it." In Ali's entire life, her grandmother had never raised her voice. The force her voice held was palpable.

"I promise," Ali said, throwing both arms around her grandmother's neck and quietly crying into her shoulder.

"It's time to go back now. I've told you all that I can. But remember, I'll be there with you through it all. You've unlocked something inside you that's been blocked for many years. The time has come to use it."

And with that, the smells of lavender, jasmine, and mud returned to their faraway place in the recesses of Ali's mind. She was being pushed from the one place she never wanted to leave again, toward the one place she feared more than anything else.

CHAPTER 14

THE WAND'S MATE

"She's waking up! Vulcan, get back, give her some room to breathe!" Lilly's voice was the first sound Ali heard. Water was spewing from her lungs as she coughed her way into consciousness.

When she blinked her eyes open, Ali came face-to-face with Vulcan. His matching green eyes were piercing into her soul, sending shivers down her body that couldn't be attributed to the icy water seeping into her bones. There was a glint in the deep green color. It was faint, but there. Could it be panic?

Vulcan's wet hair dripped onto her torso, and she could feel his breath on her skin. Barely shifting from where she lay, Ali realized that Vulcan's hand was holding her head in place, and he wasn't taking his eyes from hers. Feeling heat rush to her face, she regained her posture as best she could and sat up halfway, looking into the other three faces above her. She must have only been unconscious for a few seconds—maybe a minute at most—but the conversation with her grandmother had to have been longer than that.

"Are you okay?" Vulcan asked, his own voice sounding waterlogged. He had hesitantly taken his hand away from her head and gotten to his feet as well, stepping back from where she sat.

"I'm not sure yet." She closed her eyes and images of the sea creatures flashed behind her lids like a cartoon strip. The dolphins snapping their sharpened jaws toward the teenagers, ravenous for their next meal. The electric jellyfish sending shockwaves through her body, numbing her limbs as the seconds passed. Then the lethal beast making its way toward Ali, sending its barb deep into her skin until her limbs were too heavy to propel her toward the surface. Daring to reach her hand toward her abdomen, her fingers only had to graze the spot the point had dug into her unprotected skin before she felt prickly, searing heat shoot through her spine.

"Dammit!" she cursed, clenching her jaw and pinching her thighs to distract her brain from the pain spreading from her wound.

"What does it feel like?" her look-alike asked. Skotia flinched when she saw Ali wince in pain, putting her hand on her own stomach to mimic her twin's movements.

"There's this slow burning growing over my muscles, like it's trying to take over my entire body. It's starting in my stomach—agh—but I think my nerves are catching on fire at this point."

Skotia's face paled. She turned away from the group, but Ali could see her body dry heaving at the thought of the pain.

"Here, eat this." Gavin came forward and held out a few crackers that Ali readily took.

"I hope you don't mind. I found them in your bag," he added, looking toward Vulcan quickly before continuing to pull items from his pockets. From the looks of it, he'd found more than just crackers.

"No, of course not. Why would I mind you rummaging through my things?" Vulcan responded, dryly. Whatever glint in his eye Ali thought she saw earlier was long gone, replaced by his usual wolfish scowl.

"Well, I was trying to find these." Gavin showed them the wrap of gauze and bandages in his hands. He knelt down next to Ali, lightly putting pressure on the spot the dolphin had punctured her. When Gavin pulled his hand away, she could see specks of red marking his fingertips, which he hurriedly tried to hide.

"It's really not as bad as you think," he announced. Ali suspected he gulped halfway through the statement to try to hide his nausea.

"Better or worse than the time Lilly pushed you off that fence when we were playing manhunt?" She cracked a smile, relieving some of the pent-up tension gathering in her jaw.

"Definitely better. Don't you remember he was crying for days after that?" Lilly joined in, her own eyes lighting up at the memory.

The two girls laughed as Ali gently lifted her shirt, giving Gavin room to wrap gauze around where she'd been attacked. The thought of the three of them playing manhunt brought back a simple moment that had been lost in Ali's memory, a time when the most the three of them had to worry about was the grade on their history exam.

Things were much different now.

Once reality reminded Ali of the present, her laughter fizzled out. Instead of running through their neighborhood on a warm spring night, the three were trapped in a labyrinth of tunnels that had a mind of their own. Instead of looking for each other in their neighbors' backyards, they were desperately searching for a light to guide them toward refuge.

With a firm tug, Ali felt Gavin secure the gauze to her skin. Even though it was still pulsing at the wound, the area around it was less irritated, and she had full mobility in her torso.

"Thank you, Gav. That helped a lot," she said with a soft smile, patting Gavin's hand with her own.

"How did you know how to do that?" Vulcan asked, his shoulders broadening as his eyes landed on Gavin's hands around Ali's waist.

"For lifeguard training we have to get certified in first aid every year," Gavin answered, gathering the remaining gauze and bandages before handing them to Vulcan. "A few weeks ago, I had to teach the new lifeguards everything to know about emergency care. You'd be surprised how many people don't know how to apply a tourniquet correctly," Gavin stated, matter-of-factly. After a quick glimpse at Vulcan's raised eyebrows, Ali wasn't sure if he understood the concept of a lifeguard. Now wasn't the time to discuss semantics.

"That's rather impressive." Skotia was also studying Gavin's technique. She gave him her nod of approval, causing him to turn a bright red.

"Uh...thanks. It's nothing really...I can show you sometime if you'd like," he stuttered, clumsily stepping away from Ali and rising to his feet.

"Well, I'm just glad I'm getting some feeling back," Ali groaned as she began moving her muscles in circles and flexed her fingers. Still wracking her brain to remember what exactly happened under the depths, she vaguely recalled a bright light blinding her before the animal finally released its near-fatal clutch.

But what was the light?

"Can someone please explain to me what exactly happened down there? What *were* those things?"

"I don't know what you both saw under there. We couldn't make out a thing from up here, but those *things* that jumped out of the water were maldauphs," Skotia explained, grabbing Ali's hand and helping her to her feet. Ali looked her doppelganger in the face, patting herself dry while she waited for Skotia to explain the creatures who had an appetite for human flesh.

"They're a prehistoric Infernian creature who has made a home in our history books and our folklore. When children are younger and parents don't want them wading too far into the rivers, they warn them that the maldauphs will snatch them up as a snack," Skotia described, mimicking small children diving into the waters with her hands over her head.

"Wait, parents let their children into the water with those things?" Gavin squawked. Ali was worried his eyes were going to fall out of his head with how wide they had become.

"Well, no one has actually seen one before, but the thought of being eaten alive bite by bite was enough to keep every toddler on dry land." A shudder ran across Skotia's profile.

"Well, for being prehistoric they looked pretty alive to me," Ali noted. "But at the end there, after its tail stabbed me, how did we get out?" she asked, looking directly at Vulcan.

Instead of meeting her eyes, Vulcan shifted his weight side to side and looked toward the other three in their group. They weren't meeting her gaze either. Clearing his throat, Vulcan started and stopped his sentence three times before finally stringing the words together.

"Ali, you don't remember...anything after that?"

"The only thing I remember is this flashing light surrounding me. But after that, I thought I was drowning. I couldn't find the strength to fight anymore." Ali tried to fight the dark memories away, but they were standing tall at the forefront of her mind. "I let my body start to sink, my limbs going completely numb at my sides as my body filled with water. I think I was in and out of consciousness, so I didn't see how you escaped." Her arms and legs still didn't have their full strength, but she willed them to keep her body upright.

"That light. I think it scared the creatures away for a moment. As soon as I had them off my back, I was able to swim down to you before you were too far out of reach. Once we were out of the water and onto this landing, I reached for the lever and the water started to recede." Vulcan told the story with precision, but by the way he was still avoiding her stare, she could tell that he was hiding something. He might have been trained for combat, but his tutors forgot to teach him a thing or two about lying.

"Those things were as smart as they were vicious. When the water began to recede, the maldauphs and whatever else we saw down there fled toward the underground tunnels. Once they were through, the tunnels closed themselves off and the three of them were able to reach us by the staircases," he continued, gesturing toward the barren gorge behind Ali.

Ali slowly turned her head. Vulcan's story was true—the river had vanished. There was a wet sheen left over every stone and a few puddles gathered in the sunken areas, but other than that no one would have ever known that there had been a raging river moments before. Squinting, Ali could see the tunnels Vulcan was referring to. At least, she could see their general shapes. She saw large boulders covering each one, protecting its inhabitants from flopping on the dry, cold floor until their hearts gave out.

"But, about the flash," Vulcan slowly started again. He finally met Ali's look, but now he was furiously wringing his hands until they became red. "I have a theory about what happened down there, but you have to hear me out on this one. No interruptions."

But before Vulcan could begin, a thundering roar bellowed from behind one of the blocked tunnels. Looking into the pit, Ali saw the boulder trembling from the force, threatening to give way and release the creatures trapped behind its walls.

With a look around their circle, each teenager grabbed a bag and began sprinting toward the nearest exit they could find.

"Wait, shouldn't we look at the map first?" Gavin cried, stumbling over his feet as he heaved a knapsack over his shoulders with Skotia's help.

"There's no time," Vulcan shouted without breaking his pace. "Unless you want to volunteer as the decoy for whatever is trying to eat us."

Gavin mumbled something inaudible and fell into step with the rest of the group.

"You said you wanted to tell me what your theory is," Ali yelled out toward Vulcan, careful not to trip on the bumpy terrain. "You have my attention. Tell me what you think happened under the water."

"You want me to tell you *now*?" Ali couldn't see his face, but she could hear the irritation dripping in his voice. They could barely see twenty yards in front of them, and Vulcan had to keep his head on a swivel in case any unwanted brutes popped out at them, but she was done waiting.

"Better now than after something else tries to eat us."

"Fine, have it your way," he conceded, narrowly dodging a hanging stone that had seemingly appeared out of thin air.

"I think that when the venom entered your body, something inside you surrendered itself. Something that we all have inside us—the fear of death. To me, it sounds like you accepted death in those last moments, letting the last—watch out for that ditch—bits of energy release themselves from your body."

"And? That's it?" she stammered, barely making it over the ditch Vulcan had pointed out.

"Patience was never a strength of yours, was it?" he quipped. "As I was saying, when that happened, I think your energy released that flash of light. When you were on the brink of death, whatever was in you awakened after years of being dormant, and I think that something was magic."

If it wasn't for their labored breathing and the thuds of their shoes against the floor, they would've been able to hear a pin drop. Now that Ali had her full strength back, she had to stop herself from running directly into Vulcan's backside.

"No, nope, that's not it," she denied, his words ringing through her mind. "I don't have magic, remember? If I did, why wouldn't the wand work for me when I first touched it?"

Something was nagging at the back of her mind, a feeling that she'd had before stumbling through a door in her mind that had been closed for many years. Suddenly, she was back under the water, death tapping on her shoulder, inviting her in for one last hug. It was true. When Carter's face flashed before her mind, she had let go of every earthly desire imaginable and accepted her fate.

Maybe it was magic.

A piece from the conversation with her grandmother—a conversation she wasn't completely convinced actually happened—flashed behind her eyes.

You've unlocked something inside you that's been blocked for many years. It's now come time to use it.

Her grandmother's words mixed with Vulcan's, bouncing from one wall of her mind to the next. Could this be what Grandmother had alluded to?

"Ali, I've only had magic described to me when I was a child, but that light wasn't just a lightning bolt or jolt of energy surging from the water. It had to have a source, and that source was you." Vulcan had slowed his pace to meet hers. She could feel his steely gaze making a hole in the side of her forehead, trying to decipher her emotions.

But waves were crashing in Ali's intestines, turning her insides into swirling whirlpools. The nausea began to set in, forcing her to lose her balance and reach out for something solid to lean against. Before her hand could find a wall, she felt her body being pushed off her feet, leaving her soaring through air until she felt stone collide with her back.

"What was that for?" she groaned, pain burning through her muscles like a raging wildfire.

"So that *you* can sit down and listen for once in your life," Vulcan pushed, towering over Ali with both arms crossed over his chest. His green eyes flared with power, like a soldier ordering his troops into battle.

"It's just, I can't be…I can't have," she tried to speak, slurring her words together into one incoherent sentence.

"Ali," Skotia was speaking now, taking a few steps closer to Ali. Her breathing was still heavy from the run, but she placed her icy hands on her shoulders and forced Ali to open her eyes. She stared deep into Skotia's endless dark pupils. It may have been Ali's blurred vision, but Skotia's features looked more sunken than they had yesterday, now hollowed to their bones.

"When you two were in the river, the three of us couldn't see a thing from the surface. The water was murky. But, the one thing we did see before Vulcan pulled you from the depths was a flash of light. It emanated throughout this entire cavern, breaking through the water's surface and reaching our own eyes. It was the only light we had in our darkness."

Ali wasn't sure where her look-alike was going, but the more she heard about the power this magical energy held, the longer she was convinced that it couldn't have possibly come from her own lanky frame.

"Something changed in the air. It was subtle, but a current rushed through my body and sent a shiver down my arms. There's no doubt it was magic. It all makes sense—why my dreams told me to come find you. You're what we need to stop Mateva. You're the magic Infernus is looking for." Skotia hadn't broken her gaze and her fingers were clutching Ali's shoulder with such force that she could feel her nails breaking the thin skin.

She was still hesitant to tell the others about her conversation with her grandmother, but the longer she let her words ruminate in her mind, the more Ali's inner voice was getting louder, and forcing her to think about the possibility these Infernians could be telling the truth.

Thinking back to how both women described Infernus under Mateva's reign—scared, hopeless, desperate—Ali pictured the Sorcerer. With her wand hiding in her cloak, she imagined Mateva storming through the streets of Infernus, unexpectedly barging into families' homes and destroying their livelihoods in a matter of minutes. If destruction reigned supreme once before, how was she supposed to be the savior Infernus needed? Those other Sorcerers, Cassiopeia included, had years of training before she battled Mateva. Even when she did, there was a struggle. If Ali were to even fathom fighting the woman, she would be crushed to the wind in one flick of the wand.

Closing her eyes and focusing on her breath, Ali started to assess the different feelings coursing through her. Acutely aware that the other four members of the group were watching her every move, she imagined four tall, black walls surrounding her, blocking her off from the rest of the world. Starting with the tips of her toes and making her way up to her creased forehead, Ali focused on every inch of skin.

Even though her mind was denying it, her body knew there was something different. There wasn't necessarily something out of alignment, but rather she had found the key to a treasure chest she didn't know was buried in her. Now that the chest was open, she couldn't close it. She could try to bury it deep under the sand, but the chest would keep digging itself out until Ali took a peek inside.

So that's what she did.

And inside, she found herself looking at a younger Ali who had just come from her grandmother's house after hearing another story of Infernus. Memories of making wands out of twigs in her backyard and casting spells on her neighbor's pets from over the fence came to a screeching halt in her mind's eye. Giants, goblins, and elves had always nestled themselves nicely in her dreams and became friendly faces over the years, before fading into the background as she got older and the stories stopped coming.

But now she was in the middle of her own story, and it was time to choose which road she was taking.

"Ali, think about what this could mean for you. For you and Carter. It feels...right, don't you think?" Lilly chimed in, crashing through Ali's invisible walls and placing a hand on her shoulder.

"It changes everything, you're right. I get it. But you're not the one who's being asked to save a world from an evil Sorcerer." Ali let her words roll out of her mouth before she could stop them. She balled her fingers into fists and pulled at her long hair. "You're not the one Infernus is apparently counting on for some godforsaken reason. The one who could barely leave her bed a few years ago, only to get up to her parents fighting a floor below. The one who the neighbors stare at from their living room windows, closing their blinds the second they make eye contact. The one who forced her brother to run away, not knowing it would be the last time she'd see him."

Lilly was quiet for a few moments, meeting Ali's empty stare with her own stone-cold expression.

"First of all, you need to realize you are not the same girl you were when Carter disappeared. Then, you need to remember who was there for you, every step of that way. Us. Gavin and Lilly, your best friends." She was hovering over Ali, her words slicing through the deprecating thoughts running through Ali's mind.

"We were there for you when you couldn't leave your bed. And when we all stayed late after school because you were trying your hardest not to walk through your front door. And whenever we've seen someone point at you behind your back in the hallways, the two of us have personally left an extremely sticky present in their locker the next day." Lilly's eyebrows had pressed together, and she was wagging a finger in Ali's face with every sentence. "So, even though you may have felt alone every single one of those days, we've been behind you every step of the way, ready to catch you when you fall."

Unclenching her fists slowly, Ali felt her mouth hang low as Lilly told her version of the story. She never knew that

Gavin and Lilly had done those things for her in the shadows, hiding their deeds so Ali wouldn't feel guilty about their help later on.

"Like I said, you're not that same girl. You've grown, you've changed. We've seen it. Sure, being brought to Infernus might not have been on our summer bucket list, but you need to take a step back and realize who you are. All you've ever wanted these past three years is for Carter to come back home. And now you have that chance! You need to fight her, Ali. You need to get Carter back. And if you fail, we'll still be here to catch you when you fall," Lilly was out of breath by the end of her pitch and her throat was raspy, like she was trying to hide any emotion from her voice and speak with reason.

If Ali was logical, she would've told Lilly that it was useless to try to fight for her brother back after all this time. The candle of hope she lit long ago was on its final moments, the wax overflowing and threatening to extinguish the flame. But Ali wasn't known for her logical outbursts, and every point Lilly had made resonated with that inner voice, now barging through the front door of her mind and yelling at her to pay attention to the signs.

"You're right. I…I haven't said thank you enough. To both of you," Ali started, looking between Gavin and Lilly. She kept going before Lilly could cut her off.

"And you're right that Carter deserves much more than I've been giving him. There have been a number of days that I could have been doing more. But I let my mother take over. I removed myself from the equation. As if that would bring him back sooner," Ali visualized her mother going door-to-door, pleading for help to look for Carter while she sat crisscross on her couch, numb from it all.

"Now that I have a chance to get him back, I need to take it—for Carter. He deserves that much."

No one moved. Letting the weight of her declaration sink in, Ali slowly began to nod, more for her own sanity than the others'.

"I don't know why you keep doubting yourself, Al. Look at all you've done since we got trapped down here. This will be like a piece of cake compared to those shadowvines," Gavin's joke left a crooked smile on Ali's lips. She didn't have to believe him yet to appreciate Gavin's poorly timed humor.

"Well I, for one, believe that you are capable of greatness. But, in order for you to reach that potential, we need to get started now," Skotia had a large, beaming smile across her lips as if it were Christmas morning and she'd just seen the tree packed with presents.

"I'm glad one of us has a shred of confidence," Ali whispered, low enough so she hoped only she could hear.

By the way Vulcan had raised his eyebrows, she guessed that it wasn't quite low enough.

"Wait a moment. I need to see something first before we go jumping to conclusions," Vulcan grumbled, reaching inside his pocket and pulling out the wand.

"What do you mean, jumping to conclusions? You were the first one to say that I had magic!" She couldn't believe what she was hearing. How could he change his mind after she had just agreed to possibly the worst decision of her life?

"I didn't *say* you had magic, I theorized it. And in order to further test my theory, I need to try something. My parents taught me it's almost impossible to perform magic correctly on a first try with no magical object to assist you. Since I was the one carrying the wand, it couldn't possibly be that," Vulcan was twirling the wand between his fingertips as he paced around Ali. Feeling like the prey to his predator, she began fumbling with her hands as he spoke.

"You said that your necklace has glowed quite a few times since you've been here. I need you to give it to me."

"Absolutely not!" Ali shrieked, scrambling to her feet. Her hands flew to protect the stone that hung around her neck. "I haven't taken this necklace off in years. I'm not about to give it to you when all you have is a hunch that it might—I don't even know what your hunch is telling you."

"Fine, have it your way then."

Vulcan stopped his pacing and started walking slowly toward Ali, taking his time with each step. Never losing eye contact, the scents of damp dirt and rust exuding from his clothes filled her nose. Stopping just before her face, Vulcan slowly removed Ali's hands from the gemstone and placed them both at her sides. His fingers briefly locked over her hands, giving them a small squeeze before letting go. If she were honest, Ali could barely breathe having him this close to her, but she hoped he couldn't hear how loudly her heart was beating. Not breaking their stare, Vulcan reached for the emerald and flipped it over in the light, looking for a sign Ali wasn't sure he would find.

She could hear Lilly's faint breathing on her side, eyes glued on Vulcan and Ali.

"Ah, there it is," His sly grin appeared, eyes still locked on the stone.

"What? What is it?" Ali whipped around, forcing Vulcan to surrender the necklace from his grip. She took the stone in her own hands but couldn't find anything different from the last hundred times she had followed the same routine.

"Flip it over." Vulcan ordered.

"Oh my god." Skotia inhaled sharply.

Once she did, Ali understood what the fuss was about. Carved into the back of the stone was the same symbol they had seen on the time capsule. The same symbol that was etched into the bottom of the wand. Her necklace bore the Mark of the Sorcerers, clear as day.

"But, this is impossible. I've turned this necklace over in my hands hundreds of times, and I've never seen this. Why now?"

You belong in Infernus.

Her grandmother's words echoed around her, floating through the air before being blown away by the cool breeze.

"I told you that something had to assist you to perform that magic, even if it was for a single moment. It looks like that necklace knew when your magic woke up inside you and it decided to leave you a little message," Vulcan hypothesized. Ali ignored the prying stares from the others, all trying to sneak the perfect look at the new engraving.

With a long, silent look toward Vulcan, Ali reached both hands around her neck and gradually raised her necklace over her head. Immediately, she felt a void where the stone had lain for all those years. As the twine completely raised off her skin, her chest became bare and cold. She placed the stone in her outstretched palm, curling the string on itself so no part hung over the edges. It began to glow.

Only this time, something inside the stone was beating, as if it had a heart. There was no sound to it, but Ali could feel it pulsing in her palm, one beat at a time. Like it was alive.

He might as well have been trained for this situation; because Vulcan brought the wand closer to the emerald, just barely leaving any empty space between the two.

The pulsing was getting faster. The emerald was begging Ali to bring them closer to one another.

"Here, take the wand." Vulcan held it out for Ali, which she reluctantly grabbed with her free hand.

The second the wood touched her fingertips, the green stone began to levitate, suspended in midair. Turning itself over, the emerald moved itself closer to the wand, an inch at a time. With bated breath and an unwavering grip, Ali brought the tip of the wand to touch the stone, giving it the connection it desperately longed for.

With a flash of blinding green light brighter than the last, Ali dropped both objects but only heard one fall to the ground. She blinked away the stars from her vision and saw the wand lying on the ground.

Still scanning for the necklace she hadn't heard hit the ground, she bent down to grab the wand from the grimy floor. Her pupils were still focusing, but as soon as she picked the previously lifeless wand from the floor, she detected a change in its energy. Before, it could have been mistaken for another twig off the forest floor. Now, there was something underneath the wood.

A glowing green current ran through the wand's etchings, pulsing like the necklace had done moments ago.

"It's in there," Ali breathed, shakily. "The necklace—it's a part of the wand now. The two were meant to be one this entire time." Her ears were ringing, so she could only see Vulcan nodding but not hear the words his mouth was forming.

The wood was comfortable in her hand, practically forming to her grip so that she would have a hard time letting it go. Embracing the new shift in its power, Ali silently went over her journey to get here.

The feeling of her feet lifting off the ground as she was sucked into the tree's black hole filled her body, quickly replaced with the initial shock of coming face-to-face with

Skotia for the first time. Her veins flooded with adrenaline as she recalled the moment Skotia revealed Carter was still alive, and a dark shadow hid in the corner of her mind when she watched the nightmare the shadowvines forced her to relive. Finally, she forced her body to remember what it felt to have a burst of light soar through her muscles, giving her the strength to fend off the most savage of creatures.

Whether she wanted it or not, the magic was awake. There was no going back.

Looking the four others in their apprehensive eyes, Ali coiled her fingers around the wand, a storm rising inside her.

"If I'm going to do this, I'm going to do it right," she broke the silence. "I still don't know if I can defeat this woman, but I have to try. For my brother." She turned to face Skotia and Vulcan. "This is your home, and somehow it feels like it might be mine too. If I have some role to play in protecting it, then so be it. But I need your help. I need training, and I need it now. My brother doesn't deserve to be kept by that monster a minute longer than he has to be," Ali finished, breathing heavily after every sentence.

She expected to hear protests from the Infernians, and a few from her own friends begging her not to engage in a fight she was destined to lose. But instead, all four of them were nodding in agreement. Vulcan stepped forward, holding out his hand to confirm their deal. After a skeptical moment, she stepped forward and shook it with her free hand.

"Let's begin," he declared.

CHAPTER 15

SKOTIA'S SECRET

———

Once Ali had made the pact with Vulcan, the five teenagers had consulted the map for their next move. After trying to shine some light on the tattered map, they found a passageway that seemed to connect, bringing them the closest to the core. With Vulcan gladly taking his position at the lead of the pack, the rag tag group of teenagers made their way to what would hopefully be, safety.

That was a week ago. The room they had found was similar to the ones they had camped in previously, but in so many ways it was different. Ali wasn't sure if it was the newfound magic running through her veins, but the energy bouncing off the stones was tangible, leaving a faint buzzing in her ears at all times. The last ceiling extended for eons, forcing them to crane their necks to get a glimpse of the top, but this room's summit was no more than thirty feet above their heads. Ali theorized it could be because they were heading deeper into the mountain, leaving any signs of the outdoors far behind them.

There were signs of life in the new room, but it was a life that had ended long before their time. Two hollowed-out bookshelves were leaning against one of the walls, the wood had been ravaged by some sort of insects. What she assumed were once books were barely legible. The ink had ago long dried out and cracked, while their pages had withered away to nothing. When they first arrived, Ali carefully pried open the handful of volumes that were salvageable, blowing away the dust and beetles that had made the chapters their home.

Lightly flipping the pages between her fingertips, Ali found that the books contained spells. Diagrams of wand motions flooded the pages, along with faded inscriptions next to each image. Every page was different, some contained spells for healing wounds or lighting a fire, while others seemed fiercer, like they should be used for battle magic. The jutted sparks practically shot off the page, forcing Ali to picture the spells Cassiopeia must have used against Mateva as she fought for her life. Could they be the same ones she was reading now?

"I can't make out any of these spells," she muttered through clenched teeth. The lack of light in their new home didn't help the situation, but even if she were holding a magnifying glass to the pages, Ali suspected she wouldn't be able to string together more than two words.

Their setup looked like any other, but Ali couldn't help but notice that everyone looked a bit leaner than when they first started, their collarbones jutting out slightly sharper. Even though they'd been traveling for just over a week, the group was already living off the limited rations Skotia and Vulcan had packed with them on their journey. Considering her original goal was to find Ali, Skotia had a bit more packed, but neither Infernian had planned on adding Gavin and Lilly to the trip.

Vulcan must have calculated that rations were growing scarce because Ali noticed that he was giving himself less at every meal, chewing his bites quite a few more times to make them last longer.

"I'm not that hungry if you want some of mine," she had offered one night when it was just the two of them left. For a moment, she thought he might accept her offer as he glanced longingly at her plate, but the growls from her stomach gave her away. Once he heard them, he briskly shook his head and got up from his seat, leaving Ali alone with her provisions.

After their predominantly silent meals, everyone retreated to their own corner of the cave. Separating their belongings from one another gave everyone a sense of privacy they'd been missing.

At first, Ali enjoyed the solitude. She was used to isolating herself in her bedroom at home, closing the door and plugging in her headphones until she felt sleep take over. When she had the chance to be somewhat alone for the first time in however many days, she jumped at the opportunity to stick herself in the farthest corner possible. She was more than willing to sleep on the rocky terrain if it meant she could have some time to herself.

But after a few nights, the ground started to feel a bit stiffer, sending a lonely chill into her spine when she would close her eyes for the night. Not wanting to force her friends to leave their privacy, she hastily called Gavin and Lilly over one day when she was pretending to decipher one of the spell books.

"What's up, Al? What do you have there?" Gavin asked, peering over Ali's shoulder to the pages she held open in her palms. Both Gavin and Lilly were just as shocked as Ali was when they learned she had magic, their eyes periodically growing wide and then shooting confused glances back and forth when they thought she wasn't looking. However, her friends seemed to have much more faith that she would be able to master her newfound abilities than Ali had in herself.

"Oh, I'm just trying to decode this spell for fire that is apparently supposed to be the simplest one in this convoluted book," Ali sighed, returning the volume to its home on the grimy shelf next to her. "Sometimes the magic feels so close, like it's on my fingertips and waiting for the signal to shoot through the end of this wand. But, other times, it feels as if it's left my body altogether. Like it was using me as a temporary home, and now it's off to find someone better suited for its power."

This was the first time Ali had admitted the hesitations she'd been having, but once the floodgates were open there was no holding back the deluge behind their walls.

"The reason I called you both over here was because, well, I was wondering if either of you have felt...alone? At night?" Her words cracked on the last few syllables, desperately trying to stop her voice from sharing the rest of her thoughts. Looking down at her pigeon-toed feet, she hastily continued before her friends could interrupt.

"It's just, ever since we found this new site," she gestured to the undisturbed room they had laid roots in. "The nights have felt...different. Almost like when we separate at the end of the day, there's going to be someone hovering above my eyes when they open in the morning. Or that there's someone, something, enjoying the fact that we've separated from one another, distancing ourselves night after night. I don't know if this place is finally breaking me, but..." Ali trailed off, unsure how to continue her rambling.

"No, you're right. I feel it too," Lilly interjected, reaching for Ali's hand. Feeling the quick squeeze on her palm, Ali looked up and saw the understanding in her best friend's eyes.

"We've only been here, what, a few days? But I feel it, too, like we're trespassing on someone else's home. The strangest part is, I don't think it's *someone*, but *something.*" Lilly gave Ali's hand another panicked squeeze. "Something knows that we're here and is waiting for us to leave again, counting down the days until it can return to its peacefulness."

"Agreed," Gavin contributed, swiveling his head around the trio as if something was listening to their conversation at that very moment. "It's like Infernus wants us to keep moving forward, like it knows we're not at our final stop yet."

The thought of what their final stop could be sent goosebumps racing down Ali's arms.

"Would either of you mind, I don't know, moving your things over here tonight? I think I'll just feel...safer," Ali whispered the last word, her feet rapidly tapping the floor.

"Of course," Gavin answered, wrapping Ali in a hug she was forced to reciprocate.

"I'd like that," Lilly added, joining in on the moment.

And from that night forward, the three of them slept one next to the other, each saying goodnight to each other before closing their eyes.

Vulcan and Skotia both noticed the shift in their behavior, but both Infernians had been keeping to themselves, rarely engaging in conversations unless they had to. Even though Vulcan was trying to help Ali with her training, more often than not, she would become frustrated with her lack of progress and storm off halfway through their session, hearing Vulcan sling curses under his breath behind her.

Exasperated with the lack of direction, Ali would slam the soles of her shoes against the ground as she walked away, hoping her trainer noticed the change in her demeanor. If he had been in training for his entire life, why was it so difficult for him to teach her a thing or two about her magic?

Ali's doppelganger wasn't much more receptive. Each time Ali tried to walk over to Skotia's part of the room, her twin had turned her back and pretended not to hear Ali's footsteps. But Ali knew Skotia saw her approaching; her dark pupils would flash with panic the second she sensed Ali's shadow creeping closer.

"Skotia? Do you want to try to help me get through a few of these books?" Ali would ask, trying to keep her voice as even as possible.

Without a word, Skotia would decline Ali's offer and gather her things, moving them farther away from the crowd. She didn't want to pressure Skotia into sharing her own worries about Ali's lack of progress if that was even what these new feelings were.

On a few nights, Ali had flashbacks to the first time she ran into Skotia, alone by her own fire, waiting patiently for her twin's arrival. Preoccupied with her own inner turmoil, Ali had never asked how long Skotia had been without her family, on her own in Infernus. What if she had been alone more than just those few weeks she started to search for Ali?

But Ali couldn't lend too much of her time thinking about Skotia. She had to focus on her training, or lack thereof, if she ever wanted them to take the next step of their journey.

One morning, she forced her body to wake up an hour earlier than usual, expecting to be the first one to open their eyes. After grasping for the wand she'd been keeping safe between her sheets, Ali rose to her feet. But before she could fully stretch her arms over her head and wake her exhausted muscles up, she saw another shape out of the corner of her eye.

Vulcan was sitting up in his makeshift cot about twenty yards away fidgeting with some object between his hands. She saw him tilt his head in her direction without directly looking her way, not acknowledging that she'd risen for the day. A sliver of Ali's conscience pleaded with her to ignore his presence. Cursing herself, Ali ignored the voice and began to make her way toward him.

Vulcan didn't raise his head until her shoes were directly under his nose, impatiently tapping the ground beneath it. She noticed he had been fidgeting with one of the tools he kept hidden on him, keeping them ready for a fight at a moment's notice.

"Hi." She spoke first.

"Hello," he replied shortly, keeping his eyes focused on the tool.

The conversation was off to a great start.

"Listen, I want to apologize." Ali grimaced. Apologies didn't come naturally to her. "I've been a bit…difficult these past few days. And I've been taking that out on you during our lessons."

"Now, that's not totally true. I would say you've progressed from an absolute failure to barely a beginner," Vulcan chimed in, now studying Ali with a smirk across his face. He was clearly enjoying her discomfort.

"And I'll just pretend you didn't interrupt my apology," Ali countered with a click of her tongue. Vulcan turned an invisible key at the corner of his mouth to signal his silence, but the glint in his eyes remained.

"It's just that I don't understand why the magic can't flow out of me like it did in that river. What if I'm a one-hit wonder, destined to spend my life questioning why Infernus took the magic away moments after it granted it?" Ali ran her hands through her hair, clutching her ends with air-tight fists. "It's like the lifeline inside me is flat, with no hope at resuscitation."

"Ali, listen to me." Vulcan rose to his feet and stood a head taller than her. He placed the tool back into his pocket and tilted her chin up toward him until she met his gaze. Once again, when his fingers touched her skin, her heartbeat began to mimic the cadence of a hummingbird's wings. She hadn't heard him be stern with her in a few days, so she unfurled her fingers and let go of a long breath.

"My family and I, we might not have magic ourselves, but we've seen enough of Infernus to know that the land doesn't make decisions by accident. There's a reason the magic came to you in the river, and you'll be able to find it again," he said, then placed his hands on both of Ali's shoulders, bringing the two of them just a few inches closer. She resisted the urge to let her exhausted muscles fall into his strong grip. "Maybe we need to get you back in that state of mind again, the one where you released all reservations and purely felt. Come on, while everyone else is still asleep, we can get some good practice in."

Vulcan took her hand in his, sending electricity up Ali's arm. He brought her to the part of the room Gavin had originally claimed before moving his things over near Ali's blankets.

"Close your eyes and visualize the one place you can be yourself. The place where no one is holding you back and you're free to just live without worries," Vulcan directed, his voice smoother than normal.

For the next hour, Ali did as she was told. Listening to her body, she visualized herself back in her grandmother's house, curled up under her favorite blanket with a hot cup of tea in hand. A book in the other, she let her imagination run wild with images of dragons and elves carrying out wild adventures. At times, she would lose the visualization and have to start from scratch, but Vulcan kept his patience, encouraging her to give it one more try every time she failed.

"Come on, one more time. You're closer than you've been since the river," he whispered softly.

Careful not to break her concentration, Ali centered her attention on Vulcan's deep voice. Focusing on his encouragement, Ali clenched her eyes shut as beads of sweat began to gather on her forehead. Her fingers were cramping from her tight grip on the wand, but something was finally building inside her. It felt like a warm ball of light growing from her core, slowly spreading outward toward the rest of her body. The warmth grew and she felt the wand pick up the power inside her, its own wood starting to stir in her grip. But as the light was about to make its way behind her eyes and reach her mind, Gavin's voice broke her trance.

"Morning, Ali. Wait—you're Skotia. Skotia, what are you doing?" His voice was dowsed with sleep, but there was a hint of alarm that brought Ali out of the moment.

Ali flung her eyes open, and she turned to see Skotia huddled over her blankets, barely lifting them off the ground so that she could peer underneath.

"What are you doing?" she heard herself shout, pointing the wand toward Gavin and Skotia. Before Ali knew what was happening, a ball of fire shot from the wand's tip toward Skotia.

Unable to control the flame's path, the top of the blaze narrowly missed her head, leaving a singed mark on the wall behind her.

Skotia met Ali's eyes for half a second before Ali turned on a dime and fled, shoving the wand into her pocket.

"Ali, wait! You were making progress!" Vulcan's words echoed behind her, but she could only half hear.

The heat was already rising in Ali's cheeks as she processed the last few moments. She was mortified that she had almost taken off her doppelganger's head with the magic, letting it fly from her with not an ounce of control. Frantically turning to find an escape, Ali spotted a small crevice in the wall and made a beeline for its entrance. There were shouts ringing in her ears from every corner of the room, but they were blending into one mixed blur far behind her.

When she reached the entrance of the fissure, Ali squirmed her way through the opening. She didn't take more than ten paces forward before reaching a dead end, the stone blocking any chance at escaping. Still sorting out what had happened in their room, Ali embraced the power pulsing inside her and closed her eyes once more, focusing her chaotic energy into the wand in her hand.

Red sparks shot out of the wood, shedding light on the dimly lit crevice she was hiding in. Adrenaline coursing through her veins, Ali tried to visualize the motions from the spells she'd been reading. Her wand traced the air in the only pattern she could remember. Within seconds, a patch of flowers grew from the grime-covered floors beneath her. They were no bigger than her fingers, but their vibrant reds and yellows stood out in the dingy room. They bloomed almost immediately, giving off the fresh scents of spring that Ali deeply missed.

While she eagerly tried to picture what else she had read among the pages, she was distracted by a presence behind her.

"Ali? Can we talk?" Her doppelganger was standing before her. Skotia's long black hair was pulled into a bun above her head.

Ali couldn't fathom why, but a shudder coursed through her bones.

"Yeah, we can start by talking about why you were looking through my things? What were you even looking for? I don't have anything here in the first place," she questioned, rage quickly replacing the initial guilt she felt for directing a flaming ball of fire toward Skotia. Now that her doppelganger was in front of her, she had an entire week's worth of questions to ask.

Quicker than lightning, Skotia's eyes flew toward the wand in Ali's hand. She tried to recover and began stammering about misplacing something from her backpack, but it was too late.

"This?" Ali held the wand up beside her face. "Why were you looking for this?"

Skotia immediately pressed her lips together and grew quiet. Ali crossed her arms, purposely jutting the wand from her fist.

"I...I wanted to see if it would work for me," Skotia uttered far too quickly, wringing her wrists. "I wanted to try it when no one would see, just in case it worked for me too."

"But why would it work for you? You don't have magic," Ali regretted the comment the second it left her mouth. A hurt look crossed her twin's face and was quickly replaced by something darker, her black pupils growing a deeper shade of black.

"And *you* didn't know that Infernus existed until a week ago, let alone that you had magic, so why wouldn't it be worth a shot?" Skotia was no longer fidgeting with her hands. Instead, she had taken a step closer to Ali, projecting her voice off the walls around them. Suddenly, those walls seemed to be moving, closing in on Ali as she felt her backside meet up against the cool stone.

"I didn't mean it that way," Ali rebutted, lightening her tone just a smidge. "But you've lived here your entire life. Don't you think you would've felt it by now? Or your family would've helped you with it?"

"Growing up, I wasn't always welcome in certain circles. It felt like I was living on the fringe of everyone's life—the other children in our neighborhood, my family—everyone," Skotia scoffed. For the first time since she'd entered the hole, her attention wasn't fixated on the wand.

"It never felt like I was welcome, so I found comfort elsewhere, which worked for a time. But when my family began to question what I was occupying myself with, they couldn't understand. They wouldn't even try. So when it came time to leave, it didn't take many pushes to get me through the front door."

"But they're your family. Surely they at least tried to understand?" Ali questioned, her voice small against Skotia's building fury.

"Do you think that because I've lived in a magical land, my family has had their happy ending?" Skotia asked, her voice wavering with anguish.

"Magic does not always heal. It can create chaos as easily as it can stop it."

Until now, Ali had only thought of magic as the solution to her problems. But Skotia was right—the shadowvines, maldauphs, the forest—magic had created more problems for her than she could count.

"But maybe, if a few more people had access to Infernus's magic—if magic were thrust into the right hands from the beginning—maybe the chaos would stop for just a moment. My family…maybe they'd finally understand what I've been fighting for all along," she trailed off, her gaze landing on a spot just behind Ali.

As Skotia spoke, it dawned on Ali that she didn't know much about her look-alike. What had her upbringing been like? Who were her friends? Why hadn't Ali asked these questions earlier? If anything, Ali was one who could sympathize with a lonely soul.

"But clearly, none of it matters now," Skotia quickly regained her composure, as if nothing had happened. She straightened her posture and shook the dirt from her hands. "I came here to see if you wanted to apologize for nearly singing off my hair, but I can see that's not going to be the case. I'll just go then."

And with that, she left Ali alone in her claustrophobic space, the light from her red sparks slowly dying out with Skotia's exit.

Ali's shoulders sagged low. She blamed herself for the strained relationship, replaying the conversation in her mind. She could've at least asked Skotia if she wanted to try the wand after all of that, right? Would that have helped her twin feel less alone?

Determined to mend their bond, Ali raced out of the crevice nearly as quickly as she had entered it, trampling the flowers that had blossomed beneath her feet. Scanning the cave for Skotia's black bun, Ali spotted it by her sleeping area, back toward the rest of the group. She ran through her apology a few times in her head before she started making her way toward the girl.

She didn't get far before she was cut off by Lilly, who was now fully awake and in a wild frenzy. Her hair was thrown into a loose ponytail and she was waving her hands in a frenzy to get Ali's attention.

"What is it, Lilly? Can't this wait like five minutes?" Ali pleaded, catching glimpses of Skotia's hunched silhouette from over Lilly's head.

"No, it really can't," Lilly began, grabbing onto Ali's arm for support. "The map, it changed. It showed us where we have to go next. It showed us the final path to Mateva's hideout."

CHAPTER 16

THE DRAKE'S CHAMBER

———

"I'm sorry, *where* did you say we needed to go?" Ali demanded when she heard where the map was showing.

"The Drake's Chamber," Vulcan responded nonchalantly, brushing her question off as he rolled the parchment up and placed it in his knapsack.

"And who exactly is Drake?" she followed up, holding her head high in an attempt to meet his height.

Vulcan turned his shoulder toward her, leaving her question to the wind. Typical.

Ali turned to her two friends in case one of them had picked up on an answer she couldn't hear. They both shook their heads and held their hands up to the air. Clearly, they were done asking questions around here.

"Well, are you going to answer the question, or should I tell her?" Skotia hadn't said a word since she had run out of Ali's hole in the wall. Until now, she had been packing up her supplies far away from the rest of the group, muttering under her breath in a language Ali didn't understand. Rather than pressing her for more information, Ali gathered it would be best to give her some space for the time being.

"Can one of you just tell me what's going on?" Ali fumed. "We've already had to deal with some murderous plants and demonic dolphins, how much worse could it get?" She walked in Vulcan's line of sight, making it impossible for him to ignore her. Putting her hand on the knapsack he was fidgeting with, she waited until his green eyes finally met hers, but his mouth stayed shut. Reluctantly, she turned to Skotia and raised her eyebrows in defeat.

"A drake isn't a someone, it's a *something*," Skotia began. Her tone had evened out since their fight, but Ali wasn't entirely sure they had finished their conversation. "They're said to be protectors of Infernus that worked with the Sorcerers to protect the skies, looking for any signs of danger before they were able to reach our borders. Through the years, they've gone almost extinct since the Sorcerers scattered throughout the land, so no one has seen one in decades."

"Exactly. No one has seen one in decades. We don't know that we'll encounter one, it could just be a name. There's no use for unnecessary panic," Vulcan broke his vow of silence, rolling his eyes as he listened to Skotia's explanation.

Ali wasn't convinced, especially when she saw him sharpening his blades when he thought they weren't looking.

"The important part is that this is the last passageway before we get to the core. If my predictions are right—which they usually are—this is the fastest path to get to Mateva. Or, did you suddenly change your mind about saving your brother?" Vulcan's eyes bored into Ali's soul, daring her to take back her vow.

Ali had no plans on rescinding her promise, but that didn't mean a shot of adrenaline didn't burst into her stomach, sending ripples of anxiety across every corner of her body. She clasped her hands together to stop them from trembling and reminded herself that this time would be different. This time she would be able to save Carter. This time she had magic.

Even if she still didn't really know how to use it.

"Just finish packing the bags," she snarled at Vulcan, tossing him the spell books she was taking for her own practice. One more study session couldn't hurt. He threw them to the bottom of his bag and heaved it over his shoulder without checking that the pages were still intact.

Besides a few two-headed bats and creepy bugs on their walk, there wasn't much between them and the Drake's Chamber. Standing under a tremendous archway, Ali could see the architectural details carved into the entry, making it look like it was a portal to another part of Infernus entirely. There were notches carved, or perhaps they were scratches, into the sides, beginning where the archway met the floor and reaching their way up to its zenith.

"And you're positive this is where we have to go?" Ali questioned, stretching her neck toward the top of room. This one was noticeably more spacious than their last one, sending flares up in Ali's mind. There would be plenty of room for a creature to spy on the five of them without anyone noticing.

"Yes, I'm positive," Vulcan replied sharply, unfurling the map in his hands. He let out a long whistle, letting it echo through the cave.

"Well, that can only mean something amazing is about to happen, right?" Lilly chimed in, trying to look over Vulcan's shoulder, but he hid the map from their view before she could get a clear look.

"It's a good thing you didn't want to take back your promise," Vulcan turned his broad shoulders toward Ali, smirking while reaching for one of his daggers. "The map's erased everything up until this point. Even if we did want to turn back, I doubt we would be able to navigate these tunnels from memory."

The pit in her stomach sank a bit further. Taking a large gulp of air and clutching the wand close to her breast, Ali stepped into their new room. The other four followed, their footsteps echoing off the barren walls with every step.

Stillness entered Ali's bones. Feeling only her heartbeat, she questioned whether they were actually alone in this void.

"Maybe the drake rake left." Gavin shrugged his shoulders and brought his hands to his face, creating fake binoculars around his eyes.

Ali eyed him skeptically, but she couldn't suppress the small chuckle in her throat. Looking past Gavin, she spotted a light on the far side of the cavern, about half a mile away. It reminded her of the light she had seen when she was first thrown into Infernus, the light that ultimately brought her to Skotia.

Her heart skipped a beat. That was where they had to get to.

"There." She pointed, the word was raw in her throat. "We have to get there. That's where she is."

No one questioned her. Without a word, they began to run toward the light, watching the minuscule dot slowly grow larger with each passing second.

After two minutes of sprinting, a deafening whoosh pierced Ali's hearing. She stopped running and slammed her hands against her ears, but the sound was far too intense.

The others had stopped dead in their tracks, mimicking Ali's lead and covered their ears. They might as well have been trying to crush their skulls, but it would've been worth it if it canceled the noise.

She then felt it in her chest. This time, sound wasn't shattering her eardrums, but oxygen was leaving her lungs. Wind wrapped around them like a tornado, making it impossible to catch their breath as the air escaped. As the noise got louder, the wind spun faster. But just as she started to test how long she could hold her breath, the cyclone ceased and was replaced with a terrifying screech from above.

With a single tear running down her face, Ali prepared herself for the worst and looked toward the sky.

Gavin was wrong—the drake hadn't left.

Paralyzed with the terror coursing through her veins, Ali narrowly avoided retching when she saw the creature that had made this chamber its home.

The drake had four limbs, two wings, and a long, spiny tail protruding from its backside. What stunned Ali was that it was somehow translucent against the stone protruding above it, like it was made of air. One second she saw it flying directly toward her, the next she lost it to the sky. It was solid, yet almost invisible.

But it could still breathe fire.

A flame burst from its mouth. This inferno was far more powerful than the one Ali had created with her wand. In an instant, Ali hit the floor, feeling the heat narrowly miss her head as she pressed her cheek against the damp ground.

The drake was descending. Flipping onto her back, Ali saw outlines of its talons, at least two feet long and sharper than any dagger Vulcan had on his belt. When it had almost reached the group, it extended one of its claws and hooked into Gavin's shirt before flying off. He was left dangling in midair as the drake flew higher into the chamber, making it impossible for Ali to reach him.

"Gavin!" Ali and Lilly screamed simultaneously, scrambling to their feet. For a second, they heard his screams before they were snuffed out, his limp body dangling far above them. Ali looked at the wand in her hand, desperately trying to remember anything she'd read that might help get Gavin back from the monster.

But she didn't have long to think. Another drake, a smaller version of the first, was barreling toward them at full speed.

"It has a *child*?" Lilly shrieked, looking her demise directly in its translucent face.

"Vulcan, do you have anything that can defeat these things?" Ali screamed.

"It's impossible to defeat air!" he yelled back as he frantically took every weapon off his person, shaking out his jacket until three different blades were on the ground.

Another jet of fire flashed. It wasn't as bright as the first, but strong enough to make the sweat roll off her brow.

Suddenly, the smaller drake swerved to the left, its wings opening to their full breadth. Ali followed its path and her eyes landed directly on Skotia, who was cowering in a corner, close to the door they were all trying to get to.

"Ali! Help me!" Skotia called, her bones trembling as her back pressed against the wall behind her. There was nowhere to run.

The beast's eyes had landed on the Skotia, pinpointing her as its next victim. That was if Ali couldn't save her in time. As she wracked her brain, a spell was jumping from the corners of her mind, trying to break out of her memory.

"Throw me that book!" Ali ordered, pointing to the soot-covered manuscript Vulcan had just taken out of his backpack while he continued his search for an adequate weapon.

The spell was one she had briefly seen, faded on one of the elemental magic chapters.

Vulcan did as he was told. She caught the fragile pages, its delicate binding coming loose from the force of the throw. Flipping her gaze between the pages and the drake that was now closing in on Skotia, Ali's fingers found the section she had been picturing. She closed her palm tightly around the wand and prepared to execute the spell.

But she was going to be too late. The beast was hovering above Skotia, its razor-sharp talons swinging low like the ones that had dragged Gavin into the void.

Lilly appeared in her peripheral vision, running toward Ali's doppelganger at full force.

"Hey! Lizard brain! Leave her alone. Over here!" Lilly taunted. She feverishly waved her hands over her head, creating a blur of blond hair in front of her face. It worked—the drake's snout whipped around to face its harasser. The creature picked up speed and started flying toward Lilly, rapidly gaining momentum with every beat of its wings.

"Oh shit," Lilly muttered, tripping over her feet before racing from the very beast she had just insulted.

"Lilly, run toward me!" Ali yelled, taking one last glance at the spell to make sure she had the motions right.

"Are you crazy? Absolutely not!"

"Trust me!"

"You better have some sort of a plan," Lilly said as she changed course. Both girl and beast were on a straight trajectory toward Ali.

She had a plan, and she prayed it would work.

Lilly finally reached Ali and dove behind her onto the rocky terrain. Vulcan quickly threw himself in front of Lilly, creating another barrier between beast and girl.

Closing her eyes and letting the power build inside her, Ali traced the pattern she had seen in the book in the air and pointed her wand into the drake's face.

Translucent ropes to match the beast's hue burst out of her wand, wrapping themselves around the drake's backside, suspending it in midair. There were bonds over its mouth and wings, holding its massive body in the air.

"It worked," she breathed, stunned by her own success. She struggled to hold the ropes in place, keeping both hands on her wand while it shook in her hand.

"You did it!" Lilly leaped from behind Vulcan, wrapping Ali in a bear hug that nearly brought her back down to the floor.

"Yeah, I guess I did." Ali looked at the wand in her hand, still questioning whether she was the one who had just performed that spell. "But that doesn't do anything to get Gavin back. How are we going to reach him when he's hundreds of feet above us?"

Suddenly, the now-familiar screech echoed above them. The first drake was coming back for them, possibly upset that they had thwarted its child. But there was something on its back this time that hadn't been there before. Could it be?

"Gavin?" Ali asked, stunned at what she was seeing.

Gavin, now fully conscious, was riding on the drake's back, clinging for dear life onto one of the spikes protruding from its glassy body.

"Hold on, I'm coming back down!" he yelled over the deafening wind. From where Ali was standing, it seemed like he was almost in control of the beast, its wings turning as Gavin shifted his own weight from side to side.

"He who tames the beasts will rule the sky," Vulcan mumbled to himself while he gaped at Gavin's profile coming into view.

"What did you just say?" Ali asked, perplexed by Vulcan's sudden awe.

"Ali, look out!" Lilly shrieked.

Gavin may have been controlling the drake's turns, but he had no say over its speed. Before it barreled into her, Ali steadied herself to the ground. Remembering the spell she performed on the smaller drake, she mimicked the same patterns and the binds slivered out from her wand once again. Holding the magic for a little longer this time to account for the drake's size, she pulled the ropes closer to her and dragged the creature closer to the ground until it was hovering at a point Gavin could jump from.

Landing with a thud, Gavin dusted off his clothes before staring back up at the beast who had captured him.

"Serves you right!"

"Gavin, what happened? How did you go from the talons, to riding its back, to—" Lilly cut herself off. Ali understood why; she too had been wondering how Gavin had managed to control the animal she could only deter through magic.

"When I woke up, I was in this nest thing it created way up there." Gavin waved his hand toward the sky. "At a certain angle, I could see where it was sitting. But I couldn't move. I might as well have been paralyzed."

He stopped for a moment, taking the chance to look back to the skies from where he had just emerged.

"At one point, that *thing* turned to me—I could just barely make out its nasty face—and a stream of fire engulfed the nest. I had to jump or else I would've been the next item on the menu. Once my legs finally started moving again, I pounced onto its back and held on to whatever I could find. The thing kept trying to throw me off, but I wasn't going anywhere, which, I guess, is why it took off again." Gavin's voice had an edge to it that Ali had never heard before, and she couldn't help but take a step back and look deeply into her friend's face.

But there was no time for questions because the moment Vulcan had repacked his knives, the magical cords on the drakes started to fizzle away, giving them room to stretch their wings and attack.

"Come on, let's go!" Ali screeched, leading her friends toward the light once more. There was no sign of Skotia when Ali scanned the wall she'd been paralyzed against.

"Damn it, she went ahead! She went to go face Mateva alone!" Ali cursed, picking up her pace. Now she had to add saving her twin to the list.

The entrance was within an arm's reach. With one last roar from the drakes behind them, the four teenagers launched themselves through the door and into their final destination.

Ali blinked her eyes open as they adjusted to the light. There was no sign of Skotia or Carter, but ten feet ahead of her stood a beautiful woman draped in a dark, black cloak with her hair brought up in a tight bun.

Mateva.

"Ah, Cassiopeia's granddaughter has finally returned to Infernus," the Sorcerer exhaled, a wicked grin spreading across her face. "Welcome, Alexandria. I've been waiting for you."

CHAPTER 17

THE SORCERER'S APPRENTICE

Taking a step back, Ali shook her head without taking her eyes from the Sorcerer's face.

Mateva was far younger than the Sorcerer who lived in Ali's nightmares. She thought the woman would be in her later years, slowly falling victim to age the longer she burrowed herself in the mountain. While Ali suspected age wouldn't have hindered her magic, she was not expecting a woman no older than forty to be standing before her.

This had to be one of her tricks. That was it—a way for Mateva to get inside Ali's head before she even had the chance to save her brother. She had to keep her mind straight, focused on the task she set out for.

"What's the matter, Alexandria? Did your dear grandmother not tell you all about her adventures in Infernus? Her brave conquests, defeating the ferocious Mateva before she fled and abandoned her people?" Mateva's cheekbones protruded from her face, resembling the drakes. When she smiled, her features slanted downward until they almost came to a point, much like how the drake's jaw protruded forward and threatened death with one of its streams of fire.

The collar of her cloak jutted out around her neck, highlighting the sharp angles in her face. Her fingers were wrapped around her own wand, the same one Ali must've seen in those cave drawings that first day in Infernus. It might as well have been a decade ago.

Mateva reduced the space between them with one graceful step. Quick to separate herself from the Sorcerer, Ali took a few paces back and found herself against Vulcan's broad frame. He emitted a guttural growl that vibrated in his chest. Among the chaos, Ali had forgotten that he had his own personal vendetta against Mateva. Even from her sanctuary inside the mountain, the mere thought of her had destroyed his family and life as he knew it in Infernus.

"And who did you bring on your little quest? An Infernian soldier? And two Upper Landers? How cute," Mateva sneered, letting out a piercing laugh that echoed off the walls.

Ali brought her shoulders back and raised her head high before finding her words.

"You're…you're lying. I'm not Cassiopeia's granddaughter," she asserted, keeping her voice as even as possible. "Grandmother was an Infernian, yes, but she fled long before your fight. She left before you lost your duel." Ali waited for a fierce flash to cross Mateva's face when she mentioned her epic defeat, but the woman barely batted an eye.

"Is that what you think?" Mateva's grin was spreading into one thin line across her face. "So, then you think it's just a coincidence that you're holding her wand, correct? Or that the necklace she gave you was its life force?"

Ali's eyes grew wide, letting the Sorcerer's words resonate.

"How do you know about that?" she croaked, raising her hand to meet where her necklace used to sit.

"You'd be surprised at the knowledge I possess."

The wand in Ali's hand took on a completely new light. It felt heavier in her palm, and she had a fleeting urge to throw it across the room. For many nights, she'd lain awake picturing its previous owner. What they looked like, what spells they mastered. But now that she knew its secrets, the stories she created were washing away to nothingness.

She pictured a youthful version of her grandmother holding the object between her palms, studying under the other Sorcerers as she prepared to battle Mateva. The green hue at its core glinted when she turned it in her own fingers, reminding Ali of the precious stone that had hung on her chest for many moons.

"Now if you'll follow me, you'll get to see our guest of honor," Mateva said, carefully watching each of their faces as she made her way into the fiery room. A large flame was bursting from the center of a pit, creating a trail of smoke that disappeared into the air.

When the Sorcerer saw that none of them had moved, she pointed her wand at the group. Before they could move an inch, Mateva recited a spell that Ali didn't recognize. A shooting pain shot through her, threatening to collapse her legs onto the unforgiving ground.

"Ahh!" She pressed both palms to her eyes, overwhelmed by the suffering engulfing her body. The other three, next to her, cried out in pain.

"I said, follow me. It's rude to decline an invitation, especially when I asked nicely." Mateva enunciated each word slowly, ensuring the message was delivered. Once she brought her wand back down to her side, Ali's pain subsided, but it was quickly replaced with a dull throbbing. It was Ali's first taste of Mateva's power, and she suspected the woman had barely scratched the surface.

Without another word, they fell in line one after the other, walking along a narrow strip of rock that connected to a larger landing. When she was sure the Sorcerer wouldn't turn around and strike them off the ledge with one swing of her wand, Ali turned toward her friends only to see waves of terror crossing their faces.

Gavin was behind Lilly, his hand supporting the small of her back with every synchronized step they took. There were tears gathering in Lilly's eyes that she anxiously tried to blink away when she saw Ali turn around. Ali smiled softly to them both, trying to fill the abyss of hopelessness with any ounce of light she could muster.

But any light that she found quickly returned to the shadows.

Every few seconds, Ali scanned the area for any signs of Carter's curly hair. Short of calling his name and praying for an answer, she had no idea how she was going to get him out of that room. There were no visible exits besides the one they'd entered from, and for the life of her Ali couldn't remember what tunnels the map had shown them that were coming out of the core. She had been entirely too focused on finding her brother, without any regard for how they would escape once she did.

And where had Skotia gone? There weren't any signs of her doppelganger, either. She couldn't have gotten far without Mateva spotting her, and Ali could only imagine what her fate would be if she were caught sneaking around this lair. An icy current pierced her veins as she pictured Skotia being thrown from the narrow pathway into the pitch-dark pit below.

Losing her balance on the last step, she felt Vulcan grab her loose arm and pull her body close to his. She smelled iron and wood exuding from his jacket, reminding her of the armory of weapons he had hiding underneath the fabric. Mateva's words rang in her ears.

Infernian soldier.

Is that what Vulcan was? Had she been traveling this entire time with a lethal weapon?

There were heaps of questions climbing over each other in her mind. Ali couldn't quiet one long enough before another clambered its way to the top.

How was her grandmother the legendary Cassiopeia? If it were true, why did she flee after defeating Mateva, when Infernus was already safe? When she gave Ali the necklace, did she know her granddaughter would one day need it to breathe life into her old wand?

"Stand there," Mateva turned to face them again and pointed to a spot along the wall's edge. Luckily, it was several feet away from the closest drop.

Briefly surveying their surroundings, Ali noticed that there were veins of color slithering through the walls, appearing and vanishing in the blink of an eye. There were crystals jutting out of the sides, sharply pressing into her back. The bonfire's flames dazzled off the gems, turning their light into a world of color. Sweat was building on Ali's neck, but she pled the roar of the fire would quiet the alarms blaring between her ears.

Mateva's wand was pointing at the four of them once again. Its unimaginable powers taunted them with every swish.

"Now, before I bring our guest out, or should I say *my* guest, I would like to share a little bit about my lovely home you've entered. It's only fair that you hear my, shall I say, inspiration. But, no interruptions allowed, understood?" Mateva flicked her wrist, and the next instant Ali's lips were glued shut. She tried to pry them open with her fingers, but her screams were muffled.

The alarms grew louder. How would she be able to perform any spells if she couldn't say them?

Mateva began to pace before them. With every step, her cloak followed closely behind, but her undivided attention was on Ali. She kept her eyes locked on Ali as her feet gracefully strolled back and forth across the floor, balancing her wand between her fingers as she spoke.

"As you may have heard, Cassiopeia and I trained together in our early days, many decades ago. We were both students of the Sorcerers at the time, eager to learn all there was to know about Infernus's magical secrets. When we were plucked from our homes, they dropped us in this mountain." Mateva gestured to the vacant walls around them.

"Until now, you all have been following the same tunnels we explored in our youth. You are in the Sorcerers' training grounds, one of Infernus's best-kept treasures." She raised her arms above her head. The bonfire grew taller behind her, elongating her shadow.

The memory of the Mark of the Sorcerers flashed in front of Ali's eyes. The time capsule, the map, the books—they had all belonged to the Sorcerers. Unbeknownst to her, she had been exploring their home this entire time, studying the same pathways as those who came before. Thumbing the same copies her grandmother once did as they both trained to face the same foe. Even though her lips were magically sealed, she could feel her jaw begging to drop to the ground.

"At first, your grandmother and I understood one another. Barely twenty years old, intelligent, eager to learn, and far more savvy than the boys were, we begged our mentors to help us master our powers as quickly as possible. We watched the Sorcerers duel in the courtyard, studying their footwork as they gracefully danced around one another in a beautiful rhythm." The flames danced around Mateva. Her cloak moved with the inferno, swaying to the fire's will while sparks flew from its depths.

"We spent most hours of the day together. Waking, training, studying together, day after day, month after month. At some point, others may have even called us friends." A bitter laugh escaped her lips. "But not for long. Cassiopeia had the same daft mantras as our leaders—dedicate your life to protecting those who had refused to protect you."

Ali's ears turned hot as Mateva continued to belittle her grandmother's character.

"I gave those fools an ultimatum. Either I would stay and learn the way we should've been taught from the start, or I would take my training elsewhere. They laughed in my face, claiming they would have nothing to lose from my departure." Mateva turned her back to them for a split second, giving Ali enough time to notice that the knuckles holding her wand were as white as bone.

"Cassiopeia didn't even say goodbye. So much for friendship." She spat out the last word, focusing her gaze on Ali once more. Even though the fire was still raging behind Mateva, there was now one lit inside her eyes, challenging Ali to fight its flames.

Ali allowed the rage burning between her ears to crawl its way down the rest of her skin, her wand picking up the change in energy. As her fury reached the hilt, red sparks flew from the end and onto one of the crystals jutting from the wall.

Vulcan noticed the outburst and quickly stomped the sparks that had fallen in front of him into the ground. But it was no use—Mateva had already seen them.

"I see sharing the truth about your beloved matriarch is making you angry, dear, is that right? Well, I'm sure you've already heard of the mighty victory she had, sending me back into oblivion where the world thought I belonged." Mateva was making her way toward them—toward Ali. Ali's breath hitched. She pressed her shoulder blades against the wall, trying with all her might to melt into the stone.

"Little did the world know that when the time came to finish me off, Cassiopeia couldn't execute. She dropped that pile of rocks on my head, leaving me unconscious and weak, but alive with the force field I was able to muster. She left before checking if I still had a pulse." The Sorcerer was describing the scene Ali had watched in the tunnels. If only she had known she was watching her grandmother's greatest feat.

"Of course, she didn't tell her beloved Infernians that part of the story. As far as they were concerned, the vicious Mateva was gone from Infernus, never to threaten the good citizens again. They might as well have put Cassiopeia atop a golden throne from the way they celebrated her flawed victory."

Mateva's eyes were ablaze with a distant passion that turned her green eyes a shade darker. For the first time in her life, Ali looked into a pair of emerald eyes she hated.

"But she must've known, somewhere in that heroic mind of hers that I was still breathing," Mateva continued. "Still a threat to the land, determined to strike when she wouldn't see me coming. I always wondered what would be worse for your grandmother—facing me once more, or seeing the look on the people's faces when they realized she had deceived them."

Mateva placed the tip of her wand under Ali's chin, digging the point into her skin until Ali felt it pierce her flesh. Sure enough, when Mateva pulled the wand away, drops of her blood covered the end. Using the sleeve of her cloak to wipe away the evidence, Mateva turned her eyes toward Gavin and Lilly.

Ali threw her body away from the wall and toward her friends to shield them from the Sorcerer. Mateva predicted her movements, using another wave of her wand to throw Ali's torso back against the sharp edges.

"I never lost sight of my dear classmate, even when she fled our world," she said, twisting her wand in her fingers, pointing it back and forth between Gavin's and Lilly's foreheads. "I used my little birdies in the Upper Land to keep an eye on her, should she ever decide to make the foolish decision to return. When I learned that she had been telling stories of Infernus to her kin, I had an inkling that one of you might venture to our land one day."

How did Mateva know about her grandmother's stories? What else from Ali's childhood had she watched when no one was looking? Ali wracked her brain for anything out of the ordinary growing up, but her mind went blank. Her childhood ignorance was quickly switching from a blessing to a curse.

"Over the years, I figured out which portal Cassiopeia fled from. Lucky for me, the portal never closed. I just had to wait for the perfect moment," Mateva uttered coldly. With another flick of her wand, the invisible zipper holding Ali's lips together vanished.

A gust of soot and ash rushed into Ali's lungs, but it might as well have been a cool ocean breeze. Her airways happily accepted it, gulping in as many breaths as she could in fear of being cut off again.

"The perfect moment for what?" Ali questioned. Her hand was pressed to her chest, feeling the slow rise and fall of her lungs as oxygen flooded her body.

"To lure one of Cassiopeia's kin to their rightful home, of course. Luckily, your brother found that tree at exactly the right time. You see, I learned how to navigate these tunnels with my eyes closed. I knew exactly where he would enter."

Ali lunged forward, reaching her hands toward the Sorcerer's neck. She didn't care that the woman had years of training, that she could blow Ali's limbs apart with one flick of her wrist, or that her own lanky build stood no chance against Mateva's tall frame. The Sorcerer had admitted to taking her brother, and Ali had no one to blame for the past three years of misery besides the woman standing in front of her.

"Ali, no!" Vulcan reached out and caught the fringes of her shirt, but even his strength couldn't compete with the adrenaline coursing through her.

She was a few inches away from Mateva's throat before the woman caught both of Ali's hands and bound them together, bringing Ali just a few inches from her face.

"You insolent girl!" Mateva flared, twisting Ali's wrists until they burned. "How dare you think you can reach me, let alone attack without consequence?" She threw Ali to the ground at her feet so that Ali was forced to look up at the cruel captor.

"What have you done with my brother? And where is my friend? Where's Skotia?" Ali's booming voice resonated through the room, surprising everyone, including herself.

"Your friend? I'll show you your *friend*," Mateva cackled, looking down with a sinister knowing. "Skotia, come out here now. Your friends want to see you."

"They're not my friends."

Skotia emerged from the other side of the fire, unscathed. Her black hair was draped over her shoulders and her eyes were lit with the same fiery gaze Mateva's held.

"What?" Ali pondered aloud, creasing her eyebrows as she tried to piece together the puzzle that was emerging before her.

"Skotia is not your confidant, you stupid girl. She is my apprentice," Mateva cooed, wrapping her hand around Skotia's shoulders and pulling her in for a fleeting embrace.

"You *traitor*," Lilly spat, the rage spewing from her lips. Ali's mind was still spinning in circles, as if her thoughts were on a hamster wheel that was rotating until the end of time.

Skotia's laugh punctured the air. A handful of frightened bats left their perches, flying far from the madness as quickly as possible.

"Did you really think that I would ever befriend you imbeciles?" Skotia stood tall, meeting Lilly's stare. "You two weren't even supposed to be here in the first place, and I had to tolerate you for far longer than I had anticipated. I was praying those shadowvines would finish you off when they had the chance."

"How *could* you?" Ali snarled. There was a reason she never confided in others, keeping her secrets close to the heart where they were safe. Now, she felt the sharp sting of betrayal creeping its way into her chest. Its tip slowly inched into her back, twisting itself deeper until it reached bone.

Mateva took a step back from Ali, allowing Skotia to replace her spot.

"How could I?" she sneered, kicking dirt into Ali's face.

"I'll explain how, Alexandria. Your beloved grandmother might have been the presumed savior at one point in time, but her reign is long gone. Infernus will see a new era. And it begins with the one true Sorcerer." Skotia turned her head toward her master, her dark eyes glistening with pride.

"But why did you bring me here? If you already have my brother, what do you need me for?"

Skotia raised her eyebrows and looked for Mateva to answer, sharing a telepathic look with the Sorcerer.

"Your brother has become very valuable to me these past few years, Alexandria. His power is crucial for my reign to return."

"Power? My brother doesn't have any magic," Ali exclaimed, jumping up from the floor.

"You still have much to learn about Infernus and its ways. Only a few are gifted with magic, but power can come in many forms. None as fierce as pure magic, but intense enough that it will work for what I need." Mateva scoffed at Ali's ignorance. "While my magic has kept my body from aging as quickly as others, I need fresh blood—recruits, if you will,—to ensure my legacy prevails long past my days. Skotia has generously volunteered to help me carry that legacy on."

At the mention of her name, Ali's doppelganger raised her head an inch higher in the sky.

"But, a force of one is not a viable force at all. I am not so naive as to fool myself with this wishful thinking." Mateva resumed her pacing in front of Ali, her wand dangling loosely from her fingers. If Ali were only a few feet closer, she could try to grab it in one swift movement.

"To triumph, I will need a Sorcerer underneath me. One who will be trained properly from the beginning, learning the spells my teachers refused to acknowledge, learning the spells that bring power to this land—to all future Sorcerers."

"And you think Carter is the answer to your prayer? He will never agree to fight for you. Besides, Infernus picks the

Sorcerers, not you." Ali may not have seen her brother in many years, but she still knew him better than anyone. He would never agree to betray their grandmother.

At least, she hoped.

"Infernus has had many rules my predecessors believed they had to follow. Rules are meant to be broken." Mateva's body began to sway with the rising flames, calling something up from the bottom of the pit.

"I have discovered a way to bestow magic on another without losing my own," Mateva announced. She heard an audible gasp from Vulcan, whose features had been still as stone this entire time. "I can create a force Infernus has never seen before. No longer will we be called to preserve a land whose people have done nothing for their protectors. Your brother will be the first Sorcerer created by me, but first I needed something of yours to complete the spell."

Skotia reached into her pocket and held out a silk bag, its contents hidden from sight. She bowed slightly as Mateva promptly grabbed it from her palm, eagerly taking a look inside.

"You did well," Mateva praised Skotia, patting her gently on the shoulder before returning her focus to the sack. Reaching in, she gently took out a few pieces of what looked like...hair?

Ali's mind wandered back to watching Skotia shift through her sheets that morning, picking her way through Ali's belongings.

"You were never looking for the wand, were you?"

"That's correct," Skotia sneered. "It was far too easy to watch the guilt wrack your brain when we stood in that cave. I never needed your wand, I needed a part of you."

The invisible knife in Ali's back dug a few inches deeper. She imagined the blood mixing with her black hair and pouring from the wound until she would no longer have the strength to stand.

"If you only needed me for my hair, why bring me all the way here? Why not dispose of me the second you met me in that tunnel?" A sob caught on the end of Ali's tongue.

"That was by design," Mateva interrupted, returning the strands to the pouch. "I wanted to see if my predictions were correct, if you were really as powerful as I've heard. You are eons away from wielding the same magic as your grandmother, but you still show potential." Mateva brought her fingers to her chin, drumming them along her skin as she thought.

"I cannot have anything stand in my way this time. I will be disposing of you shortly, Alexandria, don't you worry. But first, don't you want to say hello to your brother?"

Mateva raised her hands high above her head and whispered a spell in an ancient language, calling a stone platform up from the depths.

In the middle of a steel cage sat her curly-haired brother, clutching the bars around him for dear life.

CHAPTER 18

THE DARK SORCERER

———

Time froze as Ali took in her brother's appearance, barely recognizable from the boy who left her house three years ago. His hair was mangy, matted down to his face at some points and curling out at others.

His canvas clothing was covered in several layers of grime. When combined with the tattered stitching, the outfit could barely be called clothing at all. Carter's skin sagged against his bones and his green eyes had lost their spark, leaving little life to the jubilant boy she remembered. He could barely pull himself up using the bars around him, his body fighting to pull him back down to the Earth.

This has been his life because of you, Ali's inner voice reminded her. She choked back tears, trying to use the fire's roar to block out the thoughts.

Carter looked through his cage toward the new faces. He cocked his head to the side as his eyes passed from Lilly to Gavin. It seemed like he was trying to place them in his mind, from an old life, perhaps. When his gaze reached his sister, he paused.

Clearing the hair from his eyes, he pressed his forehead against the bars and reached his hand through them until he couldn't stretch any farther.

"Ali?" he whispered, his voice cracking on her name.

"Carter!" Ali shouted, finding her voice. She let it echo off the room's walls until it reached her brother. "Carter, it's me, I promise! I'm here to save you!"

Her brother's eyes lit up. He began clawing at the metal, his frail limbs no match for the steel. Ali needed him to know that his sister was here to save him, to bring him back to a life he once lived.

"Ali! Please, Ali! Get me out of here!" Carter banged on the cage, letting the noise drown out the blaze's rage. The flames created a circle around Carter's cage, bewitched to stop before they reached the platform he was trapped on.

"She will do nothing of the sort. You are mine now," Mateva boomed, looking between the siblings. "I will not be stopped. Infernus may have thought they saw the end of me, but that was only my beginning."

Mateva lifted her hands higher, and the stone platform rose another two feet, forcing Ali to look up into her brother's pleading eyes. He furiously crawled to the farthest side of the cage to separate himself from Mateva, his feeble body trembling with every breath he took.

"It is time to start," Mateva announced, focusing her gaze on the cage. Gripping her wand until Ali could see the bones protruding through her thin skin, she motioned to Skotia to follow her, leading them toward the edge of the flames and closer to where Carter sat, helpless against the Sorcerer's fury.

"Leave him alone!" Ali yelled, stunned by the resounding power in her voice. The same energy she felt in the river was returning, creating a slow burn throughout her body. But when each second was more precious than the last, she couldn't wait for her power to build.

Recalling a spell from one of the Sorcerer's textbooks, Ali pointed her wand toward the ground at Mateva's feet. She let the energy flow out of her limbs, willing the ground to give way beneath them. If it would give her just a few more seconds to reach her brother, she had to try.

But Mateva saw her move coming. With one lightning-fast stroke from her wand, she rebounded Ali's spell away from them and changed its direction. The magic's new target was the wall directly above her head.

She heard her brother scream, but his cries were mixed with the sound of falling rock around her head. Cowering where she stood, Ali lifted her hands above her head to soften the imminent blows. The first few scraped the tops of her fingers and broke their fall on her body. Bracing for the worst impact, her body was suddenly flung backward. She hit something solid but didn't feel any more stones cascading down.

Opening her eyes, she saw the solid object she had slammed against was Vulcan's body. He had hurled Ali's away from the rockslide and brought her into his chest. Out of the corner of her eye she saw Gavin and Lilly shaking where they stood, hands covering their mouths in horror.

Ali might have been safe, but there was more distance between her and Carter's cage. Not to mention, there was a six-foot wall of rock now standing between her and Mateva.

Preparing to race toward the wall, she was stopped by Vulcan grabbing her hair by the fistful and holding on firmly, forcing her body to stay in place.

"Let go of me!" She turned, clawing his wrists until specks of blood sprouted from his skin. "I have to save my brother. I'm not letting him slip through my fingers again, so don't try to stop me."

"I'm not going to try to stop you, but if you jump out there again without a plan you're going to lose. Then, everything you've come here for will have been useless. Do you want that?" Vulcan demanded, quieting Ali with the roar of his words.

A part of her knew Vulcan was right. She'd be granting a death wish if she went out there again, but another part of her knew that every moment she sat idle was another that Carter suffered. She begrudgingly shook her head, waiting for Vulcan to give a better option.

"I didn't think so," Vulcan continued, more restraint in his voice now. "Now, if you want to save your brother, we're going to need a distraction."

Ali winced as Carter's screams bellowed from behind her, but she listened to Vulcan's plan until he was finished.

"Where do we come into play?" Lilly interrupted, pointing her thumb between Gavin and herself. Ali noticed they both had stopped shaking, but something else entirely had taken over their bodies. They both held a fierceness they hadn't before; vengeful shadows danced in Lilly's blue eyes while Gavin proudly held the dagger Vulcan had given him at the start of their journey. Soot covered their faces, and there were cuts grazed across their legs, promising to leave scars later. Her friends had changed from that first day when they followed her into the forest, but she hadn't noticed until now.

"Nowhere," Vulcan asserted, cutting Lilly off before she could continue. "You two will stay here, out of sight. We don't need to turn this rescue mission from one to three." He went back to handling his weapons, passing Ali a knife she had no idea how to use.

"Bullshit!" Lilly screamed, throwing her body between Vulcan and Ali. "We did not come all this way to be told to stand back and watch. If she's going to go out there, we are too."

"I don't care what you think of us." Gavin nodded in agreement. "We may not be Infernians, but we'll fight like ones if it means we can help Ali." His voice held a slight quiver, but he was standing taller than he ever had in their own world.

"No," Ali found herself saying. Both friends turned to face her, pain written across their faces. "I…I can't lose you both. I know you want to fight, but I need you to stay here. Stay and wait for this all to be over. And then we can go home, okay? Go home and live our lives like we should've been doing this entire time." She pleaded with her friends, bringing them both in for a hug as a few of her tears fell onto their shoulders. Ali didn't believe her life would return to the way it was, but she prayed both of her friends' lives could remain intact.

Tears welling in both friends' eyes, they let Vulcan proceed with the plan.

"This knife," he said, holding up a curved blade between his fingers, "can cut through any type of metal. I'm going to the other side of this room and getting to Carter's cage from behind. I need you to keep Mateva's and Skotia's focus away from the cage. Just for a few seconds so I can grab Carter and get him out of there."

"How are we going to get out of here once we have him?" Ali asked. Her fingers were drumming on her thigh, anxious to start moving.

"Improvise," Vulcan responded coldly. Ali didn't have a better plan, so she slowly nodded, hesitant to think about the outcome if this didn't end on their terms.

"Ready?" Vulcan asked, putting both hands on Ali's shoulders. "You can do this."

Not trusting her own voice, Ali locked her gaze with Vulcan's and took his hands from her shoulders, turning her back on the group and heading toward the rock wall that awaited her. She heard Vulcan's pace pick up behind her, his footsteps getting more distant with every second.

Holding her wand in between her teeth, Ali began to scale the wall her own spell had created. The wall wasn't terribly high, but the explosion of rocks left her with few places to hold, leaving her fumbling with her grip until she found a clear route that would bring her to the top. Once there, she hoisted herself up so that her eyes peeked over the top but kept the rest of her body hidden. At some point she knew she'd have to start Vulcan's distraction but figuring out what that would be was another ordeal.

Looking toward the pedestal holding Carter's prison, her heart sank. Carter was lying in a heap in the center of the steel, semiconscious, with one hand hanging limply over the side. His green eyes were barely fluttering open.

"I thought I was going to be the first Sorcerer you created?" Ali heard Skotia ask from below. She lifted herself a bit higher, trying to get within earshot.

"You will be the first I train, dear. But you need to have patience. The boy must be changed first before we can move any further, then we will get to you. You have done well, and will be rewarded when the time is right," Mateva replied, barely giving Skotia a second glance.

Had Ali heard Skotia correctly? Why did she want to be a dark Sorcerer?

Before she had time to entertain the questions, Ali watched Mateva turn her full attention toward Carter. Wrapping Ali's hair around her wand, she closed her eyes and moved toward the cage, shooting a jet of black light toward Carter.

Even with Ali's limited knowledge, she could see the magic was unstable. The jet of light was quivering from Mateva's wand, barely able to stay intact as she poured her energy into it. This was new magic for Infernus, and by the chill that had just spread across the room, it seemed that the land didn't welcome the Sorcerer's spell.

As the black beam hit Carter's chest, a blood curdling scream echoed through Ali's bones. This was it. She needed to create the diversion now, or she would lose her brother forever.

Letting the pain of her brother's cries ring in her ears, Ali jumped from behind the heap of rocks and sent a stream of lightning from her wand, aimed directly for Mateva. To Ali's surprise, she hit her target, knocking Mateva off balance and disconnecting the spell from Carter's body. His shrieks stopped for a moment and his body returned to his slumped state, leaving Ali to wonder if he had finally lost consciousness.

Mateva fell to the side and lay motionless. Her wand slipped from her hands and rolled toward the edge of the landing, teetering toward the growing pit of flames.

Ali's magic wasn't strong enough to defeat Mateva. If she were going to win this battle, she would have to strip all power from the Sorcerer.

Ali's and Skotia's eyes met for half a second, then both girls bolted for the magical object.

As she sprinted toward the wand, Ali saw Vulcan's silhouette across the flames. He was almost at the back of the cage, but the fire was closing in on Carter's platform, promising to swallow him whole if Vulcan didn't act quickly.

Channeling the days when she would sprint through the forest, hurdling over branches and narrowly dodging fox dens, Ali willed her legs to move faster, increasing her cadence for the last stretch of the race. Skotia had a step ahead of her, but she'd overcome worse odds.

She was at the wand a half second before Skotia. She dove toward the ground, reaching her fingers until they felt the thin wood in her palm. Before Ali could bring it close to her chest, she felt a large force slam into her side, forcing the wand from her grip. Skotia pressed her foot into Ali's stomach, pinning her body to the ground as she hastily grabbed the wand from the stone floor.

"How does it feel to know you will have lost your brother a second time?" Skotia's jagged grin matched the animosity her black pupils. The sole of her shoe was pressing harder into Ali's core, leaving her to squirm for a freedom that would never come.

"Why are you doing this? How could you do this to me? I thought you were my friend!" Ali cried, trying to claw Skotia's foot off her body.

"You foolish girl, thinking you stood a chance." Skotia avoided her question, twirling the wand between her fingertips. "You really shouldn't believe everything you're told, Alexandria."

"Huh?" Ali muttered, raising her eyebrows as she tried to decipher the meaning behind Skotia's words.

A high-pitched cackle escaped Skotia's lips. The noise was at least an octave higher than her normal voice, taking Ali aback.

Then she began to change.

Skotia removed her foot from Ali's stomach, but Ali was too stunned by what she was witnessing to move her body off the floor.

Her look-alike's appearance began to change so that she was no longer Ali's double. Skotia's features morphed from

Ali's lanky build with her jet-black hair to a short, brunette bob that barely reached her shoulders. Her complexion was covered with freckles while her cheekbones rose high into her face, giving her the same thin face a jackal might have. Skotia's new frame wasn't as lean as Ali's, but her strong build created an extra threat of brutality.

The only thing that stayed the same were her dark eyes.

"What's going on? Who are you?" Ali demanded, inching backward with the little energy left in her arms. Her legs still weren't cooperating, lying weak in front of her.

"Look-alikes do not exist," Skotia explained, stretching into her new body. "Mateva has been watching you for longer than you'll ever know. Before I was sent to find you, she changed my appearance to mirror yours, forcing me to study your mannerisms day after day. She thought you might trust me on your journey if I looked like you, and she couldn't have been more right."

Skotia's betrayal stung in the back of Ali's throat. She opened her mouth to fight back, to protest, to say that she never trusted Skotia, but didn't hear a single word come out.

"Oh, how I missed this body," she purred, wrapping herself into a bear hug. "And now, to get rid of you once and for all. Say goodbye, Alexandria."

Looking up into a stranger's face, Ali braced herself for what would come next.

She did not know what death would feel like, but she imagined it was as quick as a rubber band snapping against your skin. Her pulse remained steady, but a looming sense of failure overwhelmed her last thoughts. Ali's parents were about to lose both of their children because of her inadequacy.

But it was not her own scream she heard burst throughout the room.

There was a knife digging into Skotia's back, and Gavin had put it there. The wand fell from Skotia's hand, clattering on the floor. Lilly jumped over Ali's body, swooping in to grab the wand herself.

Both of Ali's friends had defied her orders, and thank god they did.

Lilly grabbed Ali's hand and helped her to her feet while Gavin quickly backed away from Skotia, the weapon still lodged between her shoulder blades. It had cut deep, but it wasn't a fatal blow. Skotia reached behind her and ripped the blade out of her skin, letting the blood ooze down her spine. Turning to face Gavin, her black eyes raged as she held the knife above her head, ready to strike.

"I don't think so!" Another burst of magic shot from Ali's wand toward Skotia, hitting the weapon and sending it flying twenty feet into the air. Cartwheeling through space, the blade soared across the room until it landed in the fiery pit, lost forever.

"Agh!" Skotia shrieked, turning her rage on the three of them. Before she could advance, a clanging sound reverberated from the cage and diverted everyone's attention.

Vulcan had leaped across the flames, reaching Carter's cage. His knife sliced through the bars with ease. All that was left for Vulcan to do was rip off the cage's top. Ali only guessed how long it had been since Carter had last tasted freedom.

But he wasn't free yet. None of them were.

"Carter! Carter, move! Get up!" Ali implored, her voice going hoarse. She heard her brother groaning, but couldn't tell if he heard her words through the inferno's roar. Vulcan hoisted Carter's body up until his legs hung straight underneath him. Gravity threatened to take control of his muscles if Vulcan loosened his grip for even a second.

Lilly yelped behind her. Ali felt the heat drain from her face as she saw Mateva holding her best friend by the throat. She had woken from her stupor, silently moving toward them as they watched Vulcan finally reach Carter. So much for a diversion.

Mateva snatched her wand back from Lilly and pointed its tip into her cheek, drawing a fresh line of blood.

"Let her go," Ali ordered, holding out her own wand to counter the Sorcerer's threat.

"You may have caught me off guard the first time Alexandria, but that will not happen again," Mateva sneered. Her hair was no longer in its perfect bun and her cloak was fringed, but her eyes had formed slits that were exuding one thing: rage.

And with a wave of her wand, a force threw the three friends backward against the rock wall they had all scaled minutes earlier. The room spinning around her, Ali turned toward where Vulcan still stood with Carter, her brother finally regaining control over his muscles and steadying himself without the Infernian's help.

Vulcan whispered something into his ear and Carter feebly nodded in response. They both steadied their bodies, preparing to leap through the blaze toward the perch on the other side.

Her vision still blurry, Ali blinked, then saw Vulcan land on the other side, but Carter hadn't made it across.

He was floating above the platform, rising higher in the air while his limbs flailed around him. His body was connected to Mateva's wand through the same black stream of magic that Ali had seen earlier.

"Ali! Get me out of here! Ali!"

Ali's ears were ringing from her head hitting the solid rock, but she could hear her brother's cries for help above any noise in the room.

"No, no not again," Ali feebly uttered, raising her body to stand. Her legs couldn't hold her weight, and she instantly fell back to the floor. Gavin and Lilly were barely moving on her sides, unable to rescue her like they had done once before.

The flames in the fiery pit turned black, growing taller the longer Mateva had her hold over Carter's body. She was furiously shouting a spell in a language Ali didn't recognize. Skotia stood next to Mateva with a monstrous gleam in her eyes. Ali tried to will her brother closer to her with her own magic, but she barely had enough energy to open her eyes, let alone conjure a summoning spell.

The tiny spark of hope that had been growing in her since she found out Carter was alive was shrinking again, cursing her for letting it spread in the first place. The pain was different from the first time first realized her brother wasn't coming back home. It was sharper. Quicker to pierce the heart than the dull numbness that had previously taken over her body and forced her to lie in bed for days on end. Now, her lungs were ablaze, begging for a solution to the heat that was carving a pathway through her chest.

Suddenly, her brother's screams stopped. The black flames were engulfing Carter's limp, levitating body. They grew until Ali could barely see his outline, and when they died away the boy floating was not one she knew.

Carter's slender, malnourished frame had sprouted defined muscles across his back and torso. His curly hair bounced on his head, returning to its former glory, but with a deeper shade of jet black to it. His arms were still limp, but Ali could see them stretching a few inches farther down his sides. For an instant, his eyes flashed opened. They were still green, but the cries for help had left them and had been replaced with something else. Anger.

Mateva cackled as she floated Carter's body closer to where she stood, shrinking the line of dark magic between them. When he was a foot away, she cut off the spell, dropping him at her feet.

In a flash, she burst open the wall behind her, creating a new tunnel in the mountain. Hoisting Carter up like Vulcan had done on the platform, she forced him to his feet, barking orders at Skotia to lead the way.

"It is now time for us to start. It is now time for Mateva to make her return to Infernus, with no one to stop us this time," she howled. With the spell complete, the fire's rage had died down. It couldn't silence Mateva's declarations bursting through the room.

"And you, Alexandria," Mateva boasted, pointing her wand at the teenager. "You are just as pathetic as your beloved grandmother. I hope she's happy, knowing you'll be joining her on that side of the veil soon enough."

The woman turned her back on Ali one final time before making her way through the new opening, taking Ali's brother with her. Mateva's cloak sweeping behind her was the last thing Ali saw before she closed her eyes and wept, whispering a thousand apologies she only wished Carter could hear.

CHAPTER 19

WHAT COMES NEXT

———

Ali vaguely sensed Vulcan kneeling at her side, poking and prodding her body as he tried to tend to her wounds. He might as well have been tending to a rag doll, for she felt nothing but an agony that eclipsed any other pain her muscles might have otherwise felt. Tears continued to fall, but she could barely feel them streaming down her cheeks. She let them flow, destroying the dam she had been building behind her eyes for years.

After Vulcan left her side, he made his way to where Lilly and Gavin lay, just as battered as Ali must have looked. Ali couldn't imagine that Vulcan did not have his own wounds to address, but then she remembered the scars that lined his forearms. He must have been used to pain.

Her friends regained their movements, stretching and rubbing their sore muscles that would likely swell over the next few days. She felt their stares, but they remained silent.

Ali didn't blame them—nothing they could have said would alleviate the pain.

She had lost Carter again. If there was ever a day when she didn't blame herself for his first disappearance, there would never come a time where she could put the second loss on someone else. She'd failed, and now her brother was going to be a prisoner of Mateva's wrath for the rest of his days, destined to live life consumed by the dark magic running through his veins.

Ali would be content sleeping in the cave for the rest of her own days, depriving her body of the light it would eventually crave. She imagined the drakes finding her body and ravaging it to pieces, tearing her flesh limb by limb. Magic or not, she had no reason to fight back now. She continued to sit, cradling her knees into her chest and pressing her face into them, blocking out any of the sights and sounds around her.

"Ali, come on. We have to move," she eventually heard Vulcan's voice from above her. Slowly lifting her head and cracking open her eyes, his outstretched hand came into her view. Lilly and Gavin stood fidgeting behind him, unable to look at their decrepit friend.

Scanning the room around her, she realized that a future passerby, if there ever was one, would never be able to guess what had happened here. The heat from the flames had vanished, leaving a cool draft in its place. There was a hint of soot in the air, but that would soon be gone as the ash settled and dispersed. They would never know that an innocent boy fell victim to a Sorcerer's spell, no matter how hard his sister tried to save him.

Seeing no other option but to take Vulcan's hand in hers, she let him lift her body until her feet found the ground beneath her. Vulcan bent down to pick up Ali's—no, her grandmother's—wand. Ali wanted no ownership of the object, turning her eyes so that she didn't have to watch Vulcan slip the wood beneath his jacket. The magic had done nothing for her, leaving her with empty promises and a void no buckets of light could fill.

"Let me just look at the map first. I'll figure out how to get us out of here." Vulcan reached into his tattered bag to grab the parchment, fishing for it among the loose objects.

"Don't," Ali blurted out, quickly gaining their attention. It was the first time they had heard her voice, and by the way Gavin jumped they were clearly not expecting to hear her speak anytime soon.

"I don't want to follow the map. Mateva obviously found a way out through there," she said, pointing toward the tunnel the Sorcerer had created. "I want to go that way."

Ali wasn't sure why she was adamant on following the path when Vulcan could have easily navigated using the map. But she needed to see if there was any trace of Carter, something to give her a clue into where Mateva and Skotia had run off. It may be pouring salt in her wounds, but she was numb to the pain right now anyway.

Vulcan hesitantly stopped searching his bag and slung the sack over his shoulders. He gave their room one final sweep as a shadow crossed his dark features, highlighting his defined jawline. Not looking toward the others, he led the march toward the tunnel, Lilly and Gavin falling closely in line behind him.

Taking a deep breath and wiping the dirt from her legs, Ali followed the three of them.

As she stepped onto the path and saw the three sets of footprints in front of them, sights of Carter being dragged by his frayed shirt swarmed her vision. What was he feeling now that darkness flowed through his veins? Did he feel the same rushes of energy that she did when the magic swelled, pulsing through her with a force impossible to ignore? Was he still her brother, or a stranger who wouldn't remember her and the memories they shared?

"No. He will always be your brother," a distant voice answered from the far corners of her thoughts.

She shook the questions from her mind. It was useless to ask questions knowing their answers would never come. Maybe ignorance was better this time around.

The four continued their trek through the dark, musty tunnels. Dust particles swarmed the air in front of them, but they never faced a turn with multiple branches breaking off. Never had to question what route to take. This time, there was one sole path through the mountain. Mateva must not have had time to leave a maze behind her.

Gavin and Lilly limped forward in front of her, occasionally stopping to whisper something in each other's ears. Neither of them had stopped to speak with Ali, but she noticed they would periodically turn their heads halfway, checking to make sure she was still with them and hadn't run back toward the doom they had all faced.

Her friends were never supposed to be here. Skotia had said it herself—unlike Ali's capture, they were never part of Mateva's plan. They had only wanted to stop Ali from running away from her house that last day of school, navigating the forest and coming to rescue her when they heard the cries for help.

And now they were the ones who needed help. Their skin was torn and bruised, victims of Mateva's wrath, as Ali was. They had risked their lives in this new world without a single thank-you from their best friend, the one they had been trying to save this entire time. And for what? At the end of the day, Ali couldn't even say they'd won. After all this time, it wasn't worth the suffering.

At the thought of it all, the few tears her eyes had left fell swiftly to the floor, but this time she hastily wiped them away. She was tired of the tears.

And her body was tired. The aches were catching up with her now that the adrenaline had left her system, creating tightness in her joints. The pain asked her to stop the journey and take a seat against the chilled rock. While the thought of giving her tender feet a break was tempting, she ignored the throbs and forced herself forward, one step at a time.

It was impossible to know how long they had been walking. The lack of sunlight in the subterranean passages was finally getting to Ali's head, but if she guessed, it had to be at least three hours. There were no longer any broad caverns filled with vicious Infernian creatures, waiting to devour Ali whole. No mysterious pictures revealing themselves to Ali as she ran over the wall with her fingertips, waiting for the magic to ignite itself. The magic was nowhere to be found.

Then a light began cascading far ahead of them, showering drops of brilliance into the tunnel. Ali thought back to when she originally saw the fire's glow at the end of the tunnel lined with torches. This was different; there were no flames creating shadows at the end of her sight. Instead, there was a glow radiating across the entire wall, illuminating the manmade crevice.

Just like sunshine would.

The others were already jogging toward the light, desperate to catch their first glimpses of sunshine in weeks. Forgetting about the aches in her calves, Ali trudged forward to catch up with her troop. Her body craved the sun beating down on her arms, letting the rays radiate against her pasty skin.

Ali reached the end of their route and turned the corner, facing the entrance where the bright light was bursting into the cave. She paused before walking forward, unable to believe her widening eyes.

In front of her was a balcony jutting across the most beautiful landscape Ali had ever seen.

She cautiously stepped onto the ledge, careful not to get too close to the drop. She couldn't tell how far they were from the ground, but the height was enough to give Ali a glimpse into the countless vistas Infernus had. A river flowed beginning at the top of a distant mountain, trickling through the land for miles. Between them and the mountain sat a vast forest with treetops almost touching the sky. To her right, she saw the fields of giant sunflowers her grandmother described to her, their yellow brilliance cascading over the creatures hiding beneath their leaves. A castle sat in the faraway distance on top of a hill, presiding over a village Ali could barely discern. The town's rooftops looked like ants in the distance.

"It's…beautiful," Ali murmured while the warmth seeped into her bones, invigorating a new sense of life. She took a deep breath and let the salty air find a new home in her lungs. Her body was eager to replace the scents of ash and soot with the delicate aromas of freshly bloomed flowers.

"I present to you the Infernus I know," Vulcan whispered, his voice the softest Ali had ever heard. "This is the beauty the Sorcerers have protected for all these years. So that we can live among Nature, always surprised by what we will find around the corner."

Lilly had gone to the edge of the balcony, sitting so that her legs dangled off the edge. Gavin stood behind her, his eyes fixated on the castle in the horizon.

"Who lives there?" he asked, pointing toward the fortress.

"The king and queen. They haven't been seen in some time though, hidden away behind closed gates ever since the rumors of Mateva started circling," Vulcan explained, narrowing his eyes toward the castle.

"I wonder where she took Carter," Ali pondered aloud, letting the bitterness drip from her voice.

"Ali, there has to be a way we can get him back. You can't let yourself give up." Lilly acknowledged her friend for the first time since they started their journey out.

"Let myself, Lilly? Do you think I want to give up after three years of wondering what happened to him? Do you think that the thought of losing him to that woman isn't crushing me right now?" Acid dripped from her words, but Ali couldn't bring herself to care.

"Then don't let yourself," Vulcan interrupted, siding with Lilly. "If you want to find your brother, then you have to keep going. I saw what you did in that cave. Mateva might've had more power, but there's magic inside you now, and it's awake. You can't tell me you don't feel it."

Ali didn't want to feel it anymore. She tried convincing herself that the magic was dead, but if she closed her eyes and silenced her mind, she could feel the speck of power nesting itself in her core, waiting for her permission to grow.

Vulcan took the wand out of his pocket and held it out for her to take. She kept her hands by her sides, walking out farther on the balcony. Looking toward the running water below her, her grandmother's words echoed in her ears.

You have to save him from her. You don't know how detrimental to Infernus it will be if you fail.

But she had already failed once. How could she try again, now that Mateva had the weapon she'd been longing for all these years?

"Do you remember how Mateva called me an Infernian solider?" Vulcan's words punctured her stream of consciousness. Ali nodded, hoping that would be enough encouragement for him to elaborate.

"I'm not sure how she knew that, but she was right. My family has been trained for centuries to protect certain families, and territories, in Infernus. I've been trained in combat since I could walk," Vulcan admitted, his scars glinting in the sunshine.

"My parents and I aren't exactly…close. But when I was younger, I would hear them whispering about the other two Sorcerers who trained with Mateva and your grandmother. My parents would stop talking whenever I appeared in the room, but I think I can find out where they are. If we can find them, they can teach you magic. Properly. We can see if they know a way to turn Carter back." He let his offer hang in the air between them.

Reaching forward, she gingerly clutched the wand hanging from Vulcan's hand, letting its familiar grip reintroduce itself to her palm.

"If Carter can't save himself, I'm not giving up until I do," Ali promised herself, looking into Vulcan's green eyes and taking him up on his offer.

But there was still one thing she had to do before she left the mountain. She switched her focus toward the two people who had risked their lives for her from the beginning.

"You know I love both of you, right?" She tried to smile, but even she could feel it, it didn't reach her eyes. "I can't repay either of you enough for everything. For chasing me into that forest, being by my side this entire time. I couldn't have gotten this far without you."

Ali realized both her friends knew where she was going with this, but they were going to make her deliver the final blow.

"I'm not coming home. I can't, knowing that Carter is out here somewhere. You understand, don't you?" If she said it quietly enough, maybe the universe wouldn't make her leave her friends.

"Of course we understand." Gavin was the first to respond, pulling her into a hug. "But, there's something I have admit too. I want to stay."

"No, absolutely not." Ali pushed Gavin away from her. "Gavin, you saw what we had to face in that mountain. Who knows what's out there that we haven't seen yet? Who knows what we'll run into?"

"Ali, you don't understand. No matter what I had at home, no matter where my parents took me, I've never felt like I belonged anywhere. When we got here, a voice was pulling at me, convincing me that this is where I'm supposed to be. Please, Ali. I'm not done yet, I can't be," Gavin begged, looking between her and Vulcan.

Ali thought about how she had seen Gavin conquer that drake, riding on its back toward them like he was on top of the world. Then after she had deliberately told him to stay back, Lilly and he had come to her side when her hope was all but lost. Even if she told him to return home a hundred times, at this point it wasn't her choice. It was Gavin's.

"Okay. Okay, you're right. We'll do this together."

"You've got to be kidding me," Vulcan muttered from behind her, shaking his head in disbelief.

Gavin let out a fist pump into the air. Ali had contemplated giving Vulcan a say in the matter, but then figured she already knew his answer. It was better not to ask.

"And what about you, huh?" Ali asked Lilly, whose legs still dangled freely in the breeze.

By the teardrops gathering in Lilly's eyes, Ali knew her answer before she started shaking her head.

"I...I can't. I want to. More than anything I want to, but I can't, Ali. You both belong here, you all do," she said, grouping in Vulcan with her best friends. "I wasn't even supposed to be here in the first place. Remember, I couldn't see that tree even though it was feet from my face." She looked toward her shoes.

Ali reached down and pulled Lilly into a hug. They cried into each other's shoulders, not knowing how long this good-bye would last.

When they pulled away from each other, Vulcan rummaged through his bag and placed something between Lilly's fingers.

"Take this," he said.

As Lilly flipped it over in her palm, Ali saw it was a stone no bigger than a button.

"What is it?" the two girls asked simultaneously.

"It's a Summoner. Only a few exist. No matter which world you're in, if you turn it three times in your hand, it'll bring you to the closest portal to Infernus. If you're in Infernus, it'll take you to a portal for the world you need to get to. I'm not exactly sure how it works beyond that. I nicked it from my parents before I left," Vulcan confessed, blushing. "I didn't know where my journeys were going to take me."

Lilly looked between the stone and her friends. She turned her head to take in one more look at Infernus and all its wonder before accepting the token, shoving it deep within her pocket.

Ali turned to face Vulcan. There was a battle ahead of her—of them—and she had a feeling it wasn't going to be one filled with sunshine and roses. But it didn't matter. After one last shove from the voice inside her head, she stretched out her hand toward Vulcan, waiting for him to accept her offer.

"It's time to go then," he announced, taking her hand firmly in his and shaking it once.

With one last glance, she took in the vast world that lay below her. Ali didn't know what awaited her in the shadows, but one thing was certain: she wasn't letting Mateva win without a fight. No matter what it took, Ali would find her brother.

ACKNOWLEDGMENTS

Above all, I'd like to thank my family. Mom, Dad, and Austin, thank you for believing that I could make this dream a reality from day one. Thank you for accepting my love of all things weird and magical, for without those two parts of my life, there's a chance this story would've been lost in my imagination.

To my friends near and far, thank you for your curiosity in this story. Your texts, calls, questions, and jokes kept me afloat during those late nights that turned into early mornings.

A huge thank you to New Degree Press, especially Eric Koester, Aislyn Gilbert, Emma Colvin, and Jessica Drake-Thomas for helping me flesh out the words running around in my head and turn them into something I can share with the world.

Last, to my early supporters, this book quite literally could not have been brought to life without you. Thank you for believing in me when seeds of doubt were growing in my own mind; your encouragement and excitement for this novel has kept me going until the very end.

Aaron Earlywine   Alexis Shannon
Alanna Forsberg   Alisa Gopal

Allie DeAngelis
Allie Reynolds
Ally Block
Aly Powell
Alyssa Chelak
Alyssa Lopes
Andrew Hollander
Angela O'Neill
Anna Cuneo
Anthony Garavuso
Bob & Doreen Cipolla
Bridget Burke
Brittany Manchisi
Brooke Olson
Bryan & Nicole Cipolla
Camila Tobar
Caroline Hughes
Cassidy Donohue
Catie Gormley
Catie Ross
Charlotte Breslin
Chris & Jenna Cipolla
Chris & Maria Mueller
Chris Garritano
Christine Forte
Cindy Lopane
Claire O'Neill
Clara Lindland
Dana DeFeo
Daniel Quinn
Danielle Accolla
Danielle DiSilvestro

Deborah Nye
Dianne Rigano
Donna Rabin
Elizabeth Bobroske
Ella Eisinger
Emily DiSilvestro
Emily Giorgi
Emily Scheuring
Emily VanderBent
Emma Forte
Emma Grace Trollinger
Emma Hitchens
Emma Scott
Emma Slosar
Eric Koester
Franco Scambia
Gabriella Barile
Glenn Hammer
Gloria Cipolla
Grace MacLeod
Greg Ajello
Hailey Cernuto
The Hartmann Family
Jack Testani
Jamie Marinelli
Jane Ross
Jen Duncan
Jenna Kosinski
Jenna Polidoro
Jessica Jachemczyk
Jessica Nicholas
Joe and Lisa LePino

JonPaul Crichton
Jordan Farber
Joseph Schmidt
Joseph Wenger
Julia Cantalupo
Julia Martin
Julie Kirshner
Kaitlyn Sharkey
Kat Ensign
Kate Szumanski
Katelyn Mayne
Katharine Polan
Katherine Garmer
Katherine Shannon
Katie Horiuchi
Katy Gallagher
Kayla Cihal
Kori Durando
Kristen Post
Kyle Erickson
Lee DiValerio
Lianna Regina
Liz Kratky
Lizzie Ryan
The Lometti Family
Luiz Guimaraes Jr.
Maddy Odenwald
Maggie Heaps
Mairead Cassidy
Mara Mermigos
Marcelle Allen
Margaret Lindenburg

Marie Murgolo
Marisa DeFeo
Marlon Rodriguez
Martin Sheehy
Matt & Shannon Cipolla
Matthew Criscitelli
Matthew Hartmann
Meagan Leverone
Melanie Maldonado
Meredith Bowman
Michael & LuAnn Cipolla
Michael Daniels
Michael Monagle
Michael Ubertaccio
Michele Breslin
Mike Cipolla
Mitchell Lew
Moira Quinn
Monica Diaz
Mykala Healy
Nicholas Forino
Nick Nelson
Nicole Barnett
Olivia Hymowitz
Paige Turilli
Rebecca Hidalgo
Rebecca Oestreicher
Rebecca Skulsky
Reid Steinberg
Richard Nelson
Rosemary Altamuro
Sabrina Nguyen

Sam Maniscalco
Sarah Blanco
Sarah Moxham
Scott Nielsen
Scott Waldron
Sean O'Connor
Serena Takada
Shawn Gilman
Simonas Bingelis
Sophia Cook

Susan Mullahy
Sydney Gioseffi
Tamara Nelson
Thomas Keane
Todd Benvenuti
Tom Lowe
Tristan Votta
Turner Russell
Vanessa Santamaria